The Ice King

ALSO BY ROBERT WINTNER

Whirlaway

Snorkel Bob's Reality Guide to Hawaii
(nonfiction)

The Ice King

A NOVEL BY
ROBERT WINTNER

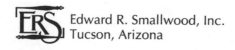
Edward R. Smallwood, Inc.
Tucson, Arizona

Edward R. Smallwood, Inc.
Tucson, Arizona

01 00 99 98 97 96 95   5 4 3 2 1

Special thanks to Kathleen Stanton for editorial guidance,
perseverance, balance, rhythm, timing, compassion, and don't
forget the old soft touch.

Publisher's Cataloging in Publication
(Prepared by Quality Books, Inc.)

Wintner, Robert.
   The Ice King : a novel / by Robert Wintner.
   p. cm.
   Preassigned LCCN: 94-067951.
   ISBN 1-881334-10-4 — cloth
   ISBN 1-881334-11-2 — paperback

   1. Jewish families—United States—Fiction. I. Title.

PS3573.163H34 1995   813'.54
                                        QB194-1773

Call 1-800-926-9050 to obtain ordering information on other
books by Robert Wintner

For Perline and Leon Wintner. And for Brother and Sissy, too.

...I swear to you that...I have despised all those overly pious people who pray out loud and beat their breasts and bow low and make crazy motions. I have hated those holy ones who talk with God all the time, who pretend to serve Him, and do whatever they want, all in His name! True, you might say that these modern irreligious people nowadays are no better and may even be worse than the old-timers with their false piety. But they're not so revolting. At least they don't pretend to be on speaking terms with God. But there! I'm on the way to Boiberik again.

—Sholom Aleichem, *Eternal Life*

The Ice King

In the Beginning

I can only tell you that time doesn't matter, that events get all mixed up until chronology flies out the window; that most people can't begin to remember what happened in '71 or '73, or '78; that it all boils down to hot and cold.

I can tell you that stories get lost in time, even the story about the time you die—people don't even remember when you died, or which stories you're in or not in, don't remember if the stories happened before you died or after. Go ahead and die, and give them a few years; they'll forget, which makes life itself suspect; it goes on so easily without you. Does it matter to a story if you were in it or not?

Of course it does, unless you were just a bump on a log anyway. But people mostly forget when. They mostly remember if something happened in the winter or the summer, because ice and snow stick, steam and sweat sink in. But that's not really remembering, that's a feeling, down to the stifling, sweltering, freezing, miserable sting of the thing.

Like summertime in Henderson, Kentucky, which was right across the bridge over the Ohio River from where I was a kid in Southern Indiana. Hotter'n a firecracker was what everybody called it, but that was a long-gone time when sayings lost their meaning too, and they were most often said by people too simpleminded to invent their own thoughts and words, but who still wanted to say something for God's sake, but they sure didn't want to offend anybody, and hotter'n a firecracker was inoffensive, acceptable, commonly said. It was safer than, say, a hot motherfucker, which could be the common saying now, times changing like they have. Nobody said motherfucker when I was a kid, leastwise not nearly so much as now, now that people are a little less simple and much more rude.

Firecrackers were one reason for heading over the bridge to Kentucky, where just past the south bank of the Ohio River, lining both sides of the road, were shanty shacks selling triple-cone starbursts, fireball flags, three-foot skyrockets, glory hallelujah heavenly ensembles with multiple reports, jumbo Roman candles—M-80s and cherry bombs and all the baby stuff like ladyfingers, sparklers, snakes, bottle rockets, cracker balls, helicopters, red chasers and buzz bombs. We threw cracker balls in the hallway at school, where the plumbing never worked right because of the cherry bombs flushed over the years. Sometimes we divided into armies and made forts and waged bottle rocket wars. I had a model airplane collection that never got old, because as soon as I got the least bit tired of, say, a Voodoo Fighter Jet, I'd rig it up with string to a high branch, stuff the jet ports with firecrackers, and light her up for her last kamikaze strafing run— *Kablammo Blamma Blammo!*

But the best ever was blowing up my replica of the *Robert E. Lee* Riverboat Queen with ladyfingers on every deck and in the wheelhouse and right at the waterline too, which called for timing and planning on fuse lengths, and I had to hurry like hell to get them all lit and get away to the end of the string tied to the bow so I could pull it through the tall grass. In the final seconds it was another sunny Saturday on the gently undulating Mississippi, as the Riverboat Queen plied my way, gently pitching and yawing until that happiest of all moments, unequivocal anarchy, total annihilation. What a wonderful oblivion we achieved, me and the *Robert E. Lee*, little gentlemen and southern ladies and ornate railings and finally the whole goddamn thing blasting into orbit. I'm lucky I still have eyes.

The other reason for heading over the bridge was Dade Park. Horse racing was legal in Kentucky, too. And since my old man knew

Mr. Bill Berry, who was the biggest jockey's agent at Dade Park, we sometimes got tips on who would win. It was that simple. I was eight or nine, focused on foot-long hot dogs on a bed of the only coleslaw in the whole wide world that was worth a good goddamn, it was so creamy and tart. You could get a foot-long hot dog with the works and about a quart of lemonade for a dollar, which was more than a sit-down dinner cost then, but Jesus, the lemonade was homemade from real lemons and you could eat and drink in your seat watching the horse races; and every now and then Mr. Bill Berry would come along and say something like *Friday's Girl,* and you would know that life was sweet and would stay that way at least for a couple more days. He wouldn't say what race because he didn't need to, because it was always the next race, and it was always to win, and he never, not once in all the years we went to the track, got it wrong.

My old man would laugh when Brother and I asked where is Mr. Billberry, but he'd laugh short, because he was on his own the days we asked, without the biggest jockey's agent at Dade Park.

Mr. Billberry was the biggest because he had the most jockeys, and he was also the biggest in size, maybe the first obese person I ever talked to. The fat rolled off him in layers. He had a belly over his belt and another belly under his belt and a third belly under that. He had big rolls of blubber on his arms and hanging off his armpits and he was wet, pitted out under the arms, all down his chest and way into his crotch and all down his back to his massive jellied ass, and he breathed like a badly tuned engine, wiping his forehead and his chins when he waddled over and told my old man something like *Gallant Dream....*

Now that was hot.

And because my old man knew Mr. Billberry, and because the biggest jockey agent at Dade was biggest because he had his eye open to the future, I was a focal point, an object of keen interest, a prime prospect for jockey school and for a stable with a winning track record. I tipped in at fifty-three pounds at nine years old, at a size called shrimpy at school, at a size that made me the last one picked for any team, touch football to Red Rover, a size Mr. Billberry called beautiful. "I got my eye on that boy, Mister. The kid looks beautiful. Starve him. Ha!"

Mr. Billberry would come around eyeballing me intensely, talking to my old man about winners and winner's circles and the goddamn Derby for chrissake, and Brother would whisper something in my ear like, "How does he reach his pee pee?" Then Brother and I would giggle insanely like a couple slobbering idiots till the tears ran down our faces, unable to stop, even in the face of a solid backhand from our old man for what could be seen as disrespect or behavior unbecoming a man. But we never got hit for laughing at Mr. Billberry because our old man saw the vision, which was me in the roses, and in the money, too. He gazed into the future while Brother and I giggled, and the big man went rhapsodic over prospects for greatness and prosperity. Mr. Billberry went on and on, like he flat didn't care about anything but the thought of me on a horse at full gallop, I think.

I hit eighty pounds at ten and stayed there two years, and the following summer was scheduled for the start of my jockey career. Mr. Billberry had already been talking for years about keeping my weight forward but not too forward, about keeping my weight low, not so much on my knees, even though that's where it looks like a jockey's weight is, but lower than that. *Lower than that?* He'd laugh and ruffle my hair, which I hated, and said it looked invisible now but I'd figure it out. He said you only kiss the horse with your knees, let him know you're there, guide him through it. *Kiss him with your knees? And guide him through what?* Through the turns, naturally, and through the changes of pace a winner needs guiding through.

Winning was simple enough for a kid to understand, especially when my old man told Brother and me we were good luck. He'd cut us in for ten bucks each after the last race on the days we saw Mr. Billberry at the track. Do you have any idea what the buying power of ten bucks was for a kid in Southern Indiana in 1957, or maybe it was '59? On the drive home our old man would tell Brother and me not to worry, because he wouldn't tell Mother we'd won. She'd only make us save it for our college educations. We decided not to tell Sissy either, because she'd only whine for her share, then she'd tell Mother.

Maybe Mother was right, because I gained eighteen pounds that spring, and we never saw Mr. Billberry again.

But then, a kid learns more from blowing ten bucks than he could ever learn at college. My old man quit school in seventh grade and he was plenty smart. He could never make a deal stick, but that didn't have anything to do with education; it had to do with luck, just like at the track—either Mr. Billberry was there, or he wasn't. I think it was diamonds that came after working the track, after I gained weight and Mr. Billberry disappeared from our fortunes. I was still under a hundred pounds, but most good jockeys come in around ninety-two, and I was only eleven or twelve and ninety-eight already, still way smaller than your average ten-year-old, but too big for a future at Dade Park. My old man took it in stride, maybe because knockdowns were such a regular part of his stride, and he knew what a man has to do after a knockdown—pick himself up, dust himself off, and take another step. That's what makes him a man, or a woman these days.

My shrimpy size was my first hard luck, and then I went and started growing—strike two was how he saw it. I think he liked my spunk and spirit, to keep on going like that after two solid knockdowns. He bragged sometimes, that I was the toughest one of all. But I wasn't tough. I was only a very small child willing to go with him, out and about, running errands, making deliveries and pick-ups, tending to business, drinks and lunch around town. Brother and Sissy wouldn't go. Brother got bored. Sissy was busy.

And every day was full of errands around town. He had a lull after I gained weight and shattered his dreams of jockey glory, as if I'd drop the twenty pounds and we could get back on course. But he got over it and didn't bear a grudge. He picked himself up and picked up diamonds from New York, which he sold in Southern Indiana at night spots I went to with him, places like the Trocadero, where guys in brown suits and matching hats drank highballs and played cards in

smoky rooms and women drifted here and there, soft and slinky, min-
gling catlike, curling a tail around a man's calf or purring up next to
him, for luck, which every man needed then, and every woman hoped
was hers to give. They moved according to a script, those women,
just like the women in the movies of those years, black and white.
The men had roles to play too, cool and aloof, ready for action, above
the need to show their success in the world, because the huge rocks
set in gold on their fingers did that for them. My old man moved easily among them, not so cool and never aloof, but ready for action. He
drifted and drank, sometimes playing a hand but mostly socializing
with focus, sometimes moving into a corner with one man or another
to pull the folded tissue from his pocket and show his wares—big
rocks, sometimes two, three carats, dirt cheap compared to retail, if
a man was lucky and could pay cash to show he had the luck.

And sometimes he'd unfold right in the center of the table, unwrap
a couple dozen little sparklers, sitting back and relaxing while the
hard-edged, easygoing players plucked every one from the tissue for
scrutiny, nodding and complimenting the clarity and color, maybe
one or two slipping a rock into a pocket. They all settled up without being asked, and I was impressed, wondering if my old man had
backhanded them upside the head too for being snotnosed little
punks, or if he'd ever had to yell at them to turn off the goddamn
lights for chrissake—*What? You think the goddamn money grows on trees?* I
doubt that he'd backhanded or yelled at any of them, but they
behaved as if they knew he could.

Diamonds and luck and money to buy both made for some juicy
times all right. Sometimes the sheer potential for violence got so
overwhelming that my old man just stood up. That calmed things
down, and he never, not once, had to pop anybody in the nose over
a diamond, not for another few years anyway.

We went once to a place in Cincinnati, a bar much farther up the
Ohio River, closer to its industrial source, where the air itself was a
browner shade of pale, always swirling with the cinder ash of progress
in what always felt like winter. The gray brown above matched the

dusty brown below; brownness filled your eyes all the way in to where the light refracted, and your soul told you, yes, brown. The dark brown, wooden floor fairly matched the dark brown bar and reddish-brown stools, and the elaborate but decrepit bar back, also in dark brown, held dozens of bottles with red-brown labels nobody read. The sauce inside was the life blood of the place, of the neighborhood, of the region, the state of being, the frame of mind on up to the firmament. The sauce kept them coming and going, kept them toasting The Kid, kept them betting in the back room, kept them alive in spirit.

The betting in the back room was a livelihood for the men who came and went. The liquor was the lubricant.

It was the kind of place a kid can't really know about, even if he's sitting at the bar counting bottles, or wondering where these guys were just before they came here, or where they would go to next, or wondering if he was the first kid in the entire history of the world to sit at that bar, or wondering when his old man would be finished so they could leave. You couldn't really know about that place if you were only nine or eleven, because stuff went on there that wasn't on TV and grown-ups didn't talk about in front of kids. I mean you could sense that anything you might need could be got one way or another somehow from someone at that place, as long as it was seedy.

I knew you could make bets or peddle diamonds in the back room. In the front room you could drink beer or liquor or talk real low like something was going down, something a kid or a member of the Rotary Club shouldn't hear about. You could keep on talking as you nodded, stared dead ahead and used inflections that asked if the listener comprehended. You could eat one of the nastiest excuses for a hamburger on the face of the earth, dirt brown, horizon to horizon, bun to center.

And if you were really hard-core Cincinnati, with so much brown in your soul you didn't know shit from shinola, you could order up a pig's foot, pickled, from the gallon jar on the back counter. The jar was half full, with a thin, light-brown film on the surface, unbroken, except where a pig's knuckle or toe stuck up. I watched a man who couldn't stand up straight, who looked like he'd been beat up more often than he hadn't, whose overalls looked so threadbare they couldn't even slow a breeze down, who looked like he'd be dead in ten minutes, or maybe died ten minutes ago, shuffle in and say, "Gimme one'em blurp glop snuk mmmneegghh, Frank." Frank served it with one of those napkins that's more worthless than single-ply toilet paper, but the guy just took it plain in his claw and stood there drooling, gumming the pig's foot. I wanted to ask Frank if he had a barf bag or a stomach pump back there, but I didn't, because those were the days when a kid could get backhanded for smartass remarks.

Over the bar in a gilded frame was a cup—a metal jockstrap in brown with a red star in the center—worn by Kid Roundhouse or someone who'd become welterweight champ of the region, who had risen above the dusty brown to infuse the region with pride, so now any man could look up from his double Scotch and think, *The Kid was one of us, and he could take it on the chin.*

I got left up front at the bar while the old man worked the back room. I was nervous at first, especially when a few of the roughneck hustlers coming into the bar looked me over and asked what a goddamn kid was doing at the bar. But they got told who I was, and where my old man was. Then they bought me Kid Manhattans or short draft beers, and they ruffled my hair or slapped me on the back, getting a big kick out of a kid like me, so little, drinking a beer. But those guys weren't the lovable bad guys you see on TV. Those guys ran the gamut from nice to nasty. Those outings ran a similar gamut, and I could always tell how we made out in the back room by the pace and tenor of our exit. Quick and all smiles meant we made enough for sit-down lunch on the way home. Quick with hard glares, down and dirty, meant walk out to the car, eyes down, don't ask. Or if we hung out and nursed a few highballs, that was the worst, because that meant the sonofabitch was a no-show.

My old man took me along as often as I'd go with him those days, maybe because he liked me, or maybe because he knew we didn't have a conventional father-son relationship and time spent together was our best shot; and maybe he thought I was lucky still, even though I'd gained too much weight to pull us out of our income slump but was still so little most people thought I was six or seven when I was eleven. Everyone else in the family was thick and overweight, and my old man told Mother to leave me alone when she tried to force feed me. "He's the healthiest one in the whole goddamn family!" he'd yell. I was small enough to have a personality complex, but I didn't have one because I didn't care, and I got fairly expert at not caring, at closing off those vulnerabilities that can kill you young or else lead you into terminal sensitivity, rendering you cerebral and sissified.

I didn't care about my physical size the same way I didn't care about every other unusual aspect of life in our family, because I was much happier out in the woods alone than I was with a bunch of fruit-faced kids playing with balls anyway. Some people said I sought solitude as an escape, that I sought those things that could not measure me or remind me of my deficiencies. I responded with silence, a silence I'd brought home from outings with my old man and from the woodlands, where a boy learns to keep his mouth shut, to let things play out. I preferred silence to the din forever rising from school, from the shopping malls, from any gathering of humans talking.

When I was eleven, softball at school fit into the regular routine, no big deal, all the kids did it. The other kids at the playground were mostly dullards with parochial parents, kids who were groomed to be the next generation of insurance agents, shoe salesmen, civic-minded dads, and that was acceptable to me; it was the way things were.

I was always chosen last, and this too was acceptable—it even seemed natural. I was known then as quiet, possibly morose, and attitude was a key social standard, even then, choosing teams for softball. I was simply distracted, distant, quiet. And after all, I was so small.

I didn't care, knowing the superior level of my outdoor skills. I was among the very best at stalking the wild salamander, hatching mantis chicks, handling snakes, raising ducks and rabbits—like Noah, I wanted two of each to come stay with me for awhile. My pressed-leaf collection was phenomenal, with perfect mountings for every specimen.

But that stuff didn't count on the diamond, so I waited with the scrubs. Sometimes I was the only scrub waiting. I didn't care, because I also knew that I wasn't that bad at softball. Sure, I couldn't hit, but I could go goofy at the plate. I could find a posture embracing a subtle, other body that threw the pitcher's read, altered his rhythm. I drew walks. No glory in walking, but I rounded the bases as often as anybody, but then points without glory, without drama, were empty. I didn't push it. I honestly didn't care, didn't try to be chosen, to be perceived as a leader, because in my heart I knew the prize was a piñata—all show, no substance but a handful of candy. I knew what these kids would grow up to, what they would talk about then.

Most of those kids had fathers with jobs like the fathers depicted in the textbooks of the day—jobs at the bank, jobs with uniforms, jobs that lasted for years. Those kids came to school with an air of propriety. Those kids played softball with a confidence based on who they were, what they would become, because their fathers told them so. They were winners; they were told as much, but I thought they were boring, without fantasy, without hope. Lines were being drawn, even then.

All the kids got chosen, even me, sometimes with a groan, a concession to Christian mercy or Republican liberalism, with resignation. I got right field, as if I were a weed that grew best there. Infield was where the action was.

One day in right field, contemplating straw grass and which type was good to chew and which was sharp or bitter, and how you had to be careful, even though nobody probably took a leak out there, and maybe thinking right down into the green of the thing, until green went blue when I went snake-eyed trying to see beyond seeing, a sound evolved. I looked up.

Charles Kniednagle stepped up to the plate. He was the biggest boy in the sixth grade, too big for his age, bigger at eleven than I was at forty. His Gothic suburban family was eminent in the area. His father sold billboards, changing the face of the countryside with a power seen as awesome. Charles' older brother was a state trooper with a stiff hat, baggy britches, a big gun and a smile that commanded respect. Charles would have been a scrub if he wasn't so big, or if his father fell into the bottle, or his mother had taken the children and moved yet again to another school district. His speech impediment was severe enough to thrust him into oblivion. But maybe not; he could hit so well.

Charles Kniednagle had thick, dark hair that looked naturally swept back, and he flung it back too with a toss of his head when he spoke, like he did then over the catcalls and vigorous hooting. Charles approached the plate grinning his big, dumb grin, and he thrust the tip of the bat toward me—"Ih goihg to right field," he said. And oh, how they howled again, his team, my team, the girls, the so-called coach.

It was a pronouncement, as grand as if heaven had cleaved for archangels with trumpets to draw even more attention to the no-glove, nobody scrub out in right field. Humiliation came my way in waves; I was embarrassed for existing, for the numbers and words that sized me up. Yet it was an exercise too, a primary event I could see much clearer with a few years of perspective. It was a turning point, a confluence of action and emotion.

At least I existed. That was new. That was something, even if I only existed in significant discomfort. Charles Kniednagle dug in. I dropped back, deep. The pitch was served on a platter. Charles had a ripple, and sure enough....

For a reason then ungrasped, with a power stumbled onto, I knew the ball could only be dropped, and when it was dropped, nothing would change. Everyone knew it would be dropped. They would cockadoodle-doo Charles around third. I would become more secure in my natural niche. It was certain, foregone, past tense. Life would go on. It was a done deal. My power was in my ability to accept this as I had already accepted so much. *Fuck it. Who cares?*

It was a line shot on a low arc taking forever, gaining meteoric power in its orbit over the playground—and it changed. It slowed down. I watched it, waiting forever for its arrival. And just as slowly, like in a dream, my hands went up, fingers wrapped around it, cradled it, eased on to the mad spin of it soft as power brakes, and it stopped. Everything stopped—hooting, cheering, Charles Kniednagle, time. I threw it in just as I would have in the shower of derision that was so certain a moment before. Silence reigned. I had caught a Charles Kniednagle line-drive homer barehanded like it was a marshmallow. It didn't hurt because of the soft cushion of adrenaline surrounding me. I had otherwise altered the course of nature. It took a minute or two for the chatter to resume, as if denial and I ruled there briefly, as if a flying saucer had landed on the pitcher's mound and then flown away, and nobody felt too good about being the first to mention it.

Charles Kniednagle invited me over to his house the following Saturday. It smelled of mowed grass, like most of the Midwest in springtime, and giant grasshoppers flew everywhere out back, near the uncut fields. Some had tissue-paper lining under their wings, but Charles never saw that; he pinched the wings off so they could be his pets. Some had stingers, so he held them tight by their middles, sometimes squeezing them until the brown stuff came out both ends. Then he pulled their legs off and let them rest on his chest, where he could stroke them with his finger and call them by name.

He chose foolish names for his mutilated pets, like Greeny. "I'll call this wuh Greehy," he said, because he couldn't make the *n* sound, saying it more like a gaping *h*.

He showed me how to play with the pinched-off legs. You can squeeze the thigh for hours and the foot flicks up. This and other wonders Charles Kniednagle shared with me that following Saturday, showing me what I'd been missing, his house was so big, so white, so infused with long-term stability, and so were his mother and father and brother. Not a bad guy, Charles, and it was good for me to realize that Charles only reflected his atmosphere at home. He was only simple-minded when the other boys weren't around, not nearly as mean.

But that was after the day that I looked up from right field to the catcalls from the bench. I didn't care. They couldn't reach me.

I most likely would have remembered catching a Charles Kniednagle line-drive homer in any event, but that day of glory for me, of humility for him, came home again a lifetime later, which was then only ten years or so, when everyone had hair down their backs and reefers rolled up in their pockets, and revolution and anarchy in their eyes and hearts. Oh it was fun, maybe the most fun of all, with the easy sex, the undying buzz, the miles and miles of open road, the sheer lack of want for anything but another high, another slug o'wine. I enjoyed a late afternoon heading into dusk, strolling down a street in complete disregard of what the evening had in store. I was high, surrounded by a hot buffet of anything you could want; I was way under thirty, so time time time was on my side, yes it was.

And out of the blue going gray, in the twinkle of the first little star, with a kind of hearty *Hey big boy! How you doing?* Charles Kniednagle shuffled boldly out from a doorway and stood there grinning. He was just as big but had taken to slouching, maybe to fit in better. We stood there nodding and grinning, checking out each other's rig, ascertaining by our bell-bottoms and shirts—ragged, with holes—and all the hair between us, that we had taken the same route.

After a moment to process the difference between then and now, between eleven and twenty-one; after making mincemeat of all the years with the password of the revolution, which was a giggle and a grin, we shook hands. Charles Kniednagle hugged me. I was gratified, because in that hug I felt warmth and more; I felt his gratitude. I felt that I had been a component of his life. Then, like two Indians of different tribes meeting in peace on the vast range of time, we smoked on it. Smoking a joint with a childhood acquaintance years later in the heart of the revolution was one of the ultimate acts of revolution. It was confirmation that all before was bullshit, hereby thrown over, good for nothing but a goof.

I wouldn't have minded chatting with Charles for awhile, but after a few seconds I could see that in fact we had not taken the same route. Charles was skinny, the methodical skinny of the speed freak, and his long sleeves were buttoned. He turned this way and that, like a thrush outside his thicket, in the open, on the lookout, as if for predators. And his body could not find stillness but rather twitched like he'd lit on a live wire, keeping time to a silent beat. He kept on nodding as we finished the joint with relish, with no words, as if smoking a joint ten years later said it all, or maybe we never had anything to say in the first place. I wanted to ask about his brother, the State Pig, because that's what we called policemen in the revolution. I wanted to know about the big white house with the perfect Mom and Dad, but I didn't need to. I knew it was all still there, that Charles could go home any time he wanted to, if he didn't die first. He put his arm around me and gave another hug. *Far out, Mah. You are wuh stohed gas, Mah. You...!*—He grinned big and pointed at me—*I love you, Mah.*

"All right, Charles!" I said, and I meant it, wishing him safe passage through the straits of crystal methamphetamine, beginning to wonder, even at that moment, why nature plays itself out the way it does, when it wants to. He walked away, calling back that now he played the guitar. That was twenty-five years ago. I still look under K in music stores every now and then, but I haven't seen him since.

Who'd a thunk it? I can promise you that life in the late '60s was more impossible to predict in the late '50s than a flying saucer landing on the pitcher's mound.

And who could have known in the late '60s how quickly the world would end? I am grateful for having known a world of discovery, a magic time, when a boy could still find the place of no place and take refuge.

Southern Indiana is riddled with lakes—lakes reflecting the sun and moon and the natural scheme of things. Lakes defined neighborhoods, the biggest lakes giving rise to surrounding enclaves.

I remember blizzard nights so dark and frozen and slashed sideways by slaking snow thick as froth—nights so shrill and forlorn, so eerie and lost as all the lost souls, that a child could be drawn in, drawn out and away from the fire. We built bonfires out on the ice over a dozen wheelbarrow loads of sand. We either picked teams or else simply flew into it asses and elbows, going for the tin can puck with our maple sticks until the teams defined themselves by who wanted to fight who and who allied accordingly and where exactly the goal lines ought to be. We went mad with it and time didn't count from darkness at five-thirty until ten or so, heavy action all the way, no rests, only the sudden freeze at the tectonic *crrrrr….ack!* when the action got too focused—too many kids on one spot. Then we waited, then we moved apart from the center slowly, listening for other sounds of mortality. I moved far and farther still, sometimes reaching the edge of the firelight, sometimes skating deeper into darkness than anyone had ever been.

And I would have gone farther if not for the weeping willow tree indicating the far shore. She was a mess those nights, her hair wild and tangled over her face, her mouth open wide on vigorous, freezing lamentations. The skate back to the fire was always full speed and furious, because the monsters were after me by then.

But the lake I remember most in summertime was not ours. Sure, we fished ours, right outside the back door, for bluegill that we scaled and cleaned, that got pan fried with green tomatoes for dinner. And we swam out to the dock with our ducks—little ducks who came in early spring, who we fed and nurtured and taught to swim, so they could be ready for the real world.

But a couple miles from our lake was a man-made lake stocked with catfish by this guy who wanted to build houses around it and sell them on the lure of the catfish, which could go a hundred pounds each in time. Maybe he planned to call it Catfish Acres, I don't know. But right after the lake was dug out, he had it stocked with thousands of baby catfish—maybe millions. They were thick as pond sludge, and at first glance you would laugh at the hard luck of the guy behind Catfish Acres. But then you thought, *Wait a minute! They just dug this lake and filled it. How'd they get pond sludge so quick?* So you'd ease on down the bank—on your butt, because it was steep enough to take a tumble, and coming home in wet clothes made you look about as stupid as anyone could look. You slide down close and cast a shadow on the sludge, then get still as a tree and wait for its undulation to gain some flutter on the edges, and then a speck or two of sludge would break off and move away, but then it would skitter back quick. Then you realized, my God, it's catfish. You could cruise the bank and catch perfect baby catfish with a net made from a coat hanger and a nylon stocking.

Have you ever seen a baby catfish? In a single inch they have pectoral, lateral, caudal, dorsal, and a few extra fins besides, all perfect and miniature, all fluttering magically down the sides and along the top, the lips practically talking to you through the whiskers, through the jar. And they never minded a few little crawdads on the bottom, and after awhile you could find the right water plants and stake them in some shallow gravel and watch the whole thing every day until everyone got too big, so you went back out to a lake and let them go, and maybe found a red-eared snapping turtle who could bring a tear to your eye if it got you, or maybe you'd meet one of the giant snappers that went eighteen inches across and twenty-five pounds, that could stretch its legs and neck out three feet in a snap and take off your whole goddamn hand up to the elbow if you weren't careful.

But if you could get it to strike at an old piece of bamboo fishing pole and get it pissed off enough to hang on and then drag it home, Uncle Rudy would come pick it up and carry it down to the Steamboat Inn where Uncle Izzy would supervise production on a week's issue of Uncle Izzy's Notorious Turtle Soup, which was damn near as famous as his clam chowder and maybe more so, the turtles were so hard to catch, and he could get clams easily. I only got one giant snapper that could have hurt me bad. My old man came out and shot it twice in the head, all smiles. Then we pried the bamboo stick out of its jaws, marveling at its death grip, imagining the pain if the bamboo was an arm. Then we had a highball.

I think my old man admired that in me—the solitary nature, the independence, the incessant drive to go, out and away, driving toward what was unspoiled because it wasn't yet known. I think he was blind to my limitations, because he always advised, "Anyone give you any lip, you pop him right in the nose." I was smart enough to understand the practical liabilities of his advice, but I figured maybe I would follow it some day, once I gained another couple hundred pounds or so. And of course, it felt good knowing my old man thought that I could just pop anybody in the nose. He'd been a professional football player two seasons, '23 and '24 I think, for a farm club called the Cleveland Tigers, not too far from the Ohio River.

He tried professional wrestling for a few years, because he went two-twenty at five-ten, and even though big-time wrestling was fixed then too, the wrestlers still had to take a punch every so often, and he could, and he could throw one without thinking, too.

Like the time I went to the grocery store with Mother and him, which was a rare family outing, and my old man was already nearly sixty and had had two heart attacks already because he drank so much liquor and smoked two packs a day, Pall Mall straights, and he loved fried foods and steaks. He asked the bag boy to carry the groceries out to the car. The bag boy should have done it and kept his mouth shut, because my old man always tipped big for favors like that and never asked for anything more than what he considered common courtesy. But the bag boy said sure and started on his way and then mumbled something about old farts and fat and lazy, and my old man spun on a dime, quick and smooth as Sugar Ray Robinson ever did with a solid one-two, left jab to the chin, right hook to the jaw, and the bag boy was down and out and back up in a few seconds spitting Chiclets and blood and scrambling for distance, while Mother shrieked her mantra about craziness as she scrambled for the scattered groceries with that mortified look on her face she was good at by then. My old man shook it off and carried his own goddamn bags. He was rough like that, rough in the extreme, primitive sense. But then he'd taken it too, and the only time he ever beat us kids was when we had bad manners and had to learn, like that poor bag boy had to learn, with a combination punch that came from experience.

But it wasn't all him, the rough and primitive, it was the world, and it was the family he came from, too. His old man was gentle and soft-

spoken, and his mother was known for her poise and social grace—
my old man's parents died years before I was born, so I only knew
what I was told, what I was able to glean. The family goes back over
a hundred years in only two generations in Southern Indiana; Joseph
came from Germany around 1880. Haddie came from Austria about
the same time. Joe went into the wholesale liquor business and stayed
with it. She stayed home raising six boys and a girl. He was strong
and quiet. She was strong, quiet and socially inclined, if the society
was willing to come to her. They lived in the same house in the old
section of town forever, with no pretense, with good manners, style
and grace, ignoring the sometimes boisterous shenanigans of the
boys, because that was what boys did—they went out and raised hell,
until they grew old and died.

At least that's the general impression they left behind for those of
us born after they'd already died. You lose the details when your forebears aren't around to tell you. You can piece it together, but it comes
out like a mosaic, with obvious seams between the pieces if you look
too close. From a distance it makes sense, providing a recognizable
context. I could see my old man as a child on the street like Studs
Lonigan, but not really, because a small town is different than a city—
always has been. And a river town is different, too.

So it's a general impression that you piece together, with the
biggest pieces as focal points, so the era forms in your mind as a backdrop for those events most dramatically allowing prevailing values
and intentions to surface.

I think five brothers who stuck together could make for rough-and-
tumble times. I don't think they went looking for trouble, but they
were remembered as troublesome, because they wouldn't let trouble
settle into the family circle, not on your goddamn life. They sustained
their spirit of right and wrong to the end, even when they were
wrong. But it was when they were right that got my attention, they
stayed so ready for action, even after they were older and calmed
down, kind of. A kid can relate to that, can wonder who and what
he is and where he's supposed to hang his hat and fairly well know
who and what and where at the same time.

I was seven when my old man was fifty-five. He was the youngest. Uncle Izzy was the oldest, already sixty-eight or so when he decided to reopen the Steamboat Inn. It was a great old place that had embodied the spirit of the town, or at least that part of the town, and the Steamboat did okay. It was a business Uncle Izzy knew well, but he'd shut down soon after the beginning of WWII. Business was off, and he was ready for a change anyway, for more money and less daily detail.

But twelve years later, when all the boys sat around trying to figure out why Izzy shut it down in the first place, all they got was a big laugh because none of them knew why. So Uncle Izzy got the old place back up just like it was. He brought it back to life from the dusty, dark, deserted storefront it had become. He scraped the whitewash off the windows and got a window painter to come in with fancy frontier Gothic lettering, black and white with a gleaming gold border arcing the entire front window, visible for a block in either direction—Steamboat Inn.

Uncle Izzy got brand-new Formica and chrome tables and chairs and a new showcase for the deli meats, a new lunch counter and bar stools, new salt and pepper shakers and napkin holders—the works. The floor got waxed and buffed so shiny it glistened, and the place filled up with all the people who'd lived in town for years, people who loved coming down to the river, because that was where somebody always had a line baited, and you could never know what was out there waiting to be hooked into, where society had a place and a time to happen, and the catfish stew and coffee were as good as you could get. The Steamboat was only a half block up from the water, so you could smell the river, feel the current, sense the action, and when the Steamboat filled up with people from town in top-of-the-line '50s suits and dresses, it was an event, a happening, a current all its own.

Uncle Izzy even got Paul to work the kitchen again, and Paul stands there still, striking the same dumb pose he did a hundred times in those years for Brother and me. He would lean over and greet us, palms up, grinning, with a ham sandwich on each palm. We didn't get ham at home, but the old man said it was okay—hell, yes, it was okay—down at the Steamboat. Paul had a white shirt and white pants and white shoes and socks and white hair under his white hat, and he always served it up on white bread, so the only color in the shot was flesh pink in his cheeks and in the ham, with a double load of dazzle in his grin, which was mostly gold caps along the front row, because Paul was practically one of the boys, which meant he'd seen heavy action.

And it seemed like most of the action was heavy. Many days were like the day these two guys, who also had restaurant interests downtown, came in and roughed up Izzy. Uncle Izzy by that time had lost the use of his right arm and right hand because of his stroke, but he never let that or anything get him down. He only smiled and laughed when all the brothers told Brother and me to rub Uncle Izzy's gimp hand for luck. We did, Sundays mostly, when the clan convened at Uncle Izzy's house for Hog Jo, a lazy name for hog jowls, a regional favorite, fried with potatoes and eggs by Aunt Vi, a red-haired, freckle-faced woman maybe fifteen years younger than Uncle Izzy, who lived there with him in an arrangement that was then called shacking up. It went on for years, since way before I was born, and they never married.

Mother said they didn't get married because Aunt Vi wasn't Jewish, but I doubted that, because my old man was married twice before Mother and neither of his first wives was Jewish. Besides that, I think Uncle Izzy and Aunt Vi were products of the neighborhood and its simple pleasures, which made the place rare. I think they didn't give a hoot for social convention. And besides that, nobody in the entire world thought my old man or any of his brothers was Jewish, no oy vay here, not on your goddamn life. Aunt Vi was so soft and sweet and gentle, just like Uncle Izzy was, and she stayed with him until the day he died and then stayed in the same house until she died years later.

She stopped Hog Jo Sundays once Uncle Izzy was gone, but the Sunday I remember best was the one when Uncle Izzy put his best face on like nothing had happened, because he was strong in a different sense, a quiet sense, and he knew nobody could run him out of business the same month he got back into business, not with his brothers around, even if the trouble came from a syndication of trouble there on the Ohio River. But Uncle Izzy couldn't cover the rough treatment he'd got with his usual composure because he was bruised under one eye, not a shiner exactly, but nobody said anything until the Hog Jo was way gone under enough coffee to get all the boys all jacked up, and one of them asked Izzy if he wanted to talk about it. Uncle Izzy didn't want to talk about it, but he understood practicality and unchangeable currents, like the two that ran in the family and in the Ohio River, all downstream.

It was Uncle Sammy and Uncle Rudy and my old man who solved the problem, quick and neat with no hesitation. They didn't go to the top but sent a message through the boys who'd brought the message to Uncle Izzy, roughed up the messengers in accordance with another phrase of the day—*to within an inch of their lives*. It happened downtown with no discretion and considerable noise, the brothers cruising fast on foot into one place and then another and asking loud *where*, until they found the messengers and dragged their sorry asses outside so they wouldn't make a mess and landed into them like a pack of wolves on two unhappy lambs—kicked the holy living shit out of these guys. Then they got down to indelible imprint, to the consequences of laying hands on Uncle Izzy—mayhem. Broken teeth and bones, blood, piss in pants, fractured faces and, of course, heartfelt sentiment yelled at the top of their lungs got the new message delivered and helped the witnesses pass the new message along. And there were plenty witnesses, right there on the sidewalk and then out past the curb, where traffic stopped until the beating was thorough enough to be called complete, and the boys stood there, dumbfounded at their power to dispense the truth.

My old man and Uncle Sammy carried guns after that. Uncle Rudy was the third best pistol shot in the United States Army in WWI. He said shooting was more sporting then and much harder because you held the gun down, then raised it and fired, one-handed, no hesitation. And he never minded coming in third, because he still beat out about a hundred-seventy thousand other guys. When Uncle Sammy and my old man got guns, Rudy said, "Ahhh!"

The guns seemed natural to me; not that my old man or Uncle Sammy wanted to shoot anybody, they didn't. They just didn't want to get messed up by any bad guys.

Paul set a record for ham sandwiches served the next week because people love a winner, and down and dirty at street level was how my old man and his brothers knew how to win. It was that simple; it was in fact the only game they ever won. And because it was the week of the ham-sandwich record, I remember just how much fun the old Steamboat Inn was. Uncle Izzy hung out up front on a bar stool, keeping the place covered, and he'd look to the back when we walked in and he'd call out, "Oh, Paul! Take care of the boys, will you?" Brother and I were the boys then and loved the recognition, because until Uncle Izzy said it, it wasn't official. He made us a part of the brotherhood, and we headed straight to the kitchen where Paul gave us each a couple big slices of ham on white bread, and then out front we'd get served Uncle Izzy's Famous Clam Chowder made personally by Uncle Izzy himself, and served by him, too, to VIPs like us. It was hotter'n a firecracker with spices and so hot otherwise you could go outside and blow more steam than a locomotive, until it formed rivulets that rolled down the front window but not very far before it froze into icicles. Or you could turn around and stand toe to toe breathing steam at the freezing sleet and the howlingest storm I ever remembered. Because the world was cold as the North Pole that week, and a bellyful of Uncle Izzy's Clam Chowder de Luxe was like a campfire in the snow, radiating warmth in waves against the blizzard blowing down River Street.

Uncle Izzy died a few years after that, quiet and peaceful as he'd lived. The Steamboat closed, and gone too were Hog Jo Sundays.

Uncle Sammy died a year or two after Uncle Izzy, and that broke my old man up worse than ever, maybe because Sammy and my old man were only a year or two apart. They hung out at the Elks Club together and both were nuts for fishing—didn't make a pinch of shit worth of difference if it was hot or cold, wet or dry, fish or no fish, they didn't need to ask each other if maybe an hour or six out at a lake, any lake, might be a good idea. Working a bank, casting for bass from midmorning to sunset was bliss for those guys. I went along and got set up with a cane pole and a bobber and some worms, and they made me the cook, too, which I liked because I could make sand-wiches much better than Mother could, with mustard and soft white bread and ham and pimento loaf and all that other nasty shit she'd never buy. I even drove the grocery cart and threw in anything I wanted—enough cream soda to make you puke, dill pickles, fud-gesicles, potato chips, candy. After lunch I'd hunt for frogs and keep the big ones for pets and give the little ones to my old man and Uncle Sammy, who could fairly often turn a frog into a bass. Strange days, those, just fishing and eating and drinking, no talking, and they rec-ollect like one long day.

The only time I ever saw my old man cry was in the kitchen when he took the call from the hospital, knew it was coming because he'd been back and forth to the hospital for a week, watching Sammy's failing consciousness. He just nodded his head at the news that Sammy was gone. He didn't even hang the phone up but cleared the line and called Uncle Rudy—and Harry Metcalfe, who lived on sliced tomatoes, salt and pepper, and beer, and who used to go fishing with us every now and then and was one of the brotherhood because he was Irish but put up his dukes at the first Jew-bait syllable. Oh, Harry Metcalfe could be counted on. Then the old man called a few guys I never heard of and told them all that Sammy was dead, with an air of finality that told me too that an era had ended. I can't remember Uncle Sammy, ever, without a smile on his face. He said, *Hey, Kid, come'ere,* every time I saw him, and he'd stuff a couple bucks in my shirt. Sure, I liked him. He was a great guy.

Uncle Rudy died a year or so after that, and that was no surprise either, he was so diabetic, had lost one leg that year and then the other and then got cancer. Uncle Rudy moved out of town the year before he died, moved to New Orleans, because that's where the V.A. hospital was, and Uncle Rudy had wound up as sick and broke as a man can get.

I don't know if Uncle Rudy was ever married, but I know he never married Aunt Pat, a blonde woman similar to Aunt Vi, whom he lived with for all of that part of my life. They had about a '39 Dodge coupe that was tits perfect, and Uncle Rudy never thought twice about cruising town in it, but then he had the most dramatic flair of all the brothers, could have made it big in show biz, and as it was had the biggest dance studio in eleven states—and could he dance?

I was about six the first time I saw him in black-face. Nobody complained then at the standard minstrel shows where white guys would wear pinstriped suits and straw hats and white gloves and tap shoes, and they'd tap dance with canes and sing *Mammy, How I love you, How I love you, My dear old Mammy*... and so on, until Uncle Rudy stepped forward and went wacko on the taps. The guy was red-hot. He slid across the floor like butter down a hotcake, leaving the same wake of little popping bubbles. And his white-gloved hands flew in perfect harmony with the downbeat, looking like rhythmic moths just crazy for the flames. Some of the old minstrel dancers painted big smiles into their black-face—not Uncle Rudy, because he didn't need to. His face was already painted with the dynamic of a man who'd found his calling.

He told me the world was his oyster then—back in the vaudeville and minstrel show days—New York, Hollywood, anything he wanted. All he had to do was go. This while applying makeup to me, age eleven, for the school play, a story about Johann Strauss. I played Strauss, Sr., a crotchety old fart who didn't understand the glory of show biz. Uncle Rudy made me look seventy. Then he tossed me his cane, took it back and cut off ten inches without a doubt, gave it back and said, *Now walk. No no no....* Then he showed me how to walk like a crotchety old fart.

So? Why didn't you go?

I don't know. I suppose I should have. I just didn't want to leave home.

So he stayed home with Pat and played pinochle with the boys, went over the old scores and played his piano and cruised on down to the Steamboat Inn those days Uncle Izzy made his famous chowder. Uncle Rudy was different from his brothers, with his olive complexion and his sharp beak with a hump in it just below his eyes and his curly black hair. All his life his brothers and friends never called him Rudy, only Dago, because he looked so Italian; and he only drank red wine, even when the boys were working up a good weekend buzz on Scotch or bourbon.

He told me once his biggest mistake in show biz was not changing his name—to Clark Whiting or Lonzo Cassal or something Hollywood like that. He said he hung on to his name even though nobody could say it, and if nobody can say it, then you work at a big disadvantage, because people can't talk about you. He said showbiz names need to roll off your tongue with an easy phosphorescence like Marilyn Monroe or Rhonda Fleming, or else come at you bold and strong like Humphrey Bogart or Rock Hudson.

I thought about that years later, since that makeup session with Uncle Rudy was only a year or two before the last time I saw my old man, before all the brothers were gone. It was a Sunday, maybe eight months after Mother had filed for divorce, and Brother and Sissy and I went with our old man for the day, which was the format for visitation back then.

He took us downtown to where he was staying in a cheap hotel that was much cleaner in the room than out in the hall. The place had a bed and a wardrobe and a table for mixing drinks. The window overlooked an alley. I mixed him a highball, and I remember how much more sense a highball made there, overlooking that alley. I pulled the curtain back so we could get a better shot of the alley. Sissy said something about me always messing things up. Brother wanted a soda.

The old man made a small project out of fetching some ice and some glasses so we could each have our own cold soda. We sat around and talked, and the old man showed us a few things, like some brochures on the aluminum siding he was trying to get excited about selling in Oklahoma, or a racing form he'd been going over for what looked like some decent prospects that evening. He hung up some pants and straightened up his kit. He was down to a couple bags by then. Then it was time to go home.

We drove home without saying much of anything, and he pulled up to the house and Sissy got out, and Brother and I would have followed her, but, looking straight ahead, the old man said, "Wait a minute." We waited, figuring he'd say something sentimental, which wasn't easy for him, but he felt compelled to say those things sometimes. It was like the way he signed his letters *Daddy*, even though we never called him Daddy. We all sat there in the car and waited until Sissy was inside, and he said, "Don't ever change your name."

It's a hell of a request to two brothers, eleven and twelve. We looked at him. "Why would we change our name?"

"Oh, you know," he said. But we didn't know why a boy would change his name, and maybe the idiotic look of childhood was effective for once. "You know, your mother. Her family."

I laughed and said that was stupid, because I'd never change my name. And that was that—the last time we ever saw him, so long, out of the car, wave goodbye and gone, forevermore.

My old man had a nickname too, but it only stuck twenty years or so, from the time he was eleven and fell down and banged his head on the curb and couldn't remember anything, including his name. He guessed maybe it was John. So all his big brothers called him John, even after he got his memory back; and I could always tell who went way back with the family, because those people would call my old man John.

I read somewhere that few people realize the amazing parallels between their lives and the lives of their parents. I banged my head, too, in high school wrestling. After I got so good at a particular move called the guillotine, I got cocky and started practicing it on guys a weight class or two above me. I met my match when I put it on a guy five weight classes up. He stood up and laughed, and then slammed me to the mat. I sat up and didn't know shit and stayed that way two days until they gave me drugs in the hospital, and I slept eighteen hours and woke up in the middle of the night asking, "What?" I suppose my wrestling and my old man's wrestling and his pro football were the highlights of athletic prowess in the family.

My old man survived one more heart attack, but then the next one got him. By then Mother had packed us kids up and moved us way across town. The divorce was final by the time he died, and he'd gone down to Oklahoma on an aluminum-siding project after that last visit. I was thirteen already.

My old man's funeral was the first time I ever visited a cemetery, and walking up the grassy lane between the rows I didn't think anything of it one way or another—cemetery, park, a walled-in place with a bunch of gravestones. The day was gray and dreary and threatening rain, but it wasn't eerie or scary or anything dramatic like I'd seen on TV. It was only a place—a place we had to go to and stay in for awhile, for a ceremony, before we could go home.

But I stopped suddenly in the procession when we passed Uncle Rudy. He'd told me he was the third best pistol shot in the United States Army in 1917, and then I read it again on his grave marker. And there he was. I hadn't seen him in a long time and sent some childish thoughts his way, but only briefly before I was encouraged along the way, because we had to hurry.

My old man's funeral was a dreary, perfunctory occasion rather than a dreary, sad occasion, mostly because all the brothers were dead and gone and moreover had ceased as a formidable faction some years earlier. Then they died. My old man was the last, leaving only his sister, Aunt Florence.

He and his brothers had played hard and fought hard and left a trail of harsh recollections. My old man was a member of the Elks Club for thirty years or so, but not one Elk showed up at the funeral; maybe because they kicked him out for popping Dave Begner right in the nose, and then the jaw, when Dave Begner dropped about a three-carat diamond on the floor at the Elks Club. Dave Begner had plenty dough, but he wouldn't pay because he said it was glass or it wouldn't have broken like it did. He called my old man a bullshitter in so many words, leaving my old man no alternative but to serve up the knuckle sandwich, hot, quick and fresh, the way the boys were famous for. Uncle Sammy quit the Elks after they kicked my old man out, and I didn't want to go back there anyway, fuck them and their Thursday night dollar-buffet that was more and better things to eat than we'd had all week.

Most of the old Steamboat crowd showed up at the funeral, but then they were already present in the cemetery. Friends of the family had mostly defined themselves as friends of Mother's, and since the divorce was a year ago, they didn't come. The year before my old man died began with the cease-fire between him and Mother. They became divorced and stopped yelling, maybe so they could figure out where the last eighteen years had gone to. The year ended with my old man's death in Oklahoma.

Social pressure in a small town can work like toxic waste. Divorced people then were tainted, stigmatized, deficient, unable to succeed in something or other. Mother had put the word out; she had had no choice in the matter. She strived for a public perception of us that would factor in some sympathy, some understanding, maybe some support in our effort to proceed as a family. That's why we had to hurry, I think, so we could get on with the new order of things.

My old man's funeral was to mark an end and a beginning. It was an end to a reality we had never grasped, a family that never succeeded. We would begin later that day making our way in the world, Sissy, Brother and I working toward our college educations and success.

Mother knew this in her heart. She told us it would come to pass, as if encouraging herself, whistling in the dark. The family fell apart years earlier; nothing had changed. But on that day we marked time, and everything that had been became far away, long ago. It was a difficult past we buried that day too, and the ceremony bore down with expedience and acceleration, so we could beat the weather and get on with our lives.

And so it was only us kids and Mother, Aunt Aileen and Uncle Louie who weren't really our aunt and uncle, the new rabbi and his wife and a few people Mother asked to come.

Aunt Florence, my old man's only sister, came up from Oklahoma City and aluminum siding. Uncle John, her husband, couldn't make it, he was so busy with impending success. The old man had died just as they were getting things going, Aunt Florence said; for once, things were going just fine. Aunt Florence was confused, there at the cemetery for the funeral of her last brother. Mother wouldn't look at her or speak to her, but held her accountable for the way things turned out. Aunt Florence was only one of them. She didn't know what to do, like a child lost in a cemetery, surrounded by familiars who couldn't help.

The new rabbi pinned black ribbons to Brother, Sissy and me, then he cut them with a razor. Aunt Florence wasn't paying attention and asked the rabbi to cut her blouse and not her sweater, because her sweater was brand new. Brother and I giggled.

The new rabbi made tsk-tsk sounds and said, "Now, boys, this is no time for cutting up." His pun was too juicy to let slide, and even Sissy giggled.

Then we followed along the general flow of the day which was down and dark, gray and cold and raining, with an overwhelming sentiment of how important it was for us to hurry to get done before the thick, black sky gave out with the deluge we all knew was up there. So it was chop-chop at the funeral parlor, one-two-three, let's get rolling to the cemetery, where Mother, Brother, Sissy and I sat on folding chairs right there, graveside, beside the casket, while the new rabbi said his usual stuff about life and death and so on, and it was done in ten minutes, all rise for mourner's *Kaddish.*

Well, everything seemed to me like one more day, like this is what happens on a day like this, and then you go home and whatever happens on a day after a day like this will happen tomorrow. I brought into play the virtues of solitary strength, independence from social norms, values that reflected manhood. It wasn't so tough, and this stuff really wouldn't have been too hard to imagine if I'd ever tried to imagine what it would be like, and so we all stood up and went to spew a little *Kaddish*.

But don't you know the skinny, stunted kid in front got stuck real bad under thick black skies—surrounded by Uncle Izzy and Uncle Sammy and Uncle Rudy and my old man with dirt on the lid already and days of fishing and days at the track and the Steamboat Inn and anything you could ever want in show biz—got stuck so bad the sky cleaved right then and there and turned the *Kaddish* into mush, nothing left but a kid verging on manhood and confusion, choked up fit to die and bawling as loud and big as his old man ever was.

That set them off, every last chop-chop, one-two-three, hurry-hurry goddamn one of them; set them off and set them straight, that this was my old man we were laying six feet under; set them off choking and sobbing maybe more for me than for him, and maybe more than me. But that didn't matter, because it all slowed down then, slowed down and started to look, sound and feel like a funeral for chrissake, and not some goddamn pit stop between gas and groceries.

I didn't go back for thirty years.

❄　　　❄　　　❄

Invasion of the In-Law People

If we hadn't moved, I told Mother for years, I had no doubt, none, zero, that I would have gone to the state university, most likely studied law, returned to the place of my birth and applied, for the first time in generations, my father's family's gift of gab in a gainful, recognizable, lucrative, professional manner. That hit home. In her heart she wanted a lawyer.

In her heart she had wanted a doctor. She gave up on doctoring when Tuffy, our dog, got sick on a bad rat and nearly croaked. When the vet punctured a fold of Tuffy's skin with a turkey baster and squeezed in two quarts of glucose, I faded white and fainted dead away. I was eight or nine, and a major frame from Life Comix is the one where I'm coming to, with a nurse dabbing her wet rag on my forehead, and Mother hovering just behind her, mumbling prayers for points and a future infused with safety and good health, and following up with, "Never mind, you'll be a lawyer."

She went through a brief stint, maybe a year or two, knowing in her heart I would be an engineer. It only made sense, I got so pale at the sight of blood, and blowing up all my model airplanes and riverboats meant that I was good at demolition, or something advanced like that—it must have. Surely it couldn't mean that her son was a borderline pyromaniac, a marginal anarchist already. Could it?

It was the year between the divorce and the funeral that Brother and Sissy and I actually felt a sense of relief, because the yelling had stopped. Maybe I subliminally missed the noise, so I blew up all my models, motivated dreamily by an inner need for violence, a hunger for the attention of worried elders. Maybe not. I don't know. I suspect I was just a kid who enjoyed blowing the shit out of my old toys, and Mother thought I was a genius.

When I announced that a man on TV had said the All American Soap Box Derby was open to all boys between eleven and fifteen, and that I had decided to build a race car and win, she knew I would win, I'd so thoroughly displayed my genius in engineering. And she began telling everyone that engineering was the field of excellence God had had in mind all along.

The Soap Box Derby was more innocent then, in '60 and '61, before the little guy who won the whole shebang in Akron, Ohio, got busted for cheating. The little guy didn't just cheat, his race car had been wired to an electromagnet hidden in the nose. The switch was a button right on the top edge of the cockpit cowling, so that assuming the position—the race position, it was everyone else who took it in the ass—the little guy pressed the button with the front of his helmet. The blocks on the starting ramps that held the race cars in place were made of metal; so when they dropped forward, the little guy's car got sprung forward, launched, so to speak, and he got the jump on every other little guy in the All-American Soap Box Derby Grand Championship. Akron, then, was like Mecca to boys in the United States of America. Then came the fall, which was taken as a sure sign of the times and put everyone in a funk. It was a milestone in All-American history, possibly notable as the end of innocence, at last.

None of that involved me, though. After the big bust and a thorough investigation, the little guy's car was estimated to have cost about twenty thousand dollars, once you factored in hourly rates for the wind tunnel tests, the forty-layer, clear-coat, custom-epoxy finish, just like on the new Corvettes then.

The body on the little guy's race car was cold molded, a professional lay-up by the United States of America Armed Forces, where the little guy's dad worked. Both the little guy and his dad really wanted to win. The guy on the news, who reported the scandal, said with a long face that they had missed the whole point.

Not me. The real limit on cost when I was a kid was twenty bucks, and your old man wasn't supposed to arrange wind tunnel tests or cold molds or any of that perfection crap. Your old man was supposed to help you, to tell you how things are built, as necessary.

I didn't have the twenty bucks, and my old man was out of town by then. But I'm certain that if he'd been available to help me, he would have mixed a highball and sat down and told me anything he knew that might be of service. That was according to the rules. And even though some people questioned his moral turpitude over the years, he was a far cry from the civic club, Mr. Community guy who taught his kid how to win the whole thing by cheating.

I only had twelve bucks, but that was enough to get started. I paid eight for a two-inch oak floorboard, and four more for all the hinges, eye bolts, L bolts, screws, cables, and stuff, because that was way too much hardware to steal. I stole the plywood, though, with Tuffy, at night. He was lookout.

My old man sent me four bucks more and promised to be there to see me race.

For six months Tuffy and I spent every extra hour in the garage figuring the thing out and bolting on parts, or bolting on parts when I couldn't figure it out. Brother came out to the garage sometimes to smoke cigarettes and mess my stuff up, because he was getting fat the same year I was building my racer. And smoking cigarettes in the garage was a statement; it said he didn't give a rat's ass about anything; in fact, it said, his indifference was so thorough that he could go ahead and get fat and still not care. Sometimes he even inhaled.

But my rebellion was in the racer. I would win the All American Soap Box Derby like a kid out of nowhere and go on to be famous, and rich, and then, you know, I would be a hero forever—me, the littlest anarchist, with cheerleaders and ticker-tape parades all the time and everything. Brother's smoking didn't help my rebellion, with all the smoke mixing in with the sawdust, and nobody really knowing how to nail one of these things together anyway.

Tuffy and I stole a steering wheel from a junk-yard Studebaker before learning that you didn't use a real steering wheel from a car but an Official Soap Box Derby Steering Wheel from your Official Soap Box Derby Wheel Kit. Everyone said I was such a dumb shit. Wind tunnels, cold molding; I was laying out sections of Masonite cut with a handsaw, looking forward to the day I could paint the sonofabitch, with a brush, because I thought that was how things got painted. I didn't even know you had to be careful choosing the paint, because sometimes in fine print under the color they put *Flat*, in case some dummy wanted paint that dried dull as dog shit. You had to get *Gloss*. No big deal, we scored some gloss paint with the money we made from a few extra nights out stealing soda bottles that were good for four cents each then on the deposit.

But the money problem couldn't be solved with soda bottles. The money problem was worse than the giant, clunky, Studebaker steering wheel, which was only an embarrassment. The money was an obstacle. Official wheels were another twenty bucks. That's why you needed a sponsor. I got one, the 500 Platolene gas station next door to Diamond Avenue Liquors—my old man had gone into the packaged liquor business after diamonds. It didn't work out so good, and the divorce came at the tail end of the liquor business, but even a year later the guy who ran the 500 Platolene gas station was still calling to see if Mother was okay. I don't know if she wanted to go out with the 500 Platolene guy or not, but she was acutely aware of the social consequences, because the divorce wasn't final, but it was pending, and that was back when more people didn't get divorced than did. Besides that, she probably figured the old man would shoot him, no pending about it. Still the 500 Platolene guy called, like guys have through the ages and will into the future. So I waited by the phone, then I hit him up for twenty bucks. What could he say? No?

A few months after that it was done—gloss black with a big fireball on top and 500 Platolene decals under the cockpit. I got some of those brass letters you nail onto your mailbox post and nailed Comet on the back, both sides. It wasn't bad, and not too crooked, but I was still worlds away from wind tunnel testing, cold molding, and clear lacquer finish.

I only took the thing off the sawhorses a week before the race, only rode it down the driveway with Brother pushing to test the steering and the brakes at three miles per hour. Everything was perfect, I thought—I hoped, because frankly the thing scared me shitless. Brother said we should run it down the street, but I said no; I didn't want anything to break until it was absolutely necessary.

So on race day, with more and bigger butterflies in my stomach than could possibly be healthy for a kid, with Mother and Sissy and Brother and everyone I knew watching on the side of the road called Casson Hill, assuming the position, I knew as close to nothing as I've ever known. Win and lose didn't mean shit, I just wanted to get to the bottom of that long, endless, forever, goddamn hill.

I'd never even heard of a critical concept of racing—wheel alignment. And getting to the bottom took on new meaning about ten feet off the ramp, when Comet pulled hard left, and I had to pull hard to the right, but not as hard as I pulled, because I was only eleven and didn't know any more about driving than I'd seen in cartoons, so my racing debut was mostly on two wheels, clearing the roadside of pedestrians faster than Godzilla did when he clomped right through downtown.

My old man waited at the bottom of the hill. He didn't run out of the way like everyone else. He stood there with a thumbs up. I lost. What a relief.

During the year after my downhill debut, Mother told everyone I was going to be an engineer, because I was so gifted with my hands. I built another Soap Box Derby racer the next year, way smarter by then, knowing exactly where to steal the plywood, saving time not stealing a steering wheel, getting the sponsor money with a phone call, because the 500 Platolene guy hadn't given up, still wanted to know how Mother was doing. And I had learned on a single morn-

ing, my first race day, that The All American Soap Box Derby is not
for boys but for frustrated fathers. Twenty bucks my ass. You either
used fiberglass or you were out of it—that shit cost fifty all by itself.
But you couldn't show all the receipts—you had to cheat, kind of. So
you had all these guys and their fathers showing up with little race
cars that looked like miniature Maseratis and Jaguars, built for $19.89,
with the father saying, "Gosh, we had eleven cents of room left over.
Uh ha!" Right. Cheating sonsabitches. That was cool—by then I was
pushing twelve and had my paper route and plenty money, enough
for a racer and a half if I wanted it.

My second racer was sleek, rounded instead of squared, with an
extremely threatening skull and crossbones on top and flames all
around it; I was radical by then. I knew about wheel alignment then,
too, kind of, so I took an extra few minutes to eyeball real careful so
the back wheels looked pretty damn lined up with the front wheels.
The bigger problem, as always, was the weight issue. You were
allowed two-hundred-fifty pounds total, but most of the boys went
one-fifty and could get their race cars to go a hundred pounds easy.
The first year I didn't care about weight, I only wanted to get it done.

The second year was different. I nailed about thirty pounds of
eight-penny nails into the floorboard and then made some enormous
fins out of scrap oak, and then loaded all the empty spaces with
screws and bolts and stuff. I still only went two-twenty, but what the
hell else could I do? I weighed over ninety by then, which made me
part of the weight-rule anachronism, requiring the puniest kids to
drive the heaviest cars. My race car was a small tank, and I really
didn't have time the second year to look too far into brake technology; anybody in my way was going down.

My second Soap Box Derby was my last, in my last summer in
Southern Indiana, and I drew a first heat against a kid who was already
fifteen and a heavy favorite to win the whole thing. He was so big, so
tall, so old, so manly and with a racer so... so everything right that
the run down the hill was only a formality. He walked over to me
before our race. He looked down at me and ruffled my hair and told

me not to worry, just run the best race I could, and when it was over he would show me everything he knew so I could do better next year. I told him to save it for later, and maybe I'd be happy to show him a few things.

He laughed, and he got way out front right away but I couldn't have cared less, because last year I only learned about fear; this year was the face of death, because two-twenty and fiberglass was so much faster than one-eighty and Masonite, I not only cleared the roadside of innocent bystanders, I looked like Joe E. Brown yelling, "Whoooooaaaaahh!" as my asshole slammed shut and the whole pile of boards and bolts and nails and screws and oak trees and official wheels set up a vibration, accelerated into a rumble, threatened delamination, and went from there to a terrible vision; I knew I was going over, going airborne, going up in flames.

It wasn't so embarrassing, losing so bad to such a favorite, and nearly dying. I practically kissed the ground once I got the goddamn thing to stop—to stop dead from forty miles an hour at three inches above the pavement, all heavy boards and fiberglass and bolts with no suspension, no airbags. I had the shakes at the bottom, or a half-mile past the bottom, because I followed the instructions on the brakes, but never really got the hang of that either, and the back edge of the cockpit put a gash across my back from the pressure of both feet jamming the brake pedal up front.

My fiberglass work needed refining too, since most of it that year ended up on my skin and what made it onto the race car had these funky air pockets that swelled up under the epoxy.

My old man waited at the bottom again and came over and picked me up like I was only six or seven and kind of embarrassed me about that. I expected him to tell me to go pop that fifteen-year-old sonofabitch right in the nose, but he didn't. He only said that was the finest thing he ever saw in his whole life.

The kid who beat me went on to win every heat that day, except the last one. He lost to a kid whose father really knew how to cheat, whose racer looked insured, like a little bitty backyard project put together by NASA. But the promise was kept; I got shown some cheating techniques that made my eyes bulge, that made me know instantly that I could win, next year. The kid who beat me was fifteen, so he could not race in the All American Soap Box Derby again, ever. I would be his legacy, his heir. His biggest advice, though, was, "Boy, you got to align your wheels." And he said he would show me how, just call him up. Was I excited?

But the old man died six months later, and we moved away from Southern Indiana. And Mother finally got the picture, that engineering was not nearly as promising as the law. A man should study the law, especially a young man as gifted as I obviously appeared to be.

I can only surmise that Mother's focus on the doctorhood or engineering or the law came from first-generation immigrant values, from a hunger for legitimacy, for a lucrative profession that could be respected by society. That notion was simpler then, before anyone questioned the intelligence, honor, or respectability of doctors and lawyers. But Mother's hope for a lawyer in the family was based on her belief, her perception, what she knew could be. What she possibly denied was that a formal profession would be unlikely for a child with so little exposure to formality, to structure, with so much exposure to free form.

It's hard to imagine a parent as old as my old man if you didn't have an old parent yourself. He was born in '00, forty-eight years before me. I suppose it doesn't make that much difference now, but he was pushing sixty when I was a child, when all the other kids had fathers half that age, fathers with well-defined careers, fathers who were extremely civic-minded. I didn't care. I would rather have hung out in bookie joints on the river, or at the track, eating hotdogs, drinking lemonade and beer and carousing with guys who had real life written all over them, rather than listen to a gang of suits talk about the great community we lived in while stroking profits for all they were worth. I knew the score—I didn't fault anyone for pursuing money, only for what they gave up to make more money.

And I sure as hell would rather remember stalking timber rattlers with my Ben Rogers bow and my dog. We got so far from home you couldn't see anything but green, and decades later those still moments rippled only by a leaf rustling, a breeze stirring, a great dog reading a scent arc as clear and memorable as if they hung on the wall matted and framed. I was luckier, I think, than the boys who sat in on Rotary meetings and learned all about shaking hands, then listened to their fathers' friends talk bullshit that was more easily forgotten than not—and don't think a kid doesn't know when it's solid bullshit coming down.

But everyone in Mother's family pounced all over the age issue from the outset to the end, loved to sling the rhetoric in innocence and loathing—*Isn't it a little late in life for him to get a job? When's he going to make something of himself? What is it exactly that he did, all those years?*

They asked with sincere, acute concern—Flossie, her son, his wife. His wife was The Devilment. Mother gave her that name; it fit, and it stuck.

They asked as if steady income for my old man would somehow make a better life for them, as if a real back-breaker of a dull-ass job, one that a man could only hate, was what separated my old man from honor. They wailed, as if they cared about more than pointing out the terrible, woeful, lamentable, incurable choice that Mother had made.

Mother understood their motive, which was dominance and positioning for Flossie's dough, but it took Mother years to see that it was Flossie and her son, not just The Devilment, who focused on keeping her down. Because Mother was loyal to Flossie and Flossie's son, loyal to a fault. She had grown up with them, was raised in their language.

So questions of purpose and gainful employment were first asked about my old man, and then years later they were asked about me—by The Devilment and her devilish cohorts. Then I knew I had inherited the family business. I faulted these people for being spiritless, for being so far from the God they so superficially strove to please. They were petty, dull, lifeless, without imagination, and they flat insisted that you be the same way, under them, because they'd started before you.

At the time I first heard the cross-examination on the value of my old man's existence, however, the questions were gnats on a dog's ass—easily shooed away. My old man got to Mother's family in a way they couldn't tolerate. He ignored them, couldn't see them, couldn't hear them. And it wasn't a show. He honestly and sincerely had so little regard for them that they alone could never get a rise out of the hottest temper in the Western Hemisphere. Flossie wailed and moaned, bit her knuckle (not really) and tore her clothing (not really)—this, out of nowhere, as if a major catastrophe had just come through the front door, all because life was what it was, and Mother was married to my old man. He couldn't even understand his mother-in-law, except that she wanted something big, and she ranted and raved about deference, respect, jobs, hard work, pain, toil, sacrifice, money, and all the things she wanted to see more of and all the things she wanted less of, if she was ever going to give her approval. She assumed the world needed her approval.

My old man figured she was up to something vile, but it was a harmless vileness, one that was so petty it couldn't even qualify for a pop in the nose, and *that* was small. He sluffed her off too, gave her a nickname: Flossie. She hated it, so it stuck. I now have a fat, red chicken named after her. Flossie the chicken is just as greedy and keen on pecking those closest to her, but she has a more even disposition and is certainly less calculating, more attuned to nature.

The other Flossie was born in 1898, making her a peer of my old man, but it was an equality that never worked out. While he cruised both sides of the Ohio River hustling up a buck or two here, a good time there, she was just off the boat from Austria. She remembered her first words off the boat, in America: *Gib'm zein inzuts sucre.* She remembered them ad nauseam all through my childhood, just so Brother and Sissy and I would know how the world works. *Give me back my sugar,* she demanded of the man on the dock in '05 or '09, because he wanted to look at the bowl of sugar she'd carried all the way from Austria, unless she stole it from the galley—which seems likely since her son stole paper towels from public bathrooms and tiny bars of soap from airlines to carry home to his family as one more score against a society he knew was out to fuck him—matches, toothpicks, swizzle sticks, napkins, cheap pens, towels, ashtrays, anything that wasn't nailed down was what the dirty rotten world couldn't keep him from taking home, by the handful if the conniving bastards weren't looking—this, even after the time of Mercedes.

But back on the boat years earlier, young Flossie knew in her heart the customs man wanted to steal the bowl of sugar from her, so she stepped foot on America wailing and lamenting.

Gib'm zein inzuts sucre was a certain communication among Mother's family in public when they wanted to convey to each other that the dirty low-down bastards were present. The dirty low-down bastards were all the people in the world who were not part of Mother's family, who would try to steal your sugar sure as they would need to breathe, and if you don't believe that, who cares? Because you're just one of them anyway.

Another catchall for the rest of the world was: *Remember the lady on the streetcar.* This phrase evolved soon after Flossie came to America and one day rode the streetcar with her mother, and only one seat was left. Don't you know Flossie said, "You take it."

"No no," Flossie's mother said. "Don't worry about me. I'll stand up in the dark. (And the cold—and the pain, toil and sacrifice.) You take the seat."

"No no, you take it," Flossie said. And so on in selfless volley until a big black woman, a *schwartze grosse* of all people, took the seat. So Flossie and her mother had to stand up the whole way, because the lady had taken what was rightfully theirs, right under their noses, because they'd become so wrapped up in concern for each other, they flat forgot to grab the goods quick and secure the goods against a world that waited beak and claw to prey upon them. Oh, they learned their lesson that day.

Of course, it was a lesson for the ages, and even when Flossie reached the skeletal phase of life she still harped at her family, *Remember the lady on the street car!* Flossie admonished her audience regularly, just before taking what she would sooner have the others take, if the lady wasn't forever and always looming, ready to swoop and steal what the family never hurt anybody to get.

I grew up with it, too, learning how to keep a wary eye in front, a wary eye behind, and a wary eye to either side, and maybe that's good, because wary and aware are from the same root, but then aware is so much more benign than wary, so much freer from paranoia. I was out in the world for years before I realized that the world could open its arms in sweet embrace every bit as easily as it could steal your shit and knock you down.

Ah, life is rich with paradoxes for a family like that one. Harking back, it's hard to remember when Flossie reached the skeletal phase—oh sure, she shrank down good at eighty, and another notch or two at ninety, but she was always close to the bone in the spiritual sense. Among God-fearing people, those who understand the awful void and terror, she stood above the crowd—above her family, too, on this score—so He would know for sure and for certain that She was most righteous of all.

She mumbled prayers first thing in the morning to last thing at night, and for all things in between; every time she ate, took a leak or a dump, looked outside or heard a sneeze in the distance. She threw away a wad of dough every time she baked. I asked her why one time, and she laughed, still mumbling the incantation for throwing dough away. She said it was for the poor people in Israel. I looked down into the trash and asked what good it would do them in there. She stopped laughing, clucked her tongue, hit the remaining ball of dough with vengeance and a rolling pin and said, "Go. Go see what Mommy wants." Mommy didn't want anything.

All I got from Flossie was a nonstop example of praying and baking. A small child taking her at face value could easily see her as she wanted to be seen, as fulfilling the spiritual needs of her family. But as

the child grew, Flossie's needs gained dimension; she needed deference, then tribute. She was as guilty as a missionary for her intoler-
ance to those different from herself—for her indictment of my old
man, because he failed to conform to her dogma. And she advised
Mother relentlessly over the years that he was poison, no good, rotten, a bad choice, and on and on. But I can't remember anything
Flossie ever showed me or taught me that bore me up in a time of
need, that instilled strength in the face of extreme hazard.

She baked in the selfless wee hours, hard, crusty bakery sprinkled
with sugar—this for sweetness, so nobody would forget the source of
sweetness. We sometimes watched. Sometimes we wanted to help,
but she would shoo us off in urgent anxiety, "No! No no. Go. Go
away." If it was morning, she would give us orange juice, in exchange
for the prayer over orange juice.

With extravagant fanfare she would prepare a rare cultural delicacy,
grievens or *grievenous*. She pared the skin and fat from the chicken, separated the pure fat, melted it over low heat and stored it in the fridge
for later when she would rewarm it to higher viscosity, and spread it
on bread and then sprinkle it generously with salt. Oy. This is *schmaltz*.
Its popularity waned after the discovery of its direct correlation to
massive coronary.

She diced the remaining fat and skin and fried it in a pan with salt
until it shrank and shriveled. More decocted pure fat resulted, but was
it wasted? Not on your life—it was added, carefully, to the schmaltz
jar. The pieces of skin and fat left were then fried a little longer with
another moderate salting—and a diced onion, if it's a little bit fancy
you'd like to get. In lay terms, it was a slice of tough bread oozing
with chicken fat, heavily salted with more fatty pieces of chicken skin
on top. And, if you were really loved and cared for, then the fat
dripped off all the edges at once and ran down your chin and forearms almost as fast and thick as it rolled down your gullet. It was eaten
fast for minimal waste, and to allow time for more before the angina
kicked in, and tradition allowed for maybe a cold Coca-Cola to cut
the grease and heartburn.

I didn't think Flossie was out to give us coronaries any more than any other grandmother who sought to give their families a special something to eat, like, say, bacon-grease gravy and biscuits, yum. I thought she was only doing the best she could in hard times, until years later when I saw her objective, her assessment, her ability to discount Mother as a human being. Then I thought she was out to give us coronaries from the beginning. Most bad blood tends to be retroactive like that.

Besides serving up the greasy dough balls, Flossie served up pride in her son. Flossie's son would have been a Golden Boy. God and Flossie knew it, knew he could be a major league pitcher, or... or... or... Well, he could have been, if not for all those bastards cheating him out of his chance. And, well, he had to take care of his family because his father had croaked, and anyway, games were for kids. He in fact had the same difficult childhood I had, and many boys had. The difference was, he took his difficulty as a personal affront from the world, turned away from its benevolent potential, never tried, never left home for any longer time than it took to make a sales call— that was his adventure. And call he did, on all of that small corner of the world and all its cheating bastards. He knew the best revenge. He was, after all, Flossie's son.

He became the person he would be at an early age and showed his fearful, devious essence to me when I was only thirteen. Maybe a child knows some things for once and for all time; maybe it was only me. I could view Flossie's son from any angle and clearly see that a day would come when only one of us would remain standing. I could easily dislike the guy, but knowing we would face off was not a rational knowing, it was instinct, as easy as feeling the barometer drop with no gauges around. His presence from the very first days after my old man died was the presence of ill will, of foul intention, of decomposition of blood ties.

Mother moved us to St. Louis soon after my old man's funeral, even though I swore to God I wouldn't go; and if she made me go, then I'd leave as soon as I could. The days of migration dialogue between

Mother and me remain the most vociferous exchange of our lives, highlighted by tantrum, yelling, stomping, threat, hiding out and, in the end, surrender.

She weakened; I went. What can you do at thirteen?

The difference then between St. Louis and Southern Indiana was between suburban sprawl and deep woods. We arrived in town a week before my first day of high school.

Flossie's son—Mother's brother—lived in St. Louis. My old man never liked him, and moreover never respected him, which is difficult for a child to understand, since anyone older was supposed to be respectable. A few years fix that understanding, and maybe I knew intuitively what my old man didn't like: Mother's brother had no soul, was greedy and nervous with the instinct of a sniveler, an ass-kisser, and had no personality at all, except for that stereotypical behavior that often gives Jews a bad reputation. His only bright moments, those events that put a sparkle in his eye and a smile on his face, were in the stories he told of struggle and survival in the mean streets, the bloodthirsty jungle that was suburbia.

Mother's brother was in the rag business; buy low, sell high. Say, for example, Hymie Glick tried to fuck him out of twelve bucks on a three-hundred-dollar order. He'd pretend not to notice, and he'd smile with profuse gratitude to Hymie Glick and all the Glicks, and then he'd short-count Hymie eighteen bucks, or else add on a carrying charge. In retelling the story his face would gain color, grow animate—Oh, the Glicks never *dreamed* of the kind of operator they were dealing with here.

Not that he invented this behavior; he was too dull. But since it was an accepted stereotype, and since the petty meanness of the effort came natural to him, he accepted it as natural; he had to accept something as natural.

My grandmother taught her son the stereotype, brought it with her from Eastern Europe. My old man never respected her either, she was so much holier than everyone else with her *oy yoy yoy* litany, her dawn-to-dusk incantations that brought her closer to God and thereby a little bit higher than everyone else; and especially higher than a crude lush like my old man, especially when he called her Flossie; and extra especially when he called her a crazy bitch Jew whore, which was a common sentiment of many men toward their mothers-in-law for many years.

My old man mostly kept it to himself, except for the time she took Brother and me to Services on a visit to St. Louis and got so involved in the fray of point-scoring with the other top contenders for God-proximity that she lost us. We were four and five, and we walked home twelve city blocks crying our eyes out because all the cars kept honking at us, maybe because we crossed all the busy streets against the lights.

So the stage was set early for the play between my old man and his in-laws. Flossie's son bore a mutual and intense disrespect toward my old man, more intense, because it was motivated more by fear than rational values. Anyone with half a wit could see the temper and the fists on my old man from a block away. I remember laughing as a child when Flossie's son would show up, and he would always remind me of our dog getting caught on the couch. They'd both grin, show fang good-naturedly, tail between the legs, the dog and Flossie's son.

So maybe the conflict between us and Flossie's son was foregone; maybe he only waited for his chance to claim dominance. It was hard to believe, because we were only children, after all. But the day came when we sat down for lunch at Flossie's son's house on that very first week in St. Louis, a few months after the funeral. I thought it was just another day, just another lunch, but it wasn't. It was premeditated.

The subject of money came up. Mother still needed milk on the table for her children.

Flossie's son ranted and raved about the lying, cheating, dirty, rotten, no-good *momzers* out there trying to do him in every day. He wailed. He flailed. He huffed and puffed and got red in the face, over money, as a concept. And like it was on cue, the doorbell rang—the doorbell on the six-panel, glass-inlaid, larger-than-life front door of the '50s ultra de luxe triple-split-level, ranch-style, sprawling house in the suburbs with the two-car garage with the Imperial and the Cadillac, a house similar to the other two hundred houses on the surrounding grid of streets known as Heatherwood Heaven or some such fa fa shit.

I'll get it! he bellowed, jumping up, striding to the door, swinging it open on a little boy who flinched and asked in fear if Barba could be in a bicycle race. *Oh, a bicycle race! Barba! You want Barba to be in your bicycle race! You want your bicycle race to be the best! So you want Barba in it! Yes!* Barba, his daughter, was nine, already destined to be the First Woman President of the United States of America, already showing symptoms of her family's disease, and maybe a few other diseases as well. Flossie's son would yell out, *Look at her! Will you just look at her! The First Woman President of the United States of America!* Then, all crimson-faced and pushing the edge of premature stroke, he would indicate Barba with his palms up. She would sit there smiling, pale, frail, and blemished, awkward and uncertain but knowing in her heart that yes, she would be the First Woman President of the United States of America. It was a joke, but it wasn't a joke to her, and she would scream bloody murder if anyone failed to endorse her candidacy, her nomination, her election, her benign but magnificent rule.

It's not a joke! It's not! It's not! It's not! she would shriek, much as a victim of child abuse might shriek—*He promised!* she would scream, running to her room, flailing, then collapsing on her canopied bed with authentic Queen of the Raj satin flouncing, goosedown comforter, hand-filigreed corner posts and Serta Majestic Sleeper mattress. She would flail, kick, and rant in a flood of heartbreak and tears.

She was simply flawless—*Look at her! Would you... just... look... at her!* Over and over Flossie's son would beseech those of the mortal pale to behold her perfection. She was Barba, her name contracted in infancy to better facilitate her limited enunciation. The name stuck, because perfection is impossible to improve upon. Barba went into a basking squirm when Flossie's son rallied the masses to behold her beauty. The squirm lost its roundness when the praise played out; she twitched anxiously for more, her eyes darting, seeking the source of confusion.

Barba had learned to love others as well as herself, and she proved this at age six by entering her younger brother's room at night, grasping him by the hair on his head, yanking him out of his bed, then dragging him down the hall to tell Flossie's son and The Devilment, "Dadad doesn't feel good."

She spoke truth; young Dadad did not feel good but in fact suffered rigorous readjustments of the brain. Dadad (pronounced Dah-dahd) was goo-goo talk for David, after Flossie's first husband, father of Flossie's son.

Barba wasn't exactly beaten, not like Dadad was, but she got yelled at so loud that she learned to love Dadad more gently. She introduced Brother and me to Myrtle a few years after that. Myrtle was Dadad's dick, which Barba would take out of his little shorts for him and work like a two-stroke piston, both of them giggling, until they both went wide-eyed and short of breath, and Myrtle went to an inch and a half.

Barba would vehemently deny her games with Myrtle by her teenage years, but Myrtle remained a source of companionship and good humor. Nobody actually thought Dadad suffered permanent brain damage from being dragged from his bed and down the hall by his head; they called him a late bloomer, a slow starter, drooling and sucking his thumb into third grade. *Look at him!* Flossie's son implored. *Would... you... just... look at him!*

And to think, we were the country cousins. We thought Barba and Dadad were strange, but we only saw them once a year or less, on trips to St. Louis, and we were all kids, so it was easy.

But on that day when Flossie's son stood at the front door, in the middle of another Gothic lunch and fusillade, history was made. Flossie's son cried *Yes!* The little boy at the door cringed but stood firm and finished his presentation, saying that the bicycle race cost five cents to enter, for muscular dystrophy. It was the perfect cue for Flossie's son, as long as we were on the subject of Mother's need for milk on the table for her children, as long as her (worthless) children were there to see the show:

Five cents! Five cents! You knock on my door and talk bicycle race and Barba. You want your race to be the best! And now you ask for five cents!—He was yelling again, in case those of us in the kitchen uninitiated in the treacherous ways of the world—a world he fought through every day—had not yet seen him in action. *You think you can come around here like Mr. Smart Guy, trying to steal my money? And get Barba in your bicycle race, too, besides getting my money? No! No no no! And Barba doesn't even want to be in your race!*

Then he slammed the door and came back to the luncheon table, gratified at this perfect illustration of his point, money, after touching on deceit and the dirty, rotten no-goodniks out there ready to steal you blind.

He was under pressure to help his sister, Mother, and he honest-to-God didn't want to.

Next came discipline. He said something about fat old farts and the good-for-nothing, lazy, drunken bum, and times were gonna change, oh boy, they were gonna change and so on, clearly delineating a profile as shocking and permanent on my young brain as that of a branding iron on a calf's flank.

Flossie's son disgorged an indictment of bitterness and hatred festering inside him for years, while his wife watched attentively, nodding slowly like a grand inquisitor. The Devilment watched with her nose held high, much as a new First Lady watches her husband take the oath, in awe and wonder, and maybe in this case with a dose of wicked glee. The two children begat by Flossie's son and The Devilment watched wide-eyed and slowly nodded with her, brain-soaked already, as children so easily can be, especially children from that gene pool, in those shadows.

I don't remember if I was just under a hundred pounds on that day in '62 or just over, but Flossie's son was about six feet and one-seventy easy, so a pop in the nose had the same limitations it always had.

Maybe that was when I first discovered that a good clean pop in the nose doesn't necessarily require a fist. I lost my voice, my thoughts falling into disarray, realizing suddenly, brutally, that the world was not as it had been presented these last few months—not a place where people wished you well, conveyed sympathy for the passing of your father, expressed belief that you would make it and make it big, because your mother was as strong and good as she was.

No, truth was traumatic, doled out wholesale by Flossie's son, who turned everything upside down, whose mouth hole overflowed with the dark side of human nature, the side a boy must see before understanding the many dimensions of men.

Flossie's son gained momentum, going from fat, old, drunk, worthless, to no-good sonofabitch, dead at last, thank God, *I should have popped him when I had the chance.* We could only stare for the few moments that became a chasm, a speechless, thoughtless disbelief that he was actually talking about our old man.

When I found my voice it was high and then low and then high again, but it wound up easily, let fly with no hesitation:

"You never told him that to his face, you chickenshit fucker."

It was eloquence 1, impact 10. I was thirteen, he was late thirties, and sure enough he wanted to beat me, as in beat me up, as in child abuse; Flossie's son lost his shit in a blink. He was up, leaning forward and over my way in a heartbeat for a solid backhand to the face; talk about discipline. My next move was pure instinct—point the fork up at the oncoming forearm rather than down at the cold beans, maybe only in self-defense. Bull's-eye, the fork didn't give but stuck in his arm, and the big prick was screaming mayhem and death as the undisciplined youth ducked under the table—easy for a small person—and scrambled quick out the door while the big prick grabbed the frying pan and chased after. What was he going to do? Bean me with a frying pan?

That day marked a break in blood ties, a rift that would never heal but in time would harden with scar tissue that would grow numb. All parties would adapt, except for Mother, who believed reconciliation was just around the corner, because Mother valued family above all;

filial devotion was the ultimate calling. She learned that from Flossie, who wanted to be the dowager Queen, with a maid waiting, on call.

Mother couldn't read the writing on the wall on that day of demarcation in '62, failed to see it for thirty years, hoping a day would come when both her families would sit down together and eat. For thirty years she pressed the issue, buying birthday cards for Sissy and Brother and me to sign so she could send them on Flossie's birthday, calling Flossie's son "Uncle," treating his children like they were her own. But Mother's press and squeeze led to further inflammation, suppuration and swelling, until the boil was lanced.

That fray and chase in that garish suburban kitchen was the scene of the last words I had with Flossie's son for thirty years. I knew his intentions then forever. I also knew that I would grow and he would shrink, knew for all those years that I would be ready, but I didn't gloat over prospects, even though he shrank real good after sixty-five. And don't you know I got a set of weights and some megavitamins and bided my time with discipline.

I knew as well that revenge is a burden that can drag a man down. I told myself I would surround him with compassion when our time came around. I knew the compassion line was bullshit—I wanted to maim the prick. But I knew as well that I would not need to reach for revenge, because he was mean spirited, because a man who wailed on three children who just lost their father had a capacity for evil that was yet to be plumbed. This fellow would be heard from again. This fellow would step up to the line unpushed. This fellow would reach for more. Then the scales would balance.

I only mention the fork and frying pan incident as a transitional point, one of those changes in direction a story or a life can take, affecting the entire chain of events, the outcome, the action, the consequence. The fork and the frying pan served me well—Mother said so, reminding me over the years, every time she perceived unwholesome intentions in her child, as mothers can and will. "But you won!" she would insist. I would not answer nor fathom her assessment of victory. "You stabbed him with a fork!" she would explain.

I sometimes smiled, savoring the stabbing. And I often asked her if she honestly believed that her brother would not one day try to take everything he possibly could from her.

Mother hated that, perceived it as bitterness in me rather than the inevitable truth. "Now forget it!" she often said.

"I'll forget it. Until I'm made to remember."

Maybe I didn't get it, couldn't comprehend her idea of reconciliation, but Mother was more dangerously blind.

Because all that Steamboat Inn saga and feisty brothers adventure, and fishing and drinking and show biz romance flowed sure as the Ohio River through Southern Indiana. That was my old man's side, and that was me. Flossie's son had shown an essence unimagined, incomprehensible to me until then. Stabbing him with a fork was only a childish reaction. I anticipated bigger challenges ahead, bigger stakes, better payout than when I was only thirteen and truths came in simple terms.

Mother was different from her family, who were greedy and hostile, spiritless and audibly pious. But she pointed out a loose cog in me, a strange component, a will and intensity deriving from what she called, "your father." She'd seen it before. She knew its tenor, its intensity, its rigid rule of right and wrong. Mother's subtle advice was that I grow out of it, consider a different personality.

Over and over I told her I would be nice, until niceness didn't work, then I would deliver something else. She could become frustrated with my adherence to those sentiments, but if she was right, it didn't even matter, she was so blind to her brother's potential.

❄   ❄   ❄

Rip Current

The difference between my parents and the places they came from were monumental, as different as up and down, left and right, dream and waking. Maybe Mother and my old man were attracted as opposites; whatever the case, their opposite natures resided in their children in vehement counterbalance.

Mother counseled adaptation and growth, which was not compatible with the fortitude, obstinacy, and pride ingrained from the other side. I tried forgiveness on for size. It has worked well over the years, but it wouldn't fit with Flossie's son. Flossie had property and money. Mother wasn't going to get any, and she didn't even know it.

Mother couldn't understand that anymore than she could understand my old man. I asked her a few times over the years how she ever came to marry him, and she could only look up in wonder and say, "I don't know."

She knew. She was only astonished that things turned out the way they did. The old man wined and dined her, threw lavish gifts at her feet, like the brand new '41 Ford Coupe he parked in front of the house with a pink ribbon around it, because her favorite color was pink even then. He was forty-one, too. She was twenty-three. People must have asked how she could hook up with him. I suspect that she, too, fell into the rough-and-tumble whirl, felt the raw power of a family as free as the countryside with the brothers to set things straight. I think she sensed the monumental potential of the oilfields with their

greasy derricks pumping out the first few bucks that looked porten-
tous of millions. That's how she fell for him, just like women have
fallen for men for ages, for a fantasy that looked like it might come
true.

Every now and then over the years Mother would point out a sil-
ver-haired man here, a fat, bald guy there, here an exec, there a doctor, all with poise and presence—gentlemen, closer to her age,
wealthy and established at the country club, and she would say, "I
could have married him." That's all she would say, yet her face
reflected regret, since any one of those guys would have doubtless
given her a nice house with a big mortgage that would be paid off in
monthly installments like clockwork, would have infused her life with
the stability she'd so sorely missed, with a nice lawn, with shrubs, and
decent furnishings inside with the latest in new decor every few years
and maybe a social circle with some polish, style, and professional
standing. The men she pointed out were men who had known
Mother, possibly courted her in the fashion of the day, in the city.

And here came the country, highballing it down the center of the
road. My old man said he sometimes drove to St. Louis in the morning to see a guy about some money, drove back to Indiana for lunch
and a meeting with a guy about some hardware, then drove back to
St. Louis for the seventh, eighth and ninth at Cahokia Downs, then
a spin by Mother's place and maybe dinner and a few drinks, then
head back to Indiana, home by midnight. Those were the glory days,
with a line on money and more, on vast wealth from oil fields in
Southern Illinois, where the tests were already done, the rigs going
into place, production on the verge, brave new world dead ahead. My
old man saw the opening where nobody else had seen it, then he
made the moves, put the resources together, brought together the
machinery and labor, the money and contracts, stood poised to close
on the deal that comes along every fifty years or so. He was flying
high those days, with a girlfriend just a few miles farther up the road,
who was young enough to match his new prospects perfectly.

He drove fast those days, drank hard, and kept the juggle in the air.

I often tried to comfort Mother when she realized she'd been fooled, seeing those nice, stable men she could have married. I pointed out, "Yes, but then your children would have been dull." That worked, sometimes, sometimes opening her eyes with a sparkle, to the color and verve her adventure had spawned. And she always admitted readily that the old man was good for nothing, except for the children she had. She is such a mother.

Sometimes my attempt at solace failed, and she only looked forlornly my way, as if a little dose of dullness sounded good. She'd subscribed to the adventure, unwittingly, because a girl has no way of knowing the gifts weren't paid for, the oil would never gush, the power would play out. It was like a hoax, the whole promise of marriage and happiness. She got sold a bill of goods, closed hard by one of the best, a guy who wouldn't take no, who dropped to one knee just like the heroes in the movies, weaving his fingers into supplication while his eyes sparkled with insistence, with *Take this ring or I'll break your goddamn neck,* and with soft, silken words had asked, "Will you marry me?"

Many questions arose, prospects for security among them. The old man had never had a job. Never, not once, was he obligated to arrive at a place in the morning and stay there eight hours, and then repeat the process the following day. And he'd been married twice already. I never knew who his first or second wives were or what they were like, except that neither one was Jewish and both could have been waitresses he'd met. So maybe the romantic power he swept Mother away with was balanced out by the homey, stable, respectable characteristics Mother brought to the marriage. And though she denies it now, I think she had a good time with him then, back when the money flowed like oil and affection seemed natural, with so much of the good so close at hand.

Well, it didn't work out. Mother was old school; you get married and have babies and stay home and raise them; no big deal. The husband goes to the office all day and on Friday he gets paid and so on like that, happily ever after. I think Mother soured quick, as soon as she realized that the money issue was not worked out, never had been, most likely would not be. Money supply would remain variable, down-trending. Her lament from my earliest realization that the lament had words in it, was that the old man wouldn't even give her money to buy milk for her children. We never drank much milk, so I guess the lament started when we were babies, and milk was required.

She really never got over the nerve of the thing, of events and circumstance bringing her up short of milk for her children, and the lament continued long after Indiana and the funeral were done and a whole new array of difficulties presented themselves. When Mother finally responded to our request that she keep her complaint to herself, she had settled mentally and emotionally. We'd been in St. Louis a few years by then, and the hardship of raising us by herself eased up some, once Sissy got engaged and Brother and I started on a long line of bullshit buck-and-a-half-an-hour jobs that ate up most of what was supposed to be the fun time of high school.

One time, six or seven years after Flossie's son couldn't catch me with the frying pan, he came through Memphis. Mother was on her second husband then, a match made by Mother's cousins. He was honest and worked every day as a plumber, and he never drank. He was maybe a little bit lackluster but forgivable because he died suddenly a few years into it at fifty-one, from a liver disease, leaving her nothing.

It was Vietnam time and even regular families suffered rifts then. Of course, Flossie's son took the right-wing Republican posture because Brother and I weren't going to Vietnam, and it had been twenty-five years since Flossie's son got shipped home shell-shocked after a week or two of just thinking about front-line action. For years his experience in WWII was referred to briefly as a terrible, terrible ordeal. He was shell-shocked. Shell-shocked was his reason for discharge—shell-shocked; the phrase was bandied about the family as if Flossie's son had actually been near a shell. He had not; he only got shocked. Mother admitted it, begrudgingly, asking, "What difference does it make?"

It made no difference until '68, when Flossie's son became a hawk, because old warriors were qualified. And what a wonderful compensation for the true nature of his courage.

He hadn't shrunk yet then, since he was only late forties or so. But he wasn't about to just march into the kitchen and grab a frying pan and pick up the chase again after six or seven years. I looked over to see if he still had poke holes on his forearm, stretched my neck and rubbed my own forearm, rubbed it in, but I couldn't see, and he didn't get it. I was nineteen or twenty and not yet fully grown but much bigger than I was at thirteen, and things got down real quick to dominance posturing.

Brother and I weren't allowed to smoke joints indoors, so we shared one out back and then came in to catch Rocky and Bullwinkle at five. We had long hair then, and all the other fixings of the day. And there we were, sharing happy hour with our blood enemy. Of course, Flossie's son got up and changed the channel from Rocky and Bullwinkle to the network news, the really good stuff—the napalm and bombings and body counts and first rumblings of village massacres. He stepped back from the tube, turned to face us, spread his legs and folded his arms. It was a challenge to us, to come change it back to our cartoons. And he said something about bums and not going to war like the rest of America, and some other stuff he'd heard back in '41.

We didn't have a problem with the scene because we were stoned to the gills; and back then, the mere color and movement of a thing was just another form of Rocky and Bullwinkle. Still, Mother's curlers were so handy on her dresser, so we went and got them and I had my hair done up so it would look nice for dinner. That unfolded his arms and let him sigh in disgust, but we'd ruined the war on TV for him, and he let Mother know as soon as she came in what a travesty and crime was occurring under her roof.

"Not now," she told him.

Dinner was served way before my hair was done, and I really had no choice but to sit down with my curlers still in. I asked Mother if she thought it would be best if I used a scarf, like she did sometimes when her hair wasn't done and she had to hit the grocery store.

She laughed and said, "Do what you want, but you're not using my scarves."

Brother said he could take the curlers out and still hold everything in place with a hit of Spray Net.

Mother said, "It's hot. Sit down and eat."

It was soup, and like two guys working the same rig so long they need no cue but can read the other without looking, we set up a slurp calliope that was most impressive, but only for a minute before we lost it giggling, because no dope ever made you giggle like Mexican dope. Those were the days, and you can call it acid flashback if you want to, but I still can't recall slurping soup in perfect sync with Brother across the table, me in curlers, him in Spray Net, trying to out-asshole our Mother's asshole brother, without giggling again.

And then Brother pulls a pack of cigarettes from his shirt and offers me one. He'd cockroached the smokes from the bathroom, where Flossie's son had left them while he was trying to take a dump. Flossie's son didn't smoke cigarettes, except for Newport Menthol 100s while he was trying to take a dump. Everyone knew this because he told them with a hearty laugh, "It's the only way I can get a good BM!"

"Oh, God," I said. "You touched those?" Mother agreed, grabbing the Newport Menthol 100s, throwing them in the trash, washing her hands.

Mother came back to the table and said, "Cut it out now." We ate in silence. But that never lasted too long. And Flossie's son complained.

"You threw away my cigarettes."

Mother slammed her spoon onto the table in a rare show of emotion, and there she sat, dazed, confused, overwhelmed by the tedious, endless conflict, glaring at Flossie's son. He laughed. She got up and went to her room. That left Brother and me alone at a dinner table with Flossie's son, who would have stayed and eaten, if only someone would have served him.

We got up, too, and left. I fired up a joint on the way out, as Brother turned to Flossie's son and said, "Now look what you've done." But Flossie's son only ignored us, finishing his soup and moving on to Mother's soup, since it looked like he'd have to make the most of the situation once again. That was our last encounter with Flossie's son for another fifteen years or so.

That was also about the time, in '67 or '69, that I began corresponding with sweet Sue, a girl I'd known in high school.

We'd met in '63, when she was a freshman and I was a sophomore, when she was becoming famous in our school as a focal point of womanly development, and I was stuck solid, as a busboy. She was famous for her square jaw, narrow waist, wide shoulders, sassy attitude—and what a swagger. She went out with juniors and seniors when she was a freshman—this, while I had stood out among the khaki-pantsed, button-down preppies in my pegged jeans and superfly shirts, singing in soft falsetto the half-dozen Marvin Gaye songs I needed to know for my new rock-and-roll band—*Now you chicks do agree... This ain't the way it's supposed to be... Somebo-o-o-dy, somewhere... Uh tell her it's unfair, even talkin' in my sleep 'cause I haven't seen my baby all week... Can I get a wi...itness... Can I get a witness?*

I honestly didn't know what those preppy guys had to talk about, or why they would want to dress in a way that made them look alike, like they went to the same parochial school, which they did, in a sense. You don't get much real-life action or exchange in a suburban high school full of middle-class students who share vast potential for meaning and the arts. Our school had several girl students with enormous breasts, and every now and then word would run down the hallway about a football or basketball player who got to feel one of those pairs of breasts. But the place had no hunger, no curiosity, no imagination, and the talent was lacking, both in the sports arena and in the arts; those kids only wanted very badly to feel like adults, smoking cigarettes between classes in the Smoking Area, where they could engage in visible, neurotic relief, just like their parents. Most of those kids drank gallons of coffee and said hell and damn and shit in class, all of which was allowed at that high school, because melodrama was taken for real drama. Our school strove to be worldly, but it was in a suburb of St. Louis.

I never fit in, which was difficult then, a point of pride now, recalling the strongest bond those preppy boys had, which was a speech pattern designed to sound stupid. I tried it, but it only felt stupid. I finally fit in on the wrestling team, maybe because the guys on the wrestling team understood how to cop a smoke with nobody watching, how to drink a six-pack for the feel of it, how to get into trouble and not care. But high school in general was significantly inferior to what I'd anticipated.

I guess I was as well-known in high school as sweet Sue, a wide-eyed girl with an electric sparkle, perfect teeth, a raw hunger for laughing out loud and anarchy. She was easily the craziest of the pom-pom girls and quite a package, so pretty, so nice, yet so full of spirit. She was as far away from me as uptown is far away from Hoosierville. I only watched from a distance, stranger from a strange land. I shot pool at the student community center most afternoons, because all the hoods and greasers hung out there, and they let me alone most of the time.

Sometimes she and I talked in the hallways, because she liked me, because I made her laugh, because the events of the last couple years had stacked up so deep inside of me that ventilation took the form of bad attitude. Bad attitude fit me much better than the button-down melodrama of that place, like it was meant for me, like it was my style. Truth is, it was; I liked it, felt good in it. Maybe I still do.

I was scheduled for accelerated algebra in ninth grade—in Indiana. But the divorce, the funeral, the move, the Nazi relatives, the dull, preppy boys at the new high school made for a stacked deck. I think the only healthy, sane thing to do was to let it all go, all the well-meaning advice, the teachers, the counselors, the prescription for a normal life in St. fucking Louis—in one ear and out the other is where it belonged.

I liked a pool table, looking down some long green, where life boiled down to simple angles. By the second year of high school I made it into remedial geometry, surrounded by dimwits and chronic failures. Some of the kids in that class had failed fifth grade for chrissake. The teach was a horny, constipated woman who completely understood what caused all evil in the world—testosterone.

She asked questions like, "Class. If the hypotenuse equals the sum of the two sides of an isosceles triangle, then why can't side C be the shortest distance between point A and point B?"

The answer was usually easy, something like, "But it can!" Teach was anxious to paste a gold star on a forehead, but the dummies in remedial geometry just sat there chewing their pencils, wondering how in the hell they were going to make it through the rest of life.

I didn't like gold stars, so I would say something like, "Maybe point A just doesn't care." And all the low achievers would crack up, and I'd get sent to the sophomore counselor's office, who happened to be the new wrestling coach and a personal friend of mine.

I was a problem. Word got around, I'd give the lip to anyone because, like point A, I just didn't care. Some girls take notice of that sort of thing. Sweet Sue laughed out loud when she heard the principal had asked why I was late again, and I told him, because my mother made *farfel* and *tsimmes* three days ago, and he'd be late, too, if he had to take the dump I just took. I made her laugh regular through high school, and when I got to be a senior, she said yes, she'd go out with me, on a date.

I got a head cold a day or so before our date and should have canceled, but I wasn't too sure I'd get another shot, because I was sure she only said yes in the first place for lack of a better offer. And I guess it had come down to first love, she made my heart pound so hard. I wanted sexual experience as badly as the rest of the boys in high school, but not with Sue. With her it was only time—time together that seemed unfathomable.

I could hardly breathe, which was okay through the movie, but then we got to the pizza place on the hill. Besides sniffling and sneezing and looking like a red-nosed reindeer, I discovered that I didn't have enough money to pay the check. She laughed at that, too, and covered me with a five spot. It worked out well, the fever and sniffles so effectively keeping me from even thinking about second base, not even an outside feel much less a dry hump. Females are always so touched when their dates reflect zero hormones until exactly the right moment. Short on cash was endearing, too. It must have been.

We corresponded infrequently for the next three years, then we wrote frequently, maybe because pen pals pick up the pace when their needs rise directly; maybe it was only time, only natural. We wrote through my reefer/co-ed/revolutionary days, through her days at a far-away university, and when I saw her again, she'd filled out, up to full womanhood. Her father had told her he wouldn't pay her way through college anymore, because he thought it was a waste.

I agreed with him on the worthlessness of college, but I didn't think he was sincere. He only wanted out of paying for his daughter's education. He was stiff as a corpse and had just remarried to a woman who hadn't had enough of anything, so money for college was out of the question.

That was about the time I got arrested in Daytona Beach, bringing to the surface my potential for a troublesome life.

Mike Dowd and I got the idea we would spend our lives sailing the Caribbean—got the idea in mid-Missouri. So we headed down in my Volkswagon hippy van. Our college educations were officially over, I'd already proven to be unfit for corporate America, and the war in Vietnam made the world a big waiting room for guys our age then. We could wait around for our invitations to Vietnam, or else we could make contact with the world of adventure we'd read about and analyzed in college. We wanted the high life. We planned to drive to Florida, where the ocean was, where we would sell the hippy van and get jobs on sailboats and sail around. We left a month after classes ended, because I had to get a job and get burned out, so I'd know for certain my deficiencies for the workplace. Then I had to get a wisdom tooth pulled. Otherwise we wouldn't have waited.

Beyond tooth extractions and a little premature burnout, we were free as the wind and way too stoned to give a rat's ass about the future. We were twenty-two with the real-world experience of eighteen-year-olds, over-educated and with no more student deferrals. So it was hit the high seas or crawl through the swamps. Our decision was natural.

We made Daytona Beach late the third day and decided to park on the beach and sleep there and the next day we'd see about a sailboat to get on, so we could begin our lives of adventure. We bought some bread and hotdogs, a can of beans and a can opener and sat in the sand eating a most reflective meal on the sunset of our childhoods, the eve of our real lives. I said I didn't want to get on just any old boat. I wanted a really neat one, like the one in James A. Michener's *Adventures in Paradise.* I felt that our prospects would be much stronger for intrigue, glamour, and beautiful actresses on the high seas if we could get on a really neat boat. I didn't say so, because our quest suffered too much from self-consciousness, and our fantasy was clearly understood.

We were only country boys who didn't know much but who realized that the whole program was a trap to steal your spirit. So we didn't mind looking and acting foolish, if foolishness could lead us out of the land of bondage. We ate and smoked, smoked and ate, pondering tomorrow, when we would sell the van and sign on. When the first stars twinkled, Mike said, "You know, the Moody Blues say thinking is the best way to travel. But most people would still rather take the bus."

"Not us," I said. And we turned in.

But at 3 A.M. the cops shook the van and woke us up and got us outside, hands up, legs spread, cuffed and jammed into a patrol car. All
the other vans that had been on the beach at sundown were gone.
The cops found our hash pipe on the front seat, but what really got
them lathered up was the drugs in my pocket—pain pills, for my
tooth hole.

We got hauled down to the station, where the cops got way down
into anxiety depression, once they verified that the drugs were only
painkillers for a tooth hole. Well, they had us caged already, so they
changed the charge from illicit painkillers to narcotics paraphernalia—the hash pipe. They laughed, telling us not to worry, because a
couple smart guys like us with college educations would be out of the
swamps at Raifford Penitentiary in three to five years maximum, and
we were young enough that our stretched-out assholes would shrink
back up some once we got out.

They gave us a list of lawyers we could call, and they said our asses
were history if we didn't get a good one.

Who's a good one? we asked.

*Why, this man right here is probably the only man in DeLand County who can
save you now.*

The man was Maurice Ligner. We called. He was all hope and
glory—*Oh, gee, we gotta get you guys outa there quick.* It was Friday which
would work out great, he said, because the bondsman couldn't see the
judge until Monday anyway, which would give us time to get our
money together. We would need a thousand dollars each to start. But
we'd already used our single phone call, we said. *Don't worry about a
thing,* said Maurice. *Le'me talk to the boys.*

We spent the weekend in a cell, and the other guys were cordial,
eyeballing us up and down but not threatening. The guys in for a year
or so were trusted to work the cells, bringing meals and orders. The
leader of the trusties was a sharp-featured black from Miami called
Cisco. He stole cars, robbed service stations, fenced jewelry, and he
was open to new ideas. He was counselor and therapist, too, for suburban white guys getting their first dose of reality. He had the cure,

H, cheap and clean—well, reasonable and fairly pure anyway, and it was only stepped on with mush, nothing that would hurt you.

We were disappointed and depressed, so much so that Mike thought the cure would be worth trying. "Not that I expect it to cure us," he said. "But look. We were out for an adventure. Here we are. I think we should give serious consideration to the experiential aspect. I know you can't get addicted with one injection." Cisco had the works, too, and he promised us brand new needles. AIDS was still years away, but still he sensed that suburban white guys liked things brand-new.

"I don't think so," I said. "I think we could die in here."

Mike nodded. "Yes. We could. That's what makes it a rich experience."

We debated the cure a day and a half and would have taken it by Tuesday, but we got out Monday morning.

Maurice showed up immediately after brunch in a twelve-hundred dollar suit and a valise that never got opened. He looked like Jan Murray, wavy hair plastered back with pomade, and he carried on with the cops like a game show host; later he would show us how the game was played. He got us out and arranged for a patrolman to get us to his office, we were so dirty, and anyway, his Porsche only had two seats.

His office had no shingle, only a sign that said *Honest lawyer, one flight up*. Maurice Ligner and the Daytona Beach cops had a small industry going, preying on kids and their parents for thousands of dollars on petty bullshit stuff. The first grand was to get started, to get us into Maurice's office. The next thousand dollars each was to ensure our innocence, and once he spoke with Mother and learned what a promising genius her son was, he put the quick close on her for another grand, to *expunge the record*.

That is, for the third grand, each, someone would remove the file that said we had been charged with a felony, and a grand was dirt cheap, considering that no law school in America would admit a student who'd been charged with a felony, Maurice said. *And just think how much money a lawyer can make*, Maurice said. His law degree from Okefenokee U hung askew on the wall in triple-matt and a dramatic wood frame.

We got put up at a sleazy motel, and I called Mother from a pay phone to tell her not to send more money. We were out, and that was all I needed. I would be out of there by sunrise, as soon as we got the van out of impoundment. I told her Maurice Ligner was a *schnorrer*, a *goniff*, a cheat, and I didn't want to be a lawyer, not now, not ever.

Mother said, "You talk like a crazy man. What did you eat?"

"When? What did I eat when?"

"You get that… truck or whatever it is and you drive it home. You hear me?"

Mother sent the money. It was all she had. She never asked Maurice what the felony charge was because it didn't matter. She paid it quick.

I came home in defeat, with no prospects but the invitation, the swamp crawl. Sweet Sue was there, too, pondering a life of drudgery as a waitress, a college drop-out, because her father would no longer pay.

I asked her if maybe we should share a place down in Columbia, Missouri, where I'd recently finished college and she could finish as well, at the state university. It would be much cheaper than where she'd done her first three years, and I'd help her out since I couldn't do much else anyway, with Vietnam and everything. I'd always had a crush on her, and I remember her then as a fantasy fulfilled, as an untouchable beauty suddenly within reach, as my new prospect for adventure.

We didn't marry until '73 or '74, after shacking up a couple years. Those were the days of women saying yes to guys who said no, and to most other guys, too. But the sex thing with her was different, call it first love, contact above the flesh or beyond it, or something.

Meanwhile her penny-pinching father, who'd changed his name from the original Jewish to the camouflaged suburban, was making a go of it with his new wife, who looked like Victor Mature, especially when she got sloshed and drooled Jew jokes from her gob. My in-laws resented me; I was the two things her father wanted away from—Jewish and broke. I suppose slipping the Hebrew National to his daughter didn't boost my stock. I wanted to tell him that whatever he did, he should try not to think about that part of the situation—ah, but I knew he'd take it the wrong way.

I'd always heard that in-laws could be difficult, and I'd certainly had a good opportunity to observe conflict at that level. Still I was amazed when the wicked stepmother would get all drunked up and hateful. Maybe she knew why she didn't get the high hard one nearly as often as she wanted it—knew that it had to do with manhood compromised, lasting trauma, resentment and regret, or something, and the Jews were to blame for that, too. Maybe she was only a nasty drunk.

When I try to remember something likeable about Father-in-law and his wife, Victor Mature, I can only come up with their love for animals. They had a dog named Sparky, a mini-Airedale, who bounced up and down like he had electric springs in his feet, plugged into 220. Sparky barked and shit on the rug like he had springs in his yap and his asshole, too. Sparky was nervous and dumb, and then dead and replaced by another furry little pogo stick named Sparky. "What a cute, furry little guy," Father-in-law said.

Sweet Sue and I split up maybe six or seven years later, because what looks so familiar, so convenient, what feels so much like home, changes like everything else. And two people in their early twenties have no idea who they will be in their thirties.

I'm not saying my marriage could not have worked; it could have, with tremendous sacrifice, chemical imbalance, square pegs banged into round holes. But why pursue what becomes unnatural?

I did inherit the family business, my old man's approach to life, which is based on the corollary that it's for living, out on the edge with the best view and the best odds on making it with some semblance of spirit left over. Sue was beautiful and talented, maybe like Mother once was, and trapped, more or less, in a low-income, zero-mobility life with a guy who pored over stories every day—a story-

teller. She couldn't relate and certainly couldn't *believe* that all my effort
would turn into money some day. She was only practical.

We had two sets of friends; I found hers cleaned and pressed, conventional, predictable, so nice, so d-u-l-l. She thought mine droll,
unkempt, worthless, bums, colorful maybe, sometimes, but bums. Sue
had a job those days, working promotions for a G-rated state park
in town, for events I considered aggressively wholesome. The place
was fun for the whole family, unless you had any imagination. I kept
my assessments private, because she busted her butt, doing her best;
she brought home the bacon those days, while I whiled away those
days, honing stories. Sue thought I was goofing off, denying reality,
killing time with my worthless friends most likely, and though she
came home most days to a clean house with dinner on the table, she
asked, "What did you do today?"

I told her, "Pages 130 to 142," or I would offer some oblique insight
on dialogue or flashback or something. She stopped asking. We both
knew the score. Just like the oil wells my old man staked his future
on, my gushers were only fictional, my drilling compulsive. We came
to the fork in the road, politely, not really understanding how the
other could actually want that kind of a life, but willing to tolerate the
other's calling as we parted, maybe because of old love, lingering
fondness.

By then it was '78 or '80 already and feeling way past time for
another move. Mother said good, at last, I could move back to St.
Louis. I told her a few times, those first twenty years or so away from
Southern Indiana, that she'd made a serious error in judgment by
moving me away from my natural home—that in my childhood you
could blindfold me, put a pillowcase over my head, spin me around,
roll me down a hill, lead me every which way through a bunch of
somersaults, take me for a drive in the car, and I could still point due
north—with the blindfold still on—and if that wasn't a natural, mystical bond with the land of my birth, the land of my ancestors, then
what was? In St. Louis I couldn't even point downtown without a free-

way sign to show me. Because I had no bond to the place, mystical or practical, so it wouldn't be St. Louis that I'd be moving to.

Mother said she'd buy me a compass if I was getting lost around town, and besides, she said, I never smoked that LSD in my childhood. But I told her that moving from Southern Indiana was the first step in a lifetime of wandering for me, that her ongoing anxiety over all the places I lived in, all the packing up, cutting ties and moving on, all the displacement, the disconnection, the lost friends and wayward path that looked for twenty years like the indelible path of my destiny, all of it began with that very first dislocation, leading to disorientation and disenfranchisement.

She would never agree, but she was so proud of my rhetoric. She said, "You know it's not too late." Her plea was understood, her desire unrequited. "It" was my obvious—to her—destiny, law school for only three short years, and then her dream come true.

And it wasn't just your average lawyer she had in mind. She wanted her son, the lawyer, in very expensive suits, very expensive shirts, exquisite matching ties, because a man who dressed like a page out of *Gentlemen's Quarterly* was a man for all the world to see as... a Success in Life!

I always felt that her greatest drive was for the unbelievable opportunities a lawyer would have to wear expensive clothing. Mother loved fashion; she could hardly wait until the world could get a load of her son, the lawyer, in sartorial splendor. Wouldn't that be something?

I had a different agenda than playing Mother's mannequin while measuring years in dollars. I tried to make her see that the law was a prospect *before moving away from Indiana*, but now it was not. "I could have been... lieutenant governor by now," I told her during that strident lament over my wayward ways. That hurt her, because she believed it—believed that a kid like me could have avoided stealing pop bottles and mop buckets, could have avoided picking black walnuts for a living after college, would not have yearned for adventures at sea—if only we'd stayed a couple hundred miles up the road in Hoosierville.

All my errant ways—those things she moaned and groaned about—would have been displaced by another approach to life, in which I, behind my desk, preened, polished, button-downed, bow-tied and hardly ever saying fuck or shit could have shown people just how nice I was—and what a genius, too. If only she hadn't moved me from my home in '62. She shut up, at last, pondering her error.

But regret pangs weren't my objective. I only wanted her to ease up on the angst over my life. She was still ready for the Success in Life to begin—the brilliant career, the unfathomable gratitude of a needy society, the fame, the fortune, the praise and respect of... of... *the entire nation!*

Short of that she would have been happy to see me move back into her place, or at least to a place of my own in the same town, where she could know for certain that I would not starve to death, which hazard concerned her daily as long as I was out in the cold, cruel world. Maybe she longed for the old days of mothering, but I don't think so. I think for Mother the nest never emptied, that the blinders ensuring her faith in the sheer, innate genius of her children also guaranteed her permanent perception of them as children, say around nine or ten years old, dirty, hungry, in need of a bath and a hot meal and certain watching over.

"I don't get it," she said over and over again. "Moving again? Why? Why moving again? I don't get it. I don't understand. A rolling stone gathers no moss. So why? What are you running to?" I tried reasoning with her, explaining that I wanted no moss, that I'd been wrenched from my true home and that I would wander the world until I arrived home again, and that was the deal. My defense fell on deaf ears. She said I talked crazy.

I could shut her up briefly with might-have-beens, one time playing out the scenario to the governorship of the state of Indiana, outlining my campaign precinct by precinct, assessing strategies for the soybean vote, the corn belt, the live-crickets-and-nightcrawlers faction, the catfish minority, the industrial north. But in mere minutes she got the picture and asked why, why, and why?

Another sure thing she loved to regret was the lost potential for a law partnership with an obnoxious little twirp from our town whose father was rich. I asked Mother what she meant by rich. Mother said, "He's a millionaire. A millionaire!"

My old man once said the twirp's father didn't have all that much money, and besides that, my ass would have made that kid a good Sunday face. I had giggled and spread my cheeks.

Sure enough the little twirp grew up to be a lawyer in very expensive suits, shirts and ties, who never generated too much money in the way of billings but did inherit enough to look like he made a ton of dough, and boy oh boy oh boy, Mother still knew, years after the fact, that the twirp was now raking in what should have been mine, only because he had the kind of father who could provide the financial backing a father should provide.

And there was the rub for her, the wicked irony she wanted most to correct. Mother considered it the cruelest act of fate that I faced hardship with no support, financial or otherwise, from the outset— me, her baby, the one blessed with a genius beyond that of the vast majority of twirps from our town. And now look; on the road again, moving away from another place that, to her, looked perfectly acceptable as a place to *establish roots*, moving on to... to... to what? To some vague notion? To some cockamamie idea that everything will be better in some faraway place with no family, no friends, where I didn't even know anyone?

And girls; what about girls? When would I find a nice (Jewish) girl and settle down and be a *mensch*, with a family for chrissakes?

Mother always had a unique aptitude for expressing the conditions of my life in terms of woe, profiling me as helpless victim, perennial waif, sickly, weak, broke, mentally vague. Oh, she knew how to push my buttons, utterly blind to a young man's idea of freedom, his yen for adventure, his get up and go for limitless horizons. She was just as blind to the suffocating restraints imposed by her mother and brother, as if constraint was what children should conform to. She wasn't mean or self-serving like them, but she couldn't see why I couldn't find happiness right there in my own living room, with a nice television set and three good meals a day, or five, and a few snacks. But no, I had to run—run, run, run—"And so where are you off running to all the time?"

"Yes," I said. "It is painful to think what might have been, if I hadn't been pulled up by the roots! By the roots was how I got pulled up!" She nodded slowly in recollection of the Exodus from Indiana, maybe in consideration too, of what might have been. "Painful," I said, "Especially when you consider that my ass would have made that little twirp a good Sunday face."

That one shut her up again, because my old man's epithets had an enduring way of quelling her old laments. They were often so base, so cruel, that they took her back to their utterance even twenty years after. They shut her up and glazed her over, leaving her dumbfounded, possibly shocked, that life and its random events would put her on the receiving end of: *Why don't you go blow yourself up?... Every goddamn dime I give you, you piss it away baking for the whole goddamn town... Awww, kiss my ass.* These unlyrical maledictions conveyed my old man's frustration from the beginning. Mother was the target.

But Mother only shut up for a minute at every phase of life, and she had a few toxic rejoinders of her own. *Bum! You're a bum! You won't give me any money for milk, for your children!* And so on, until she demanded to know again why I was moving again. So I reminded her again that I could have been United States senator from Indiana for chrissake, if only she hadn't torn me from my roots. We got each other going on transience and politics—oh, she longed for a showcase winner in the family. It was only unmitigated success, tons of money, a lavish wardrobe and a refrigerator bursting with good things to eat that would prove to the world and to Flossie and Flossie's son that Mother's children had risen above the poverty, hardship, and instability of their youth. Mother was focused on health and well-being, she said, but it was success, through her children, that she longed for—family, comfort, pride; all those things she never had.

I chided her again for wanting it both ways; she wanted the world to see the suffocating hardship her children had endured, she wanted the world to exalt her second-rate children.

"I never said you were second-rate," she said.

"You don't leave much room for doubt, with every single person you feel compelled to tell your story to, about your poor, suffering, helpless, can't-make it-alone-children. I'm way ahead of the game, goddamn it. Now how many people have you told that to?" And there I was, yelling at Mother again, like father like son.

"What was I supposed to do?" she asked. "I was beside myself with you kids." She said she had to be both father and mother to us kids. Just as the years in Southern Indiana had been difficult, the first years in St. Louis were spartan, uncertain, unstable. But after the divorce we could sit down for a special lunch of cold cuts, kosher dills and cola on a Saturday or a Sunday and not worry about the old man coming home and staring, then glaring, then growling, then yelling that the goddamn mortgage was three months unpaid and we're eating kosher meats at triple the price.

Mother kept a kosher home, because Flossie went snake-eyed and demanded it. That had been another bone to pick, another struggle for control. Flossie knew the score, knew how to keep things hopping at our house, as if they needed help going at it every chance they got, reminding each other at ten decibels what a lousy goddamn life they shared while Sissy and Brother and I sat and waited for the storm to pass, while the cola went flat.

Mother worked as hard as any single parent ever did when we moved; bringing home cold cuts that could cost a half-day's pay was her small victory, like a kid who blows his savings on his first crummy car, for the freedom of the thing. And she did love the greasy, salty taste.

But Mother didn't know what to do with us kids because she couldn't allow herself to do nothing. Her mothering compulsion required new clothes each season, expensive groceries so we wouldn't forget what the good things tasted like and every now and then an outing, a movie or the zoo. She worked hard and saved nothing. She continued to squander money on gifts or bakery for others, but it was much less money now. Her giving was still mostly misplaced, but at least she proved a point, which was her honest inclination to give.

Mother's biggest project those years, though, was seeing Sissy through college. Sissy always got good grades, so she got scholarships, but cash requirements were still steep and out-of-pocket. Mother wanted Sissy to have a degree, but most of all Mother wanted Sissy to have her Mrs. It was an old and tired joke that got wore out all over again when it was Mother's turn to coach Sissy toward the winner's circle. Mother was always open-minded, except toward the pursuits of her children. She wanted doctors and lawyers for sons, a suburban housewife for a daughter; she wanted Sissy's Mrs. Then she wanted grandchildren, so the normal life could begin.

Brother and I suffered the usual run of goofy college guys trying to get into Sissy's pants on the couch late after the date. One time we hid and watched and were fairly amazed that the guy couldn't get in there with lines like, "Aw gee, come on, wouldja?" Then finally Jerry came along and met with Mother's approval and Brother's and mine, too, because he worked so hard all the way through college and then spent all his money on a brand new '65 Pontiac 2+2 ragtop with the big block 421 engine and four on the floor, and he'd toss us the keys when he wanted to get into Sissy's pants, sometimes right in the middle of the afternoon. They got married in July, a month after graduation.

That was a relief for Mother, but then it was short-lived, because Brother had discovered the wonders of liquor and drugs and the underside of the city all night long. He became a devotee of the Gothic, the perverse, keenly attracted to people of the night, especially those with physical deformities, whose outlook on life was happy as that of a well-adjusted Martian. It was a pursuit he would cherish for years, until he was thirty and decided to get his college degree, then a series of advanced degrees. But I think the research most applied to his students now was learned on his own, out in the real laboratory, seeing firsthand the consequences of this choice or that one.

I finished high school a year after Brother and hit the road, like I always said I would, not from vindication but from pure lust for horizons. What could Mother do but worry, work harder, try to catch up and wonder when things would improve? When would her sons settle down and make something of themselves and their lives, after all she'd been through?

"Both a mother and a father," she often said, reminding us of the ante on the table, of the sacrifices made for us. Brother shut her up one year, presenting Mother with a pair of socks, a half-dozen handkerchiefs, and an ugly tie for Father's Day.

I maintained my refrain of regret for what might have been, if we hadn't been wrenched from our rightful homeland. When Mother pressed for details on my social life, wanting to know who and when and what, I told her, "Yes, I met a girl, a slut, but very nice, you know. Her name is… Goldstein or Goldfarb or Goldblatt or Golddig or something like that. Her father owns a chain of department stores and he's all upset because he doesn't have a son to take over."

I could pump Mother's pulse to 210 over 190 any time night or day with prospects of department-store dynasty, until I wore that one out, until she figured out that the very nice slut was only a tease, a figment, a cruel mirage. She wanted that one so much that I always suspected her reverence for medicine or the law was not sincere. Her generation looked up to men in authority, men in white robes with knives and clamps, men in suits who clung to their lapels while speaking ponderously, men who made more money than anyone else. But Mother couldn't really see the action in medicine or the law. In retail, on the other hand, you had the meaning of life, the give and take, the game, the bluff, the raise, the ruse, the disinterest, the walk away, the close, the tease back—my God—*the window displays!* Mother's heart was in retail. I could make her heart go giddyap over casual mention of a nice Jewish girl with no brothers to take over the stores.

I could veer off into politics for a sustained and merciless brow-beating. "United States senator? I could have been president of the United States of America!" I told her, looking maybe for permanent relief.

She only shook her head. "Then I'm glad we moved. They get shot."

"I could have been vice president," I tried, but she was already back on track asking me when, when, and when I would settle down and *establish some roots*. That of course left me with one answer, a simple, obvious one that took me years to figure out and in the end shut her up: "I don't know," I finally said. "I just don't know. I think maybe something is wrong with me. I think I could be a failure and a bum."

That brought her around to my side. "No, you're not," she said. "You'll figure it out when you're good and ready and the time is right."

"Gee, do you really think so?"

It was this kind of convolution that drove my old man nuts, because he never figured out how to work it. He never got past the argument Mother can put in anyone's face at any time over any point, pro, con, up, down. And he made the big mistake, arguing, so the background sound at home for the first twelve years of my life was a dreadful fugue of *You sonofabitch, I don't have any money for milk!* Or, *I'm trying to run a house!* Or, *I can't even buy groceries!* And other accusations of non-support.

My old man answered with: *Aw, why don't you go have a tongue sandwich and use your own tongue?* Or, *Can't I even have a drink in peace?* Or sometimes, down to the real nitty-gritty, *You spend every goddamn dime I give you on baking for other people!* Yes, it was daily and repetitious, as if each believed the other had actually forgotten what had been yelled yesterday. It was the dialogue of my youth.

And then came the horrible truths behind the accusations. Mother did spend every goddamn dime on baking for other people. And there again was the crux of Mother—she could drive you nuts, but my God, what a cook. She said she had to bake and give it away so people would be nice to her children. This was naive.

Yet if you isolate the primary components of Mother's life, Mother's story, Mother's ups and downs, it would be meal preparation and giving that would stand tall and solitary like stone columns on the facade of ancient ruins.

Of all the meals Mother prepared, the hallmark meal for me was the simplest, packed in a small paper bag. Sometimes Brother and I went together, but it was mostly alone with our dog Tuffy that I went to find the woodlands no one had yet found, yonder, in the great beyond across the street.

Sure, you can remember high points of youth, the wild, crazy times when children together can enjoy anarchy—like Saturdays at the movies, 10 A.M. to 5 P.M., twenty cents to get in, another ten cents for popcorn, another nickel for a soda, and you were looking down the barrel at seven solid hours of cartoons, *Hopalong Cassidy, The Three Stooges, Jungle Jim, Tarzan, Captain Midnight*—and then the main features, stuff like *Earth vs. The Flying Saucers* or *Forbidden Planet* or *Thirteen Ghosts*. And best of all was the theater, packed with a thousand kids screaming bloody murder, throwing popcorn and candy and cutting loose from an entire week of pressure, built up indoors, in school.

But that glory, that pressure ventilation, that Saturday revolution was small potatoes compared to the bursting exhilaration on that first morning of each summer in the first week of June.

Three months of freedom shining as bright as a pot of gold got me up at six, amped up, fully charged. Christmas was for kids; it was the first day of summer that lay under a soft sunrise, so full of promise and fun, that filled my heart with want—*ninety days in a row!* It was a wealth I have spent my life pursuing.

My lunch was prepared already, and I was out by 6:30. Tuffy and I crossed the street and headed across the field and into the trees— walked and walked where no paths showed the way, where mature stands canopied high overhead and the ground was mostly covered in shade, pine needles, and sparse thicket. We walked, stopped, listened and watched and then walked farther, soaking it up like an alky who realizes his thirst with the first drink. We walked until eleven or so and found an old dead log to sit on and opened the bag. Those lunches in bags probably weighed a significant percentage of my total body weight for years—corned-beef sandwiches three inches thick, half a baked chicken, a half-pound of carrot sticks and celery sticks, a handful of olives, maybe a PB&J and a couple deviled eggs, chips, pickles, some cake and cookies, two napkins and some chewing gum. We finished it every time, Tuffy and I, realizing even then how good Mother was at the details of giving; just look at the lunches the other kids brought to school—a single slice of fake cheese on two pieces of Wonder Bread and an apple. Get serious.

Lunch in a bag is long gone. I've seen that same forest in Southern Indiana—blown away worse than Beirut is what it looks like now, buried in an avalanche of ugliness.

Just as buried are the nobler times when a dog like Tuffy could show more spirit than most people do now—he walked the half-mile every morning with us to the bus stop and watched us get on and ride away, as sad as we were that a perfectly good day would be wasted. He hung out at home until 2:30, napping in the dirt, mostly, then walked back to the bus stop and waited. He came alive when we got off the bus, knowing we had all the way to dark to raise hell, run the countryside, have fun.

We worked the streets in every neighborhood of our youth together, selling seeds or greeting cards door-to-door. He ran alongside every afternoon on my paper route. Sundays we finished by sunrise.

Now the countryside is gone. The old woodlands are crowded and paved now, and a boy better have his goddamn dog on a leash if he doesn't want to get a ticket. Nothing remains, except poor old grayhaired Mother, who sometimes asks me if I want her to fix my lunch in a bag. I ask, *Where would I take it?*

She's only kidding anyway, when she suggests another lunch in a bag, I think.

Years later Brother came for a visit, and one day went for a bicycle ride down what now passes for a country road. He said he stopped for a rest a few miles out, near a service station/espresso bar, and sitting on a grassy bank by the side of the road, he felt a cold nose on his ear, sensed a writhing body nearby, heard the swish of a madly wagging tail. He turned around. It was Tuffy.

The reunion was fervent, until Brother turned back around briefly to pick up the bicycle, and Tuffy vanished. Tuffy would have been thirty-eight that year. But he died in '68 at fourteen. Tuffy's mother, Beanie, came in '53, but she got run over a year later, a week after giving birth to eight puppies, so we had to bottle feed them and then diddle their peepees. We shrieked when they pissed on us. I was five when Tuffy was born.

I told Brother it was only acid flashback. He said, "Yeah, but it was real." I couldn't argue with that, and after Brother went home, I nearly packed my lunch in a bag, with the grassy bank, roadside, in mind. But, nah, I was too busy for that, and besides, as soon as the sandwich was made, I ate it. What was I supposed to do, put a six-course meal in a paper bag and head out on my bicycle looking for my childhood dog?

I don't think so. I think God makes a time for seeing certain things, and you see them or you don't. What I saw way back when, was that Mother's attention to detail wasn't just a skill in packing lunches, but a compulsion to give everything available for giving. It was an obsession, an undying drive.

I had no idea that those were the last days of a world with nature close at hand. Soon after those years I went to college to avoid the draft—four years of smoking dope, taking psychedelics and trying with all my heart to get laid. It was a waste of time, in deference to a spurious social norm. It was stifling and vastly forgettable.

Soon after college I encountered my first blank marked *Education*. I filled it in: "In the woods across the street with my dog." I didn't get the job. I didn't want it anyway, because it required lying on the application.

Meanwhile, Mother's giving continued past the transition from Southern Indiana to St. Louis, continued to a fault, with no time for her own needs. She gave all she had to give just to get Sissy through college and Brother and me out of high school, and Sissy and Brother and I knew even then that we still had so much less than the other kids, because America teaches its suburban children that certain inalienable expectations from life should be met, like a car to drive and a little walk-around money, and new clothes and something other than sharing a room with two siblings.

We didn't help Mother then but instead fought with each other, hurling live blades across the dining room, aiming to kill. Sissy would scream that Brother was a fatso, because he went over two hundred pounds at fourteen, which looked even bigger when I hung in around a hundred the same year, at thirteen. Sissy had a hard time then. She was disappointed with Mother, who had so obviously failed at proper judgment every step of the way to wind up in such a pile of shit as the one we lived in. Sissy was embarrassed by Brother, who was fat, drunk, and stoned and not in the least like the cool college boys she saw every day. And she couldn't conceive of success in life with someone like me around, small but in the way, playing the radio every night too loud for college homework. She yelled. I ignored her, lifting my barbells with little grunts and squeals in the tiny gap between the cot and the dresser and every now and then chirped up that she could go fuck herself. Then she would storm out, slamming the door behind her, or else we would fight.

We fought over important things, like whose record would be played on a Saturday morning on the hi-fi. Sissy had a new LP by a guy who looked like the original nerd and sang tone-deaf songs about beatnik stuff and called himself Dylan, even though he was only another Jewish kid from the suburbs. I told Sissy to fuck off; nobody wanted to listen to her *schmendrik* beatnik kid genius, especially when I was practicing in my falsetto voice with the Ronettes, and I nearly had it down... *Be my, be my bay-by. My wuuuun and only bay-by... Wha wha wha wha....*

Sissy yelled that I was an accident, a mistake, and one day she elaborated that I was only around because of a bad diaphragm. I asked a few people what a diaphragm was and then asked Mother what Sissy meant, and Mother shrugged and asked back, "Why worry about it now?" I asked Mother how Sissy knew I was only around on account of a bad diaphragm, and Mother said, "How do I know how she knew?"

Mother made small efforts after that to let me know that I was no accident, or at least she was glad it happened, or something; she gave me more cookies or more baked chicken, which was nothing new, really, since we'd suffered the force-feed ever since when, but it was the only solicitous gesture she knew. But I liked being an accident, a low-odds fucker who'd come out on top, cleared the first hurdle and kept on coming. That was me, unstoppable.

Sissy said I was warped. I think she bore a grudge from the time a few years earlier, back in Southern Indiana, when I called her a whore, yelled it actually during one of our regular fights, fights that were normal for siblings but maybe not to the extent that we fought. That was back when Sissy was in high school and had a hard time fitting into an environment emphasizing maturity and coolness, having to come home to such a zoo. She told Mother I'd called her a whore. Mother told my old man, who asked me if I knew what a whore was. I was ten. I said sure, Sissy's a whore.

We went for a drive in the car—a '57 DeSoto, black and white two-tone with red interior and push-button drive and three tailgun lights in a column on either side, on the trailing edges of the rocket fins. The old man gave Brother and me the scoop on men and women, and what men did to women with their dicks. Most unbelievable of all— and we didn't believe it, not for a minute—was the idea that men liked doing this, liked it so much, well, that's where the whores came in. He didn't get around to women liking it; for one thing that would have been worse than unbelievable, that would have been crazy. For another thing, it was only '57, and women didn't like it yet.

Brother and I spent the standard week staring at married people and giggling at each other. Sissy looked smug. She'd known for years.

I told her, soft and low, she was still a whore. She screamed and told. I denied everything.

When Sissy grew long fingernails a few years later in St. Louis, she dug them into Brother's and my forearms because we were such little shits. Or maybe she just wanted to scar us. For years the other kids at school thought Brother and I had a strange disease, causing our forearms to break out in cuts and scabs. The forearm rash went into remission the year I gained fifteen pounds and landed a solid left jab on Sissy's chin. She never dug in again and in fact we stopped fighting a few years after that and maybe realized a few years later that siblings are supposed to help each other.

I think sometimes adversity stimulates growth, and sometimes it doesn't. It wasn't until Mother married again and moved to Memphis, and I got a job in a match factory for a dollar ninety-two an hour, which would set me up for a whole year on the proceeds of a single summer's work, that I got an ulcer. I was twenty. Too much repression was what got to me, I think. Too much denial of the world on top of me, too much struggle staying afloat, too much worry, too little money, no fun. I moved in with Sissy and Jerry for a few weeks and ate pabulum until the pain eased up. I quit the match factory; better to stay poor. Sissy ditched all the bullshit then, because it was only and always a thing of the past anyway. We only hung onto it because it never was sorted out. Fuck it, and fuck matches. The pain went away. I got my strength back, got my youth and my dream back and hit the road like I should have in the first place instead of giving in to getting ahead. I got ahead, heading out on the next leg of the trip some people have to take.

Sissy and Jerry moved to Alabama to start having babies.

Mother was forty-four then, getting old already. Still loyal to Flossie and Flossie's son, she continued regretting the rift that had come between her two families, continued urging Brother and Sissy and me to "do the right thing." She knew in her heart that the rift would go away, that her two families could reunite in the endless struggle against the rest of the world. The struggle raged fiercely in

Mother's other family, Flossie's son so valiantly slaying the bastards coming at him right and left, pouring tales of woe into Mother's ear about the difficulties of earning a decent living and supporting his family—and hers! Mother worked for Flossie's son, which amounted to another ravaging hardship for him—he had to pay her.

Flossie clucked her tongue in the background and mumbled prayers, to God, invoking more power to her poor son against the bastards, and don't forget the money, because he didn't make nearly enough to support so many people.

Mother worked for Flossie's son in the rag business as a kind of secretary and frontline sponge for the bullshitters Flossie's son had beat out of six or eight bucks last week. Mother got about sixty bucks a week for protecting Flossie's son from what was coming at him then, and she didn't mind it, except when The Devilment came down to the office and did her hoity-toity, prissy prancy number like the Queen of Sheba, or Dinah Shore, or Sister Woman, except that The Devilment's dominion was in her mind; she was not a Powerful TV Hostess, and she was nobody's sister.

The Devilment always reminded me of the witch queen in *Snow White*, her face a chiseled study in focus, intention and hunger. She focused on the mirror-mirror-on-the-wall, intent and driven to the heights of social status, the deference and respect that should come by rights with a new Cadillac every year, until the Mercedes was achieved, along with membership in the Club. The hunger was fed with two hands, inflating her ass. It got very big, bigger in rapid disproportion to the rest of her body. God works in mysterious ways.

The Devilment was wrapped tight around the center of her being, around her beady, busy eyes. For anyone sensitive to body language, she sent a predatory message, socially speaking. The Devilment wanted to know who and what you were, what you had and your prospects for having more. The Devilment wanted to know all, needed to know all, so she could adequately process the information, for filing, to use as necessary. And if any aspect of your past, your prospects, or your assets were unknown by her, she would step up to within six inches of your face, and she would ask point-blank. I remember the mesmerizing effect of her Pan-Cake makeup at that proximity, the way it moved under the surface like another subtle spirit, an evil one, with its own volition, its own foul agenda. The Devilment and Flossie's son were a match made in heaven, or somewhere.

She came on strong, all teeth, her hands and eyes in gesticulations of warmth and engagement. The Devilment had insisted that Mother call Sly, the lawyer, to find out what to do about *the situation* in Daytona Beach, when I got thrown in jail.

Sly had advised, *Leave the kid there. That'll teach him.*

Mother didn't need anyone advising her to leave her child in jail, or on an iffy bond, or in a sleazy motel, and she did what she had to do, driving The Devilment to new heights of rant and tirade over the injustice, the unfairness, the... the... the outrage of such a thing, that a no-good punk of a child would take his mother's savings and squander it like that.

Oh! said The Devilment.

Oh, The Devilment didn't really care about Mother or Mother's savings; she was only jealous of Mother. Mother and Flossie knew that! The Devilment hated everyone and everything who could possibly compete for the attention of Flossie's son.

After awhile, it just wouldn't work out anymore, the business in medium-priced clothing being so diluted, with so much nasty competition from all the bastards trying to keep Flossie's son from his rightful fortune. Mother could stay, but Flossie's son could no longer pay her. He honestly waited for her answer, because she may have wanted to stay, because Flossie's son would at least have made sure that she had something to eat.

So Mother had to find a new job. But The Devilment had a new job for Mother all lined up already; it would be so great, being a secretary down at United Hebrew Temple. It was another sphere of dominance for The Devilment, who enjoyed mutual reverence with the rabbi. Flossie's son concurred, it would be so great, getting money from outside the family, instead of continuing with the internal hemorrhage. And for what, those lazy, good-for-nothing louts, Brother, Sissy and me, who never worked a day in their lives?

It wasn't so great for Mother, wading into that swift stream where piranha were known to feed, standing there for all to see, for all to know and to ask whatever personal questions surfaced, questions about poverty, divorce, worthless children, wonderful brothers and a sister-in-law too good to be true.

No country Jews, these, and I didn't need to remind her that I'd told her so. Mother knew. She worked, paid the rent, bought groceries, and worked some more. We worked too, reinforcing our second-class status by spending the afternoons of our adolescence in worthless jobs. I worked in a print shop after school, for a catering company nights and weekends, and for a car-parking company nights and weekends when no parties needed catering.

Mother quit the temple and worked as a secretary in one office and then another, and when Flossie's son folded up altogether in the rag business, because the bastards beat him down so bad, he opened a franchise employment agency and dredged up his old lament, his teeth-gnashing, hand-wringing wail over so many people to support.

Because he needed help and he needed it cheap—front-office help to screen the scum looking for handouts. He got it, you know where. Mother worked the front office for less money than she'd ever made, but then she had the future to consider now, because Flossie's son planned to make her "a part of the organization." My warnings to Mother went unheard.

The Devilment worked a back office, interviewing the unemployed, asking them what they had, who they knew, showing her teeth every minute of every day.

We'd come a long way from Southern Indiana by then, too many horizons from lunch in a bag in a solitary woods, too far down a rough road that only led to St. Louis and a suburban high school full of kids who knew everything, but didn't know anything.

Mother took us to see where she worked once, after hours to avoid conflict. She showed us her desk, out front. I asked about the other three desks, each in its own private office. One was for Flossie's son. One was for The Devilment. One was for Dadad, since that was his phase as young hero, carrying on the family tradition of success in business. Dadad drove a new car then, because he could be anything he wanted to be, and you can't constrain that kind of potential for want of basic transportation. Mother told us, because Flossie's son told her. Dadad would go on to want to be a major network sports announcer, or, short of that, a CPA, or, short of that, the perfect heir for Flossie's son.

The employment agency had its own bathroom, with a radio. I asked Mother why she had a radio in the bathroom. She said it was for Dadad, who couldn't *make tinkle*, much less a dump, if he thought *anyone* could hear him. But the strangeness of cousins had lost its simple color. We heard of Dadad's quirk and laughed, but we laughed short. Dadad was a proven simpleton, driving a new car every day to an office where he continued to fail in potty training, where he required spoon feedings. Mother worked the front office full speed, after arriving in the old Studebaker.

Harsh little truths like those ornamented our world then. And hanging out at an ice cream parlor near our suburban apartment in St. Louis was a far cry, too, from heading up the back steps behind the Java Shop, next to the Hotel Vendome, up to the bookie joint there, where once when I was six and Brother was seven all the bookies and players and general neighborhood guys stopped suddenly and got quiet, like a flock of birds sensing predation in the same, collective heartbeat, and in the next they lit out for dear life, out the windows and across the roof and down the fire escape. Brother and I wanted to play too, but my old man said, "Stand still, for chrissake." And he was right, because the cops never bothered guys with little boys back then. So it worked out well, and maybe that's what my old man meant when he said we brought him luck. Still the window, roof, and fire-escape scramble was a tough one to miss.

So besides being hungry, those years in St. Louis were colorless, lifeless, given over to the tedium of labor for dollars, for rent, for groceries, for more labor. The years rolled past more quickly through Sissy's marriage and a couple more marriages for Mother to guys who couldn't get it any better than my old man could, and then to an unhappy juncture in her life, taking care of her mother—the Flossie one.

So the easiest time I ever had of quelling Mother's refrain of rolling stones gathering no moss, of no roots, of where and why, was about that time, when I asked her, "And just where is your illustrious career headed?"

❄   ❄   ❄

Grist for the Mill

So at age sixty-five, finished with all her secretary jobs and her two other marriages it was time for Mother's next indenture—live-in nurse, chief attendant, cook, and maid for Flossie.

Mother was born in '18. She didn't see anything wrong with her status as idiot sister, the second-rate child as long as she lived at home, about twenty years. Her role as the less-important child was couched in different terms and was common then among females with male siblings, since the one was so better suited to carry on the family glory than the other.

She ignored my old man's opinion, then ignored Brother's, Sissy's, and my opinion, spanning another twenty years, then another thirty years. It took a straight shot to the chin to wake her up, but it left her groggy.

Flossie wanted to be the Dowager Queen, with Mother, Sissy, Brother, and me as court attendants. She wanted proper deference and respect, genuflections and visible acts of self-sacrifice. But we were my old man's kids, and that shit just didn't get it. Flossie was as greedy, mean-spirited, and disrespectful as her son, who walked the earth, cruised the reef, in her image. The children of Flossie's son lost their innocence, reflected their parents, profiled gamma normal, and dove whole hog into kowtowing and ass-kissing. Mother believed in family, believed Flossie when she promised, "We'll always take care of you."

Flossie's son was executor of Flossie's estate. And The Devilment's best friend in the whole wide world, besides the rabbi, was her lawyer, Sly Albertson, who was available when Flossie's will needed writing. The Devilment never did make it into the fold, the inner sanctum where Flossie and her son ate and breathed, but she never stopped hovering just outside it, from where she worked the principals.

I can't remember the exact year that Mother tagged the wife of Flossie's son with the name, The Devilment, but the name went back in time and forward forever, because The Devilment compensated her status as outsider—yes, outside the blood bond—with gossip, rumor, ill will toward the world. Her eyes always looked ready to pop, as if the pressure behind them from such intense manipulation and maneuvering for material gain was too much for her skull to contain. She worked the spiritless tundra that was her life, and she worked it hard; the name fit.

Brother and Sissy and I expected nothing from Flossie's will, and that was okay, because my old man never was for sale and neither were his brothers or his kids. We reviled Flossie, her son, and The Devilment, were grateful for the distance between them and us. But Mother insisted on continuing contact with them, and she did have a vested interest.

In Mother's family the Holy Grail for years was The Property. The Property had been left by Mother's father, who croaked in '38, or maybe it was '31. Flossie feared the greed and treachery of everyone who was not herself, her son, or her dead husband. I can't imagine her marriage to her dead husband beyond the understood body language of pain and suffering—hand wringing, teeth gnashing, a sad prayer for every other minute in the day. He died, earning himself unequivocal reverence as one who was God-like. After all, he had bought The Property in the first place.

Flossie's distrust was based on her profound insight into human nature, and when she remarried twenty years after her first husband croaked, she knew full well that her second husband's children were human. They would try to get her, to get what was hers, sure as sundown. So she quitclaimed The Property to her own children when her second husband croaked—this in a rare, weak moment, a slip-up, a mistake perhaps resulting from years of non-communication with her daughter's children—Sissy, Brother and me.

And maybe it was a case of out of sight, out of mind, but the goddamn quitclaim got recorded before the Forces of Evil realized the property could conceivably fall to Mother's worthless children. This lapse in defense occurred about the time The Devilment's ass passed XL and opened up in the stretch, headlong for XXL.

The quitclaim on The Property was more than an oversight; it was a blunder, a karmic debt. Flossie's son figured it out one day in '86 while counting his sheckels, wondering what to sell high, what to buy low, when it came to him in a blaze. We now speculate on his dazzling epiphany by his haste, his urgency, his life-or-death approach to the cure. He convened the principals, in theory. They included Lawyer Sly and The Devilment and Flossie, at Flossie's condo. Mother was invited too, so she could prepare something nice for a little snack for everyone and maybe a little something to drink, to wash it all down. Flossie's son liked his chicken salad with mayonnaise—*with mayonnaise, not mustard!*—and his tea had to be scalding hot, maybe to remind him of the world.

These details came from Mother, who, after preparing, serving, and clearing was given another quitclaim deed to sign. *Come on, come on, come on, Sister. We haven't got all night!*

This new quitclaim was *exactly* like the old quitclaim. It only needed signing again for re-recording to make it right, because the old one wasn't recorded right, and it got sent back, and now this new one had to be signed for recording or else nothing could be right. The Property could be in jeopardy, and anyway, it was only a technicality, only another document just like the last one.

But Mother smelled a rat. I don't know if her undeveloped instincts toward her mother and brother finally broke loose, or if Flossie's son or The Devilment made some comment about Mother's children and their pitiful lives, or about their own children's knack for genius and prosperity. Or maybe Mother finally saw through the jive, the lies and theft, and she knew the old document was fine.

She said, "No."

They were gentle with her, at first, understanding her misunderstanding, nurturing her in her confusion, easing her with soothing explanations, as you might calm an emotionally disturbed child. Mother was the emotionally disturbed child to them, even at sixty-eight.

But Mother was sick of that shit, and standing firm with a resolute *No* was possibly most soothing of all, like scratching an old itch. So they ganged up on her, her own mother swooning into God tongues, The Devilment cackling incantations, Lawyer Sly spewing monotone statutes across the room, Flossie's son huffing and puffing and saying what was what.

I don't know if Mother would have guessed their motivation. She'd learned by then that anything The Devilment or her lawyer, Sly, or Flossie's son wanted from her *that* badly was most likely another injustice.

She didn't have to guess for long though, because the big, incurable problem with the old quitclaim deed from '84 could not be contained, so thick was the fear and loathing in the room. The problem was that Brother, Sissy and I had ceased all contact with Flossie, her son, and The Devilment for over twenty years, not even thank-you notes for the birthday five-spots sent by Flossie for the first few years after Indiana. So how could such a line of claim to The Property be allowed to exist any longer? Because even though Flossie and her son and Lawyer Sly and The Devilment love love loved Mother, and cared for Mother's own best interests, because they were her own flesh and blood, well, some of them were, well, it just didn't make sense for one minute to let Mother continue under that kind of liability, all set up to get taken advantage of by her unstable children, who, let's face it because we're all adults here, were just plain no good.

And, lo, into the night they wailed, they moaned, gnashing teeth, wringing hands, and with her head bowed long after the witching hour, Mother once again said, No.

It didn't sit well with those people, after all they'd done for Mother, that she should try to cheat them like this. They let her know how bad she was, spoke down to her like she was the retarded sister who could find happiness doing floors, if she would only let those who had her best interests at heart take care of her, and save her from the evil that no one wanted to discuss but everyone knew was waiting to pounce on Mother. The evil was, of course, her children.

Similarities between Mother's family and Cinderella's family were painfully apparent. But the legal, emotional pressure Flossie's son applied was not apparent. Mother kept these things secret, fearing hostilities, thinking that her continued denial to bend would protect her interests.

Migrations, fortune, chance, and a sailboat, at last, had taken me to Hawaii by then. I spoke with Mother regularly, and though she was careful not to disclose her tormentors, she sometimes slipped with a complaint, a question, a subtle yearning for help. I asked every time what was going on, and every time she said, "Nothing. I just want to know."

Mother was left to her own devices, which weren't much more than cooking and giving—and worrying that Flossie's son would cheat her out of everything, and worrying that if she told me, I'd maim Flossie's son.

Flossie's son came once a week to the condo where Mother was full-time attendant to Flossie, came for the weekly wail over the world and its evil bastards, including The Devilment—everyone had her number. When Flossie and her son were alone, truth could emerge. The Devilment was outside the blood bond, seen as one more conniving, evil manipulator out to get what wasn't hers, never had been hers, never could be hers, because Flossie and her son knew what was going on when The Devilment first worked her treachery to trick Flossie's son into marriage. You better believe a free ride on his hard work and sweat and blood was what she was after all along. Well, at least Flossie knew it, and she banged it into her son's head, making him see the truth, even though The Devilment let him stick it in there at least twice.

Mother's role in these covens was to prepare a six-course lunch for Flossie and her son, salad, soup, little sandwiches with no crust, crackers and chopped liver, fruit and cheese and dessert, and she left, so they could be together, to talk assets and evil intrusions.

Mother was wising up even then, but only at the speed of a glacier. And, it wasn't long after the heavy pressure failed to get Mother's signature on the new quitclaim to The Property that Flossie's son committed his ultimate sin, his worst error.

He let himself come unglued over Mother's failure to give Flossie an enema, or Mother's failure to cut all the crust off his sandwich, or Mother's failure to appreciate all he'd done for her, or Mother's failure to keep Flossie's condo clean enough, or something. And he managed to have Flossie off somewhere on a day that he came into the condo, all lathered up and yelling at Mother for her failures, and he pushed her—once, twice, and three times—knocking her down. This, when Mother was nearly seventy years old.

Can you imagine what my old man would have done to him? We're not talking within an inch of his life here, we're looking at ten, twelve feet past the end of his life. My old man never hit a woman, even Mother, who pressed more of his buttons than a woman should press on a man.

I would have flown in directly, but I only heard what Flossie's son had done several years after it happened because Mother did want to keep whatever peace she had in life, and because, after all, Flossie's son was her brother, she said.

And Mother continued the following week, preparing lunch for Flossie and Flossie's son.

Meanwhile, I was out in the world, the world of evil bastards, good Samaritans, average pedestrians, the teeming refuse yearning to be free. The road of years and miles went up and down and all around, in and out and down again and way down, and up, up, up. I applied what I knew, what I had inherited, which was freedom from doubt, freedom to go and go again, and the knowledge that everyone out there gets knocked down, and most everyone out there gets knocked down again, and if you're lucky, your knockdowns will come fast and furious from many directions when you're young. And I suppose the greatest family legacy to me was the confidence that comes with knowing knockdowns are part of the game—the most important part, as long as you get back up, brush yourself off, and get back in the action, a little bit smarter this time, this time applying what was learned down in the dirt.

Twenty-eight years after leaving Southern Indiana, the wandering ceased for me; the roots took hold again far far away in a place that once again looked, smelled, and felt like home. Twenty-eight years, twenty-two different places, probably around fifty different hustles. I felt like Mr. Boll Weevil, looking for a home, when I finally found it and settled in and relaxed and took a look back eastward to where *the situation* had been on hold. *Okay*, I said. *Now let's see what we got here.*

You can imagine my shock and surprise, my disappointment and sadness, discovering that Flossie's Son had managed The Property ever since when, but since the '84 quitclaim had not yet given Mother her half of the rent. *Oh my*, I thought.

I thought about a clean pop in the nose and I called my own lawyer with instructions to go for the knockout. "What do you mean, the knockout?" he asked.

"I mean get the bastard on the ropes," I said. "And when he's on the ropes hit him hard in the kidneys, try an uppercut to the chin, box his ears, wallop his head until he falls down, and then, when he's down, kick him in the ribs, kick him in the head until blood comes out his nose and his eyeballs and his ears, then kick him in the ass until...."

"I think I understand," the lawyer said. (And I hadn't even yet learned about Flossie's son knocking Mother down. Can you imagine the booster rockets that kicked in then?)

"Look," I said, "I don't want to get emotional about this."

"I can see that," the lawyer said. "Why don't you just relax and let me see what I can do."

"Fine," I said. "Call me next week."

And I guess this lawyer was good, or maybe it was only one more synchronicity, because no sooner than a smidgen of pressure was brought to bear, Flossie's son decided to sell The (goddamn) Property to the first offer that came along. Not that Mother or any of us outsiders would have known of other offers. And sure, Flossie's son tried to get Mother's signature on another paper, a formality was all it was, telling the escrow people who got the money and how much, except that Mother smelled another rat. "My own brother! Did you ever?"

Mother was never lucid in the technical jargon of tax, real estate, contracts, or anything that happened outside the kitchen or the department store. But her instincts were sharp, and moderately sharp went to razor sharp, went to blood on a soft touch when she realized at last like a child discovering the joke is on her, to her status within the Flossie hierarchy—not casual but official—she was the handmaid, idiot sister.

Mother said she would sign this new paper—said it sweet with a smile but with a vengeance, too, unforeseen by Flossie's son in all the bastards who'd come at him over all the years. Mother said she would sign the new paper at home, because even Mother was getting smarter by seventy.

The new paper was instructions to escrow, disbursing all proceeds of the sale of The Property—half a million bucks—to Flossie's son. Oh, it was an oversight, and what? You think he wouldn't have given her her share? You think he wouldn't have taken care of her when she needed it?

"Your own flesh and blood!" Flossie wailed, bobbing and weaving like a penitent before God. "Your own flesh and blood!" Flossie sobbed, squeezing her fingers bloodless, as if life itself was seeping hopelessly out of her grasp, as if all her good works, all her good deeds and thoughts, all her prayers—to God Almighty!—were coming to naught. Flossie wept. Flossie whined, "Your own flesh and blood! Your own flesh and blood!" Then she driveled into gobbledegook, her secret code linking her direct on the Hotline, to God, who would surely make this terrible mistake right.

Mother was dazed, more dazed than when she realized she'd married the wrong man, this was so much more sudden, so much more singular, so much more difficult to resolve. How could she have been born into the wrong family? How could?... How could?... She worked it out in her way, her brow knit into the question voiced at last: "How could he do that?"

Maybe Brother and I gained tolerance with age. We didn't bear down or feel any need for one-up, for the reminder that we'd told her so, so many times, so many years, told her that she had been born into the wrong family, had been born into a family suffering a curse, and that she, luckily, was a freak of nature. By the time she came to see the truth in what we'd said for years, we kept our mouths shut, because Mother, then, was her own worst inquisitor.

So The Property was set to close escrow and the whole sick affair ended—or at least that was the line Mother and her children were supposed to accept. Hadn't we bled Flossie's son dry? Hadn't we taken what was naturally his?

God knows Mother and her children wanted the affair over—well, except maybe for the fun part, the continuing litigation on the stolen rent money. Oh, it wasn't all that many dollars if you look at it as a monthly outlay, except that it would have resolved Mother's poverty, would have brought her up from the hand-to-mouth scrimp and scramble that defined Mother's life from the time she was only a girl of nine until the time she was only a girl of seventy.

As it was, Flossie's son had taken all the rent money for himself and his Mercedes (leased), for The Devilment and her lifelong dream of membership to two clubs instead of only one, for Dadad and his new Chevrolet (leased), and for Barba, long past presidential aspirations, but still in dire need of extensive wardrobe, travel, and many specialists to meet her needs.

As it was, the monthly outlay came to a decent hunk o' dough when you tallied up all the months between '84 and '91. Repayment would require another major capital outlay for Flossie's son. A trial would be a spiritual gift from me and my old man to him—allowing him a day of atonement for his sins.

I admit that I relished prospects for embarrassing truths made public, for civil victory and possible felony indictment. But I was just as happy relishing another fantasy about to come to pass. *Oh boy*, I thought. *A trial. Now Mother will get to see me in court after all.*

It was a new era, a unique situation in which the players and facts and evidence became ordered and accountable. And it was more; volition and justice were coming home as surely as the planets followed their orbits. The characters could rise or fall like suns and moons, could sing out or wail laments, could at last discover who in the world they were, what kind of people we had become.

Mother was in for the biggest surprise of all, eclipsing a former self, molting, casting off the old shell, and at her age, growing more in her seventies than she had in all the years before. For years she had been prone to small fits when the internal combustion was more than she could handle. She often blew her stack when Brother, Sissy, or I would make a joke about Flossie or Flossie's son. Brother did a great imitation of Flossie threatening to die. Sissy might ask if Flossie's son would be able to steal enough paper towels in time for the holidays. Or I would ask Mother how much longer she thought Flossie could live.

Mother would blow her stack, because she'd stayed blind to the source of the trouble, because the bindings on her brain confined her to repression and subservience no less than foot bindings hobbled Chinese women in the last century. She was seventy before she cut those ropes and learned to walk, resigning the role of Gothic Cinderella in a mere span of moments, which was something to behold.

Her awakening wasn't sudden, but it was. She knew, but she fended off the knowing. She hated what Flossie's son had done to her, to her

belief in filial devotion, to her faith in what a good daughter is supposed to do. Maybe the faith was too strong—she continued preparing little quartered sandwiches with the crust trimmed off when
Flossie's son came over to discuss "business" with Flossie. Why?
"Because," Mother said. "They have to eat."

But Mother was too tired to fend forever, and in that time between
the sale of The Property and The Trial, she understood the most difficult lesson of all—her lifetime of faith had been misplaced.
Realization left her speechless, or down to phrases anyway, dazed
into depression; she stared, as if catatonic, as if in search for the lost
truth.

Truth was, her children's harsh indictment of her blood relatives
had been accurate. She learned that Flossie's son had been lying
through his teeth on every grin and promise, that the material legacy
of her family would be denied her.

"After all these years," Mother said, over and over, because the con-
tent of those years was simple and understood. Devotion, duty and
performance defined her role in her family, no questions asked; until
the big question had come out of nowhere like a mystery punch that
floored the champ. The new quitclaim and the effort to steal all the
money on the sale of The Property were a one-two combination that
opened her eyes and made her see: She came from bad blood.

The ensuing litigation on the stolen rent money brought Flossie's
son up to his full potential as a parasite.

"What are you trying to do?" Flossie's son wailed in her face. "You
just want your children to get this money, don't you?"

"Don't you?" Mother asked, quick and clean, like an expert
swordswoman removing a head with dispatch.

She got weaned away at seventy from the small-minded covey she
was born into, and though it was nearly thirty years by then since my
old man died, I couldn't help but feel that his spirit was present, too,
for the grand awakening, because he always loved her. I cannot discount the possibility that she loved him, too, once—got swept up in
the few months of romance that usually precedes a marriage, with

prospects of fun, affluence and mobility forever. But she could never forgive him for no milk for her children.

But shit, a hustler gets lucky or he doesn't, and even though she drove him nuts, just like she drove me, he wanted her back, ran into her on the street there in Southern Indiana halfway through that year that began with divorce and ended with death, dropped to a knee just like he had in '41 when all the world shone with promise. The second time was more realistic; he said nothing would change, could he come home? I think it got to her, because she couldn't say no. But she couldn't say yes. She only walked away.

That was the last time they met or spoke, and though the sentiment of the moment got to her like no other moments I ever saw or heard about, she went right back to her grief-driven, hard-boiled assessment of my old man and the whole clan—womanizing, squandering lushes—every one of them.

My old man was a building contractor after oil, before diamonds, when I was about three, or six. He built very fancy houses that reflected his view of the world. Both shrank, and as he sold them off we moved into smaller and smaller houses that he'd built, a new, smaller house every year. Our moves paralleled the old man's and Mother's capacity for civility to each other, so that years later, arriving at the moment of rejection of the man on bended knee who had fathered her children, Mother could no longer fathom the potentials of love. The main currents of love, nurturing and exploration, had come to cross purposes so long ago that they were already as dust.

So she laughed scornfully when I reminded her of the spirit, the zest for good times, the honest adventure in the hearts of the clan, and don't forget its current descendants. "You call it whatever you want," she would say. "I know what I know. No good for nothing."

But then the day came after all the years and years of filial duty and selfless devotion leading to a dog's breakfast, which she lapped up whenever Flossie or Flossie's son would feed her. And with every feeding came the question: *Don't we have your best interests in mind?*

What finally showed Mother the light was the day Flossie fell down for her bimonthly seizure and wouldn't shut her yap until the ambulance showed up and she got stretchered down to the hospital with her two full-time attendants—Mother and a nurse. Flossie hated stretchers and wanted one of those things she'd seen in books, a sedan chair, one that you can sit up in, with four fellows to carry instead of only two.

It was a Saturday, Mother's customary day of furlough, often spent at Brother's house for the relief. Flossie was only ninety-two then, and called on the phone to wherever Mother went, to say that she felt bad, but don't worry because today she might die; yes, perhaps today. This, to inspire Mother to rush home to the sterile museum of an apartment she and Flossie shared, rush home to plead with Flossie no, not today, pulleeeze!

And Mother ran home at every cry of wolf, too, until she was sixty-eight or so—the phone would ring, and there was Flossie, just calling up to say goodbye, because Mother had been gone a good two hours already, and today would be a good day to die. And Mother would say, "Aw shit," just like my old man used to say when a goddamn fucking duck would dive on his bait.

But Mother got tired near seventy, wore out, and fatigue sometimes offers insight; she figured out Flossie was running her around so she stopped running home, stopped begging Flossie not to die.

So Flossie would call back a few minutes later and say so meek and mild in a lilting whisper from the other side, "Where is the silver polish? I can't find the silver polish." Not that she wanted to polish the silver, but she wanted "the new girl" to do it. The new girl was not a nurse, because everyone knows you don't really need a nurse, not for what they charge. Steal your money is all they want to do, when you can get a "girl" for a fraction of the price, and a "girl" won't be so hoity-toity, too. Why, who ever heard of paying somebody by the hour and just having her sit there? And who do you think was paying for the air-conditioning while the girl sat there? Did you ever?

Well, if Flossie wasn't going to go ahead and die, then the "girl" might as well be polishing the silver—it was that or sit on her lazy ass watching soap operas. The nerve of that miserable, conniving bitch.

Then came the day it was simply time for more—more attention, more deference, more tribute. So Flossie waited until Mother got over to Brother's house, then she went into a seizure, this time laying herself gently on the carpet and twitching and demanding an ambulance and the hospital. Mother still got weak then over prospects for the ambulance and the hospital, so she asked Brother to drive her down after the "girl" called. The "girl" had no name, because she changed more often than the pages of a calendar. This "girl" was sixty, a professional home-care attendant. She quit the following week.

I was in town on a visit and not inclined to join the fray, but I did when Brother promised an outing to remember, and besides, we could smoke a joint on the way. "Oh no," Mother said. "You're not smoking that stuff with me in the car. I'll be sick."

"Go get in the car," Brother said. "We'll smoke it in here."

"We've got to hurry!" Mother said.

"For what?" Brother said. "She'll be dead a long time."

We arrived at the hospital just before the ambulance, and in came Flossie on the stretcher with "the girl"—Flossie saw Mother and wailed, waving Mother over so Mother could tend to something or other.

I hadn't seen Flossie in about twenty years and could only stare, she'd so dramatically approached the bones.

Then she looked right at me and yelled for the doctor, "Right now! I'm ready to die!" She yelled way too loud for anyone to believe she would actually croak. But she stopped suddenly, clutching her jaw, and she shrieked at the attendants, "The cheese! Get the cheese! Get the cheese out! It's killing me! Get the cheese!" Flossie had a cyst on her jaw. It filled up with a unique smegma that she thoroughly enjoyed having squeezed out by somebody, although none of the rotten bastards cared enough to do it right.

The hospital drama got thick when Flossie's son came down, once Flossie was subdued and sedated. He strode in with accusation, passing judgment that Mother had been negligent in her care of Flossie, and Brother was nothing but a bum, because bums run in Mother's half of the family, and on and on, until Flossie's seizure was incidental to the threats and accusations flying around the emergency room.

I stood straight, still and silent, and when Flossie's son came as close as I thought he would come, I stepped toward him. One step, that was all. He stopped, which caused a strange tickle in my brain, a thrilling anticipation that perhaps, he knew, he understood what had not died.

Mother was learning new postures, other than the putty posture of her entire life until then. But we hadn't seen the measure of her resolve until Flossie's son displayed his loud-mouthed arrogance at the hospital. She stood up straight, stepped up in front of Brother and me, as if she still needed to protect her children, and told Flossie's son to shut up. Then she told him where to get off. Flossie's son would have got physical but Brother and I were there. Brother was up to two-ten already, much bigger than me, but hardly bigger than my intent. I was further encouraged by our odds, seeing how thoroughly Flossie's son had begun to shrink.

He turned away like an old man who'd been insulted, while The Devilment debriefed the doctors. The Devilment smiled expansively, darting here and there in her acute concern for the single fragile life between her and the inheritance. She sucked up to the doctors, asking where they lived, were they Jewish, what club did they go to, had they too experienced the joy of Mercedes? She made it plain to see that she was different from us.

For weeks and months and years after that scene, Brother often broke down in the middle of anything, clutched his jaw with both hands and yelled, *The cheese! Get the cheese! It's killing me! The cheese!* He stopped only a few years later, when he instead began turning slowly, ponderously, asking anyone, anywhere, "Who'll give the enema?" Like I say, Flossie loved personal service.

On the way home from the hospital, finishing our joint while Mother processed what had become of her day off, what had become of her life, she freely answered our questions. Maybe the emotional fatigue loosened her up. She told us about the cheese and the squeezing of the cheese—Brother couldn't get enough of it. He wanted to know if Mother had ever squeezed the cheese. She told him he talked like a fool. Then she laughed, and we knew—she had squeezed the cheese.

Our little rolling confessional loosened her up a little more, and the second-hand smoke must have taken hold as well, because she said that squeezing the cheese was nothing. It was the enema that found Mother's limits.

Flossie had for years wanted Mother to give the enema but Mother said no, she would not give the enema. Flossie told Mother to ask this neighbor and that neighbor, until Mother had knocked on every door in the building and asked every neighbor if they would give the enema. All refused, some politely.

Flossie had then gone from asking to wailing, like an old Jew at the wall with a modest request, please, in return for a lifetime of devotion. Flossie had pleaded, Mother said, until Flossie's enema lament required Mother to put a foot down. "I told her," Mother said. "I won't give the enema. And I won't. She can call her son to give the enema."

"That's right," Brother said. "Let him give the enema."

"You know what she did?" Mother said.

"No," I said. "What did she do?"

Mother told us that Flossie had wailed, "You *could* give the enema!" Flossie had wailed loud enough for the neighbors to hear, so the neighbors would know that Mother refused—that Mother was a bad daughter.

"But the neighbors only bolted their doors," I said. "Right? Because if you wouldn't give the enema, they knew you'd be around to see if they'd give the enema. Because they *could* give the enema. Right? Am I right?"

"What a fool I've been," Mother said.

"Yes," I said, "You keep saying that, then you follow up with more foolishness."

"Not this time," Mother said. "I can't give the enema. Even if I wanted to, I couldn't."

"But you don't want to, do you?" Brother asked.

Mother said her position was not rational, not arrived at; it was heartfelt. And she had wearily reiterated no, she would not give the enema, because she could not give the enema. Well, Flossie was beside herself, so stuffed with baked chicken and matzo balls and gefilte fish and little sandwiches with the crust trimmed off. She had in fact gone with no enema until the newest "girl" gave her one and then quit—the cheap, no-good-for-nothing bitch. "And she was Catholic, too," Flossie had said. "They usually hang on for awhile."

That was last week, and the problem was again unsolved this week, leading to the seizure and cheese backup.

Flossie was already ninety-four by then, and the rift between Mother and Flossie's son was two years old, evolving into clear realizations for Mother. She had continued resisting what begged to be known, that she was not only outcast, she was a nonentity in the material legacy that was due her. For the last two years she had asked, "Why would he want to do that?" As if the answer was too unbelievable to be true.

"Why would he do what?" Brother would ask.

"You know, try to get me to sign a new paper."

"Which paper?" Brother would ask. "Do you mean the new quit-claim deed paper, that would have taken The Property from you? Or do you mean the instructions to escrow on the sale of The Property, that would have given him all the money?"

"I don't know," Mother said, slipping into her daze again, regressing to, "Why would he do that?"

"Why would he do what?" Brother would ask, over and over, Mother apparently needing repetition to let the truth sink in.

So Brother and I accompanied Mother back to Flossie's place, so Mother could prepare for Flossie's return—more soup, more baked chicken, more snacks and sandwiches—this within minutes of calling herself a fool. But it had been a day of change, of still newer insight on Flossie's character and the intentions of Flossie's son. Mother couldn't break her old habits, but she was beginning at last to understand that she came from bad blood.

So, returning to the gloom, to the low-oxygen, heavy-mothball atmosphere that was Flossie's condo, she found Flossie's will, because she always knew where it was and had wondered lately what it said, even though she'd been told over and over what it said. She read it aloud.

It left a half mil or so to Flossie's son, and then to his children Barba and Dadad. It left Mother's children five hundred bucks. It left Mother nothing.

It was her day, her hour, her moment of epiphany. It was ugly and painful, she'd avoided it for so long. Mother grew up with a cast-iron rule that all the world should be mistrusted, peopled as it is by immoral, mean, unfeeling and, most important, unrelated sons-abitches. Immediate family was supposed to be at the other extreme, to lie down and die for, and Mother would have—she spent her adult life pushing her children to *do the right thing*. Over and over, over the years, she pleaded for Sissy, Brother and me to call Grandma on her birthday. *Do the right thing. I only want you to do the right thing.*

Mother got her eyes opened wider the following day, showing Flossie the will and asking, "What is this? What does this mean? How can you do this?" Mother was livid.

Flossie was meek; in meekness she manipulated. "Your own flesh and blood," Flossie whined. "Your own flesh and blood. He has your best interests at heart. Your best interests. Why wouldn't he take care of you? He's always taken care of you."

Well, the strain between Mother and Flossie's son then got down and dirty. We'd revised the cash disbursement instructions on The Property, the document initially drafted by Flossie's son and put in Mother's face for a signature—*Now! Quickly! Come on come on come on!*—in which all the cash went to Flossie's son, thereby protecting Mother's share from her wicked children.

The close of escrow on The Property was as strained as any litigation, any feud, any meeting of warring factions. I was compelled to be on hand in case of a sudden need for an upper cut to the chin. After all, Mother's fair share was in the balance, and moreover so was an adjudication of the past, another prospect for satisfaction.

Mother was counseled to remain silent, to constrain herself from relating the injustice, ingratitude and degradation she had suffered at the hands of Flossie's son. She'd become weak, pouring out her story to anyone who could understand. I didn't think she could keep it to herself, not with lawyers, escrow agents, secretaries and assorted office staff there to hear what she had to say. But she did famously, honing her gaze to razor sharp and focusing it on The Devilment, who chattered happily, explaining the music now coming from the little bathroom in the corner.

"It's the most unusual thing," The Devilment tittered. "He practically runs our company, and he knows more about accounting than most CPAs, and he's a terrific sports announcer."

Brother walked over to the little bathroom and knocked on the door. "We can hear you. Dadad! We can hear you!" Flossie's son stood up, so I stood up too, and I walked over to the little bathroom as well. Brother was grinning, ready for a tag team and a lunatic giggle, just like the good old days.

What choice did I have but to bang on the door like a Gestapo agent and yell, "Cut that out! Stop it! Right now! Come on out of there! With your hands up!"

But then the escrow officer with all the documents was ready and the signing began. Dadad missed it, stuck in the bathroom on top-40 tunes, massaging Myrtle into the relax and give.

Mother signed here, and here, and here, as instructed by the lawyer, approved by Brother and me.

Near the bottom of the stack of signatures I asked her, "How do you feel?"

"I'm fine."

"Can you feel your dirty little paws on the moolah yet?"

"Almost."

"Do you feel good about that?"

"Yes."

"Good. Now, calmly look at your brother and The Devilment."

"What for?"

"Now you can tell them."

"Tell them what?"

"Tell them to kiss your ass."

Well, that got her laughing through the tension. It was a favorite saying of my old man's. I think she understood the spirit of the moment in terms of the spirit of the years, understood what coursed through the veins of her children and how it differed from what she came from. I think she came over to the right side of the family that day, and don't you know we took her in.

❄   ❄   ❄

Around the Clubhouse Turn

On that day that escrow closed, so too closed an era, ending the contention between Mother and us, because she took the blinders off and looked around and saw the truth, looked back and saw us, and maybe let up as well on her bittersweet recollection of the era she called *all those years.*

But transitions don't happen in a single day. Oh sure, the old time ended, ended once and for all, and we all used this milestone to let go a little bit more of the old stories, the old people we had been, the old places and events that had defined us. But the new time still defined itself, still took shape in its measure of the past, its look at the future. And like most transitions in life, or in this case in lives shared, an event loomed ahead that was held over from the past; the trial, in which Flossie's son would face a judge on a charge of stealing rent money from Mother.

Deposition, discovery, duck, dodge, and hide took two years, then three. Mother began complaining that it was dragging on too long, that it was too much, that it needed to end. I told her: Hush, justice takes time.

I was on an extended tour of London and Paris to see if I'd left anything in those towns, and to see old friends. But I came back to St. Louis for the trial, because I knew I'd left something there.

The trial was more than an event I wouldn't miss, it was the culmination of years of waiting. Flossie's son was in acute squirm, either digging into his pocket deep for a hundred-thousand after-tax dollars, or getting run hard around the block on judgments, collections, liens, garnishments—all the unkind realities a guy in my line of work learns about, coming up through the ranks. I feared my own motivation, feared that the vindication I longed for was more a part of Flossie's curse than I cared to admit. I wanted to pop Flossie's son in the nose, and I tried justifying that motivation as coming from my old man's side of the family. I thought of letting that go too, along with the past; Flossie's son was so old now, so shrunk. Then I stopped thinking about concepts and the way people should be. I thought best to let nature take its course, to let events unfold according to the virtues of the players. I thought The Devilment would be there quacking, but who would listen to a woman so shrill with such a large ass?

Mother cooperated far more than she ever had, keeping to a minimum her whine of, "But he is my brother. What if he doesn't have the money?"

"He can always mortgage the house," I consoled her. "Or sell some cars or get a loan. Or maybe we can get lucky on a criminal charge and lend him the money for his new striped suit."

Mother scowled at prospects for putting Flossie's son in jail. I loved the idea. Our lawyer followed a pattern most lawyers follow, which was that of becoming a disappointment. He, too, thought jail time might be excessive. I told him, "This is an exercise in excess. Excessive bullshit, excessive theft, excessive bitterness. We can prove that he stole. So why shouldn't he do a little time?" The lawyer and Mother shared a scowl then. I allowed that hard time would not be required for now. "But thirty days in the County Jail would be a nice little tidbit to chew on at the Club. Wouldn't it?"

"You're crazy," Mother said.

I didn't think I was any crazier than my old man ever was. We were only focused on immediate modification of an unsatisfactory situation. I contemplated sudden changes, so easily imagining a misplaced comment, a word, a phrase, a look I wouldn't like because it would defame my family; I imagined Flossie's son insulting me, for which I would respond in the tradition of my family, with a straight shot to the nose. I was so ready for it I could not see how it would not happen. I pondered revenge and risk.

I stayed at Brother's house, on the fold-out couch in the aquarium-and-TV room. He'd picked me up at the airport the night before after a long, most miserable time in the friendly skies, London to St. Louis. We winged farther, farther, farther north, across the Arctic Circle and the permafrosted earth, unbroken white from horizon to horizon, even at thirty thousand feet, and every few hundred miles or so a few Quonset huts, shacks, buildings, igloos, whatever, sprinkled the frosting with chocolate flecks. Here, in bitter cold and blizzard winds people were engaged in their inevitable pursuit, community. Who in the hell would live down there, and why? Each settlement looked half buried in the ice and snow, looked uninhabited except for smoke from a chimney. In only a few hours across the glaring tundra, you could easily see why these places are known for alcoholism, why liquor is key to sanity here, or to insanity.

They must have been Indians, Mongolians, Polynesians looking for new routes or escape or spices, never mind, they were the same old cavemen who trekked everywhere on earth and settled in to become native. I imagined living down there and wanted to experience it, but I could not. That was the second idea I could not grasp in a short time, the first being not popping Flossie's son in the nose, and I wondered if a significant percentage of the world's population could be more advanced than me, living in the ice, letting grudges go.

And I wondered if the people living down there were in fact the warmest people in the world, so warm they could live anywhere. I imagined that the warmth came from their hearts naturally, that they learned warm-heartedness from their parents, and from the leader of their land, the Ice King.

I wondered if anyone could become all that different from their parents, because response to life in its extremes of hot and cold—of cruelty and compassion, of right and wrong—is taught by parents, usually by example. Most babies look up soon after birth and bond with the big creatures nearby. Most children grow up to serve a standard. Maybe down there it was a standard of warmth.

I'd read of monks in Tibet who become reclusive, solitary among the icy peaks, the frozen whispers, whose hermetic life and continuing meditation are supported by disciples who bring water and food from time to time. I wondered if some people may search for years along a similarly barren, chill trail, to find a place of solace and repose, a place of resolution between the generations.

I ordered a brandy, contemplating the earth below, with its flecks and curiosities, its collective imagination and all its people trying to sort things out. I'd known for a long time that I was a disciple, that the standard was one of fair play, but that a dark, human potential, revenge, resided as well in the line.

But meditations ended on the verge of the light—it was time to shut the windowshades for a slam-dunk basketball competition, reruns of *M.A.S.H.* and *Nightcourt*, and then a bad movie, as if that pabulum was a better view than the heavens.

After the glitz, the reruns and trash, the windows stayed shut, maybe because the folks forgot they were ever open.

St. Louis was thirteen hours later and came on with a compression in the head and chest that felt like poison and lint balled up and packed into my nose and lungs. Brother had a joint rolled up and waiting in his new truck because a joint for reentry had become a tradition, maybe because seeing immediate family only once every year or two, seeing the aging process on first glimpse, is a reality too harsh to take straight up. We cut mortality with a joint, eased in with a few jokes.

Brother brought Sissy's son along, J. Woodrow, home from his second year at college. We sat in the front seat, J. Woody between us, not moving, staring ahead, until Woody said, "Let's go." Woody, the nephew, thought Brother and I were nuts, which was somehow gratifying, confirming that our generation gap was multidirectional.

"We want to talk to you about your drug problem," Brother said.

"I don't have one," Woody said.

Brother turned to him saying, "We know," and he lit the joint. Woody said he didn't smoke the stuff, and he especially didn't smoke it during the week. So we passed it over him until Brother asked him if he understood the potential for bad blood in the family. So Woody had a few hits, got blasted with his uncles, bonding so the next generation would not need to suffer a feud like the last generation.

At the airport parking-lot gate, Brother gave the attendant his ticket and peeled off a couple bucks, and Woody leaned toward the window and called to the attendant, "Hey, how do you get a nun pregnant?" The attendant had been taking tickets and making change for years and didn't lose the count. Woody yelled, "You fuck her!"

Brother and I laughed, hopeful at prospects for a young heir. "Hey, what's the worst thing about being an atheist?" Woody asked. We gave up. "No one to talk to when you're getting head!"

"A good college education," Brother said.

"Only the best," I said.

"Fucking right," Woody said. "Four grand a semester."

St. Louis in January is colder than Labrador. The wind howling outside sounded like lost centuries returning to haunt the frozen night; little gusts sounded like new time dying in quick flurries, and at night the dull gray town looked a darker shade of gray, lit weakly with anti-crime lights in bilious amber, and by the soft glow of millions of TV sets tuned mindless, prime time—and by the lights of all the buildings where all the people would go tomorrow to work or shop, work and shop until they died.

I asked Brother what was new. He said he worried for a long time that Mother would die before Flossie dies. Now he thought he might die before Flossie dies.

Brother's suburb looked like Smallville, that little town made famous by Lionel Electric Trains, laid out perfect on plywood, with a train station and a guy holding a lantern going in and out, in and out. The biggest action on Main Street was the Hobby Shop; it sold little cars and boats and airplanes that really ran, as if movement itself was a commodity, exotic, amazing, imported in miniature.

Thoughts like these are best left unspoken. And stoned to the gills, not speaking is easy, possibly natural.

And stoned to the gills allows forgetfulness too, easy as a second nature. So I forgot that Brother's new truck was a foot higher off the ground than a car, so I fell out at the end of Brother's driveway, fell into the dirty snow, the yellow and brown slush with its half-dead, icy stink rising like cold ammonia up my noseholes while Brother and Woody laughed and laughed, and Mother stuck her head out the door and frantically asked what was wrong.

It dawned on me there in that foul moment that I lived in the snow and ice after all, no imagination required. Maybe another truth was struggling to reach me. "My slip forked," I said, picking myself up, preempting further ridicule with, "Jesus, what a great town this is. It's got everything." But my weak attempt at saving face was overridden by Brother, yelling at me to get my goddamn suitcase so he could pull into the garage. Mother began with her hurry up, come in, sit down and eat, while it's still hot.

Inside would have been uneventful, but Woody wanted to share his adventure. He swooned, kind of, hands out like he was ready to fly, and he giggled and said stupid things like, "Geez, those colors."

Brother and I laughed at the silly kid. Mother didn't get it. So Woody lit up the roach and sucked on it big time, like he'd seen Hollywood people do in the movies. Mother still didn't get it, she was so focused on serving the perfectly browned potatoes, the overboiled broccoli, the baked chicken and carrots—her specialty—with a few chops, in case anyone wanted some chops, the squashes, greens, more potatoes, this time twice-baked, and the soups, especially the beef-barley, an old favorite. "Don't eat that. That's mine," she said, indicating an older, smaller, leftover bowl of soup.

She served it up quick and anxious that we'd arrived a full three minutes ago and still were not eating with two hands, don't worry yet about the cookies, cakes and ice cream.

Woody passed the roach to Brother, who took a hit and passed it to me with the broccoli. Then Mother got it. "Oh, my God!" she said. "You're smoking that LSD. I'm going to be sick."

Brother laughed again, and Woody got another lesson in family play when Brother said, "I'm going to be sick too. I don't know why he brings this stuff to town. Is this why we send him to college?"

Woody looked at me for help, but too late. "Me too," I said. "Four grand a semester and for what? So he can come home like a drug addict and try to drag us down with him. This stuff is poison!"

Woody cried foul. Mother said, "Put that away and eat! Now!" She served and watched, watched and served. And homecoming was then official, with one of Mother's extravagant meals.

I was up early next morning, awakened before first light by a phone call from Mother. She would be over again in a few hours but she knew I'd be up because of the jet lag, and she called to ask what I wanted for breakfast and to review the refrigerator, shelf by shelf. The fridge was jammed so packed the door wouldn't seal—a chair kept it shut. I left the phone on the bed and took a leak, brushed my teeth, took a shower, and hung it up. It rang again. Mother said we got cut off and she started again on bagels and eggs and smoked fish and coffee cakes and paradise cakes and herring and, of course, what was left of dinner.

"Why are you up?" I asked.

"I get up at five. I like to get an early start," she said.

I told her it was a good thing she called because I was on the verge of starvation and it was a miracle that she had known intuitively of my hunger, because I wasn't sure where to find something to eat.

"Wait until you're a mother," she said.

I had coffee, poking around Brother's kitchen in fair amazement at its similarity to Mother's kitchens over the years. Brother was mid-forties, already, many years independent. But his kitchen was a direct connection to the past, possibly an attachment; it reflected Mother and her instinct for nesting in hard times, as if he, too, was from the Great Depression.

"I'm from the Depression," Mother always said, when she needed to be driven to a supermarket across town she'd been to the day before because they'd had toothpaste on sale, and she'd picked up a year's supply of toothpaste for Brother and me—she mailed mine, a tube or two at a time, each package with a hurriedly written note asking, *Do you need toothpaste?* and a reminder, *You must shop the sales!* Sometimes Brother and I had two years of toothpaste if the toothpaste sale came twice in the same season. I remember once when I was way younger, trying to explain to Mother the value of cash in hand, and the false value of buying toothpaste futures. She looked at me with rancor and pity, like I didn't know nothing from nothing, like maybe a good solid Depression would open my eyes.

And, while she nailed down the toothpaste deal crosstown, she'd picked up a five-pound bag of sugar; what the hell, she was there, but the bastards got her for a buck eighty-five, and don't you know she found the same bag the next day for a buck fifteen. So, it was back across town with me or Brother protesting over the miles, the time, the gas, the wear and tear to save a few cents, but the protests were weak next to Mother's compulsion. "What? You think I'm nuts? Besides, we have to go anyway."

We had to go anyway to cop onions at twenty-seven cents a pound less than on our side of town, and if you don't think that adds up on a twenty-pound bag, well I've got news for you. Supermarket visits nearly always included return items—items purchased in faith that pricing could go no lower, when in fact downward the price plummeted the very next day or two, sometimes as much as a dollar. Brother lived there and got used to it, or at least he expected it. I never did, and when the supermarket managers asked what was wrong, and Mother told them the price was sixty cents lower across town, I told them, "She's from the Depression. The Great Depression. She's from it." Supermarket managers must see it regular; they all nod and take it back, so they can get on with their lives.

Brother's kitchen wasn't exactly small; a grown man could have taken two strides across it when it was empty, back when the earth first cooled and the sedimentation of aeons had not yet layered itself over the crust of the thing. By late in the twentieth century a grown man, or an ungrown man, could only pivot slow, finding new footholds on the marshbottom as he moved from fridge to stove.

The pantry held twelve cases of Acme Cola in an even mix of Diet Acme, Classic Acme, New Acme and Caffeine Free Acme in both Diet Classic and Diet New. His pantry was an indictment of American culture, proof of a sick society that supports a billion-dollar industry in sugar water with bubbles. Acme Cola came in cans or bottles and looked exactly like Coca-Cola but cost much less. Buying Acme was an act of rebellion, a vote for anarchy, and, as Brother put it, "Why pay more?"

Gross national product has decomposed to the literal level, causing doubt on the value of numbers when all they reflect is an exchange of money for sugar water with bubbles.

He had a case of olives and two gallons of pickled okra, enough canned goods for a crew of nine at sea adrift for a week, and two tins, five gallons each, of dog biscuits, because dogs get hungry, too. Outside the closet were foothills of bags, paper and plastic, tinfoil, rubber bands, empty jars and boxes, and, of course, many balls of string that unraveled in odd lengths, two inches to two feet, although most of the two footers were actually shorties tied together. Mother always said it's good to have some long string ready to go.

Stacked on top of the stacks of empty plastic containers was a Sara Lee Pound Cake foil container a few years old, used and washed, used and washed, used and washed a hundred times until it looked soft as old denim—it held eggs wrapped in Kleenex. I later asked Brother why. He said Mother put them there, he didn't know why. I asked Mother why she had wrapped eggs in Kleenex and nestled them into an ancient Sarah Lee foil pan. She grimaced, like I'd asked her why she hadn't changed her underwear, and when I pressed her for an answer, she said, "You talk so crazy."

Beside the tissued eggs were more plastic bags in plastic bags—bags packed full of bags. Rubber bands in jars and plastic bags in jars and jars in cabinets that could not close on all the jars. Brother had two old toasters buried deep on the counter under a Busch Bavarian clock, brown, dusty and dead on 4:30; under bags and boxes and plastic tubs of plastic forks and metal forks and odd forks and spoons and knives from a half dozen services for eight, or twelve; and two sets of Ginsu knives as seen on TV, an amazing value at not $49.95, not $39.95, no, not even $29.95, but yours today for only $19.95, guaranteed sharp for fifty years. And if you order today, you get the slicer, the dicer, the peeler and this amazing paring knife worth $60 all by itself! They were there, too. Brother had two sets because two is better than one, and anyway, fifty years rolls around before you know it. The second set waited under a five-year supply of pens and pencils, some of them collector's items already, with Presidential candidates from the '60s printed on them.

Neatly folded rags and rags and rags lay on most horizontal places, here and there among the active rags hanging from faucets and cabinet handles. Brother still had the GE iron Mother got in '37 when she was just a girl. She used it through all her lives and marriages and moves, until Brother got his own house in '81, or '86, and needed an iron, a good one. I watched her demonstrate, like a Chinaman, wadding up the shirts and then grabbing water as it ran from the faucet, grabbing it into the shirt and then ironing. But not too quick; you have to wait so the water can absorb evenly.

A banged-up, leaky, melted down Mr. Coffee showing around 300,000 miles sat front and center. A new Mr. Coffee, still in the box, sat under the sink with the rags and bags and a few more jars—had sat there since the day it arrived in 1972, bought on sale, still sat unused because, what the hell, the old one still worked.

That was the year I got my first job on a boat, a shrimp trawler out of Okracoke, North Carolina, *Edith*, one of the old PT boats from WWI, sixty-five feet long and one of the last survivors of the splinter fleet because she was all wood, stem to stern, built late in the campaign, in 1918, the year Mother was born. Jeffrey Baxter owned *Edith* and must have known a lubberly kid from Hoosierville when he saw me coming, and he must have known for sure when he heard me lie, *Sure thing, I worked on plenty boats before.* Because a kid with plenty experience at sea would have understood speechlessness, would have said with his eyes what he'd seen.

But Jeffrey'd been around and maybe slung some bullshit in his time too, so he said, "Four-thirty tomorrow morning." So I showed up in the dark and stood on the dock imagining the thousands of dawns like the one just ahead that *Edith* had sliced her way into. She had the demeanor and build of Ma Kettle and looked just as indifferent that this dawn would begin at last my salty adventures. *Edith* was massive tied to the dock, and she didn't get much smaller in the channel heading out to the sound.

Out in open water she shrank to the same proportion of a toy boat in a tub, with the same slosh and bounce. Sunrise came on gray and yellow with a pink rash over that, all reflected on the bilious swells from two directions and on my face. I was filled with diesel fumes and the glory of life at sea by 5:30 and was sick as a mangy, beat-up, poisoned dog by 6:00, breakfast time, when Jeffrey walked out on deck with a paper plate piled high with fresh boiled shrimp.

"Boy, you're lucky," I said, slinging the fake, hail-fellow bullshit, like he wouldn't be able to tell I was gray going green—"Get to eat shrimp every day! Boy!... Lucky...."

Jeffrey spoke in the Cockney accent of the hoigh-toiders, immigrants from London's East End to North Carolina's outer banks, where they stayed and fished and married each other forever more. He looked at me like I was nuts, and he said, "Maggits is all they is. That's all they is. Maggits." And he ate two at once with disgust, letting the legs dangle out his lips while he chewed, so I could see for myself just how lucky he was. Jeffrey thought anyone who peeled a shrimp had time to kill, or else wanted to put on the dog, like it was a sit-down feed or something. He ate them whole, sometimes with the heads on—"Them's the juiciest parts!" He was further amazed at the plastic tools some people used to de-vein the shrimp. He said the vein was nothing but shit, and it was high time—*hoigh toim*—them people figured it out. But what difference would it make, getting the shit out? You was still eating maggots. He shoveled a few into his gob, crushing them on one side, sorting the shmush with his tongue, then dribbling shell fragments out the other side of his mouth. The chewed waste tumbled onto his chest, and he laughed again at the sheer notion of luck on a guy like him—or me.

Jeffrey didn't even look when I lunged another heave over the rail—he knew. He only finished crunching and dribbling his plate of maggots and said, "You moit git over it. You moit not. Awroit, let's get 'em in a water." He meant the nets, and he dropped the winches into gear as naturally as a corporation man slips into his suit coat. He let the bags over and then the nets and the tickle chains, while I watched like a bump on a log, or maybe more like a spore growth, until Jeffrey realized too late just how worthless a lubber is on a boat, when I just stood there watching the tickle chain slide on over the deck and take a wrap around my ankle and then flip over the rail with me right behind. I spun in the air and grabbed the rail with both hands and hung there.

Jeffrey jumped to the big steel brackets suspended over the rail and pushed the big wood and lead doors forward on their racks to slow the nets, first port, then, leaping across the deck, starboard, picking us up a solid six seconds of slack time before I would get yanked off the rail and sucked ninety feet down by a half-ton of rig. Then he stood in front of where I'd been flipped straight up in the air and over, where I hung on from the outboard side. Jeffrey slid his fingers under my wrists and said, "Twarl yer lags gentle like. Slow down. Relax… Now." The chain unwrapped slow and easy and fell away about a heartbeat before the big doors slid off their racks, swung out and went in with a half-ton splash and a mess o' bubbles that would have surfaced with little last gasps inside. He pulled me back aboard. He didn't yell or anything, but told me to *Stand over thar* while he worked it alone.

At the end of the day he didn't fire me either, but he said he couldn't pay me on days I didn't work. I stayed on, but stayed fairly worthless. It wasn't a question of proving myself or proving anything to Jeffrey or making money. I'd given up all that proving bullshit years before, when I was nine or eleven or so, and Mother kept telling me what I was proving every time I took the bit in my teeth and slogged to victory. I'd told her so often that eighty cents an hour wasn't victory, it was slave labor, that I realized by age ten or twelve that Mother was confused on what builds character. A smart man knows when to cut his losses.

And the money wasn't in shrimping, anyway. Oh, it was big dough the year before, when a crew percentage of the take could go to hundreds of dollars a week. But that was the year before, so the year I went, every trawler from the Outerbanks to the Sea Islands focused on Port Royal and Calibogue Sounds. No, it wasn't the money.

I stayed on for the fantasy nurtured since *The Seventh Voyage of Sinbad.* I wanted to go, too; needed to go. I sure as hell didn't want a career on a shrimp boat, not after what I'd seen, but how could I handle the open sea, if I puked on little six-foot swells that weren't even breaking?

I guess I was lucky, because Jeffrey didn't mind—because Sue picked me up the first afternoon and every afternoon, and Jeffrey longed to show her the rule of the sea. I thought he was a billy goat and harmless. He told me a few weeks into it that his wife had died that year. He was thirty-one. She'd been twenty-eight—"She's purty as a picture. I swear she was. She's purty as your wife. We had us two kids. They's still up home." Jeffrey didn't cry, even as two tears rolled down his face; he only told his story as if it happened like breakfast had happened, and shrimp drivel and tears are what accompany those things. Then we got the nets into the water.

I never did get up to a hundred percent on the deck work and machinery, but I probably got to ninety-five. I could keep my coffee down, leap from rail to rail and gobble maggots with a laugh, heads on, in roly-poly waves and diesel dust.

Sue and I had Jeffrey over for dinner a few times. He wore a white shirt and aftershave every time and once brought a bushel of crabs and showed us how to dress them out live and cook them right without the guts and without boiling the taste out.

I only stayed on a few weeks, even though I'd anticipated a life of it, because it only took a few weeks to figure it was more grease, rot, salt, gut pounding, hangover, instant death, and maggots than glory or money. We had a few adventures—engine failure in a heavy ebb, when Jeffrey went below for eight hours in a hundred degrees and fixed it. I monitored the bilge pumps, running straight off the batteries, and kept a few boys apprised of our progress on the radio. We snagged a hulk in a net one day and couldn't back off and faced losing the net, the chains, the doors—half a season's work. Jeffrey dove on it, thirty-five, forty feet he figured, hand over handing down the drag cable into the murk. I don't think he liked that stuff, but he loved not knowing what each day would bring.

They mostly brought nothing. I found a couple sheets of glass leaning against a barn and cut them down and glued them up into a tank one Sunday, and the next Sunday I set it up with a filter and pump and filled it with seawater, blowfish, batfish, butterfish, sea robins, fantail file fish, upsidedown file fish, pipe fish, and once an Atlantic giant seahorse. Jeffrey was amazed at the sheer notion of keeping them alive and then putting them in a tank and watching them for their movement and beauty.

We hit a couple bonanzas, when the big nets came up full of nothing but shrimp—once when the barometer dropped two millibars in a few hours and the VHF buzzed with hurricane chatter. We had all of Port Royal Sound to ourselves that day and tore'm up, heading in at last light when the seas had built to ten feet and broke over the bow then over the wheelhouse as *Edith* plowed through and Jeffrey at the wheel looked like a man fulfilled. He said he just wished those boys would be at the docks when we came in.

Those were happy days, but I said no when Jeffrey said *Edith* would work it on back up toward home, and I could work it with him, if I wanted to. That was my biggest payout. I didn't get sick anymore. I could work it. And that counted for plenty later on.

Maybe that was about the time Brother brought home his new Mr. Coffee, on sale, and stashed it under the sink for the time he'd really need it.

Behind the old Mr. Coffee topside was the new food dehydrator as seen on TV, and surrounding it to the horizon were little plastic bags of dehydrated apple slices. Unsliced, undried apples and potatoes sat between the dried apples in plastic bags and empty plastic bags—and hand towels and face towels and paper towels. The electric socket on the counter had three extensions in the three plugs and three more plugs in each of the three extensions, all beside a tower of plastic margarine tubs and two radios, mute since '68—which was the year those radios carried late-breaking news about Richard Daly and Hubert Humphrey stealing America in Chicago, the year it came down to which side of the line you were on, and it was long hair and bell-bottoms and more LSD than you could hallucinate a stick at on our side. Two cardboard boxes of money-saving coupons in the 10- to 35-cent range, some on the bottom expired twenty-four years now, but even some that old still good, you know.

The newspaper collection filled a corner beside another stack of paper bags, and the darkness outside broke gently through the new curtains tacked up ten years ago over the old curtains. A cardboard beer case printed in the holiday design sat beside the ninety-gallon trash can. The beer case was from two Christmases ago and was empty, except for two beers.

The old Mr. Coffee squealed and moaned and gave up some coffee as begrudgingly as a wino's tired veins give blood, and I stepped outside the many-layered kitchen for a sit among the years and years at the dining room table. In stark contrast to the kitchen, the table was empty, except for the butterfly napkin holder I made in shop class in seventh grade in '61. Brother's house is an archive; he inherited everything, including the habit of saving things.

I can't think of all the crap he's saved without an overwhelming feeling of tedium, deadweight, no air. I've saved nothing, stayed light as a feather. Yet, I get out of bed on the same side on most mornings of my life of adventure and follow the same steps to the same two footprints in the bathroom, hold up the wall at the same angle and bend my cockadoodle *schwantz* down to where I mostly miss the floor. And I brush my teeth, feed the cats, shower, dress, and open the door just like every day is just like yesterday, and tomorrow. I know the days lose their delineation and instead have come to define my life in terms that will survive me, terms that don't mean shit because the change, the unknown, the adventure, the fun boils down to routine, to days, sooner or later. Some people might call it a crisis, here, in the middle of a life of adventure, but I call that bullshit, too, and I move like a man in a dream, stuck in the ooze, most mornings.

I've read we cannot know alternate realities. We come to a fork in the road, and we choose; this way or that. And I believed that theory to be true, until I wondered just where in the hell else could a road go to, any road?

And then I come home—the home that is the everlasting home, because Mother lives there, cooks daily for me there, worries that I'm not there to eat, to relax, to live. I've come home from a hundred different roads all leading back from the same place, away.

This return is different though, part of a trip that's kind of business but with a unique luminescence to it, a sweet, soft lilt of maybe, maybe after all these years, revenge. Maybe it's too bad, but now the tedium of all the days will get a reprieve, a lift, a reason to be. I think the very best family reunions should have a little court time on the agenda for settling old scores and setting things straight.

The sameness my roads led to seems a long time away from what life was back in '61, when I stood in front of the jigsaw, cutting out two butterflies with a seven-inch wingspan from quarter-inch plywood. I painted each one yellow with black trim on the wings—my idea—and though the napkin holder looks silly now, it looked sleek and artistic then, the two butterflies held in place by inch-long dowel rods at the bottom. I wonder how many other napkin holders survived from the seventh grade shop class of '61 at Plaza Park School, and how many napkin holder makers.

My butterfly is still ready for action, jammed with too many napkins, separating a pot-metal set that says *Salt* and *Pepper* and below that, each one says *Camp Cooke*.

Mother was a Girl Scout leader in '55 or '57, when Sissy was a Girl Scout. Spring and fall those years when Troop 38 went up to Camp Cooke for a weekend, Mother had to take Brother and me along because, well, what else could she do? We were six and seven or so and couldn't be left with our old man, because Mother knew it would only turn into a weekend of bologna sandwiches and beer and most likely some tawdry women to steer us wrong. Brother and I hadn't yet been clued in on the sex thing, and our little hormones couldn't give rise to much more than a giggle. We looked at the situation as a weekend of fun, plain and simple, with none of the pesky ulterior that accompanies males in their transition through adolescence. But at night all the Girl Scouts got tucked into their cabins, where they told ghost stories in candlelight or had pillow fights, and Brother and I weren't allowed to join in, even after we'd hiked and swam and all that other stuff all day long with the girls—even after we discovered an abandoned concrete ledge that was an old spillway that emptied into a ravine about four hundred feet below, and an old ratty rope hung down from a dried-out limb about fifty feet overhead, and all the girls shrieked and giggled, and so did Brother and I. Brother was already gaining weight then, up to about one-forty, and he grabbed the rope and took ten steps away from the ledge and got a running start and swung so far out everybody gasped, and the limb cracked just as Mother turned her head and saw what everyone saw, that Brother was dead meat.

But the limb didn't break and he swung back in, and just as his feet touched the old ledge, the rope broke. Mother is still figuring why that one played out like it did for Brother, still reminding him what a fool he could be. We didn't care—Brother and I were the craziest kids in the group, but that was way before Girl Scouts knew they could opt for careers and be crazy too. Still we couldn't play with the girls after lights out, for some reason, so we got tucked into our cots in the Troop Leaders' cabin, where we faked sleeping while the five troop leaders got undressed. They yakked about the day's adventures and the girls and slipped out of their dresses and their slips and carried on just like Brother and I were sound asleep and not peeping through our eye slits, right down to bras and panties; sweet Jesus you could feel the electricity in our cots.

But then Mrs. Rice, Carol Rice's mother, kind of looked over at the two little boys sound asleep in their cots, and she went ahead and got bare-ass naked. She was old, over thirty, which was much older then because nobody knew about exercise, not that exercise would have helped Carol Rice's mother. We didn't care anyway about tits and pussies then, six and seven; we only giggled. It was the principle of the thing, she was so proper and full of shit that busting her naked made the weekend perfect—she shrieked and tried to cover her tits and her pussy with her hands, but she didn't have enough hands. That was funny, so we laughed out loud.

It wasn't until a whole week later, after the fame and glory of the deed was all around the camp and followed us home that we even discussed the frightening, smoldering thicket Mrs. Rice kept in her panties. It was like any scary thing we knew couldn't really get us— it made us giggle some more.

Brother keeps our high school yearbooks on the dining room table, too, so high school days are as close at hand as a fresh napkin. Jim Bollinger was sponsor of the high school Writer's Guild, and he still grins stupidly from the back pages of the '65 yearbook. I never joined the high school Writer's Guild, because I wasn't much of a joiner, and because they were so noisy, so wacky, so zany, so confused and undeveloped, and so keen on compounding those problems. I only remember Mr. Bollinger clearing me up on the nature of writing and prospects for market success. Jim Bollinger was one of my high school English teachers and kind of a goofy guy, but maybe that's redundant. I got As and Bs from him on my compositions during first semester of '64-'65, because I liked working on a composition and making it good. But an A+ on the final—another composition off-the-cuff—got me a B for the semester. What a setup. "Hey, what?" I asked Mr. Bollinger, report card in hand. He wasn't a strong man, his fortitude best reflected by a twitch in his lips that moved quickly into a smile, and then quickly out of it, like he was afraid to stay anywhere too long.

He said he wanted to motivate me to do better. He motivated me all right, motivated me to see that it didn't mean shit, As or Bs.

A few weeks later, well into second semester and compositions thrown together in minutes with arrogance and resentment, Mr. Bollinger put a *See me!* under a C+. He said it was plain to see that I'd stopped trying, stopped thinking things through. I told him that when he gave me a B first semester, it hit home like a *Fuck you.* That was cool. I told him my compositions now were just a *Fuck you, too.* He did his funny twitch and had no more to say.

The following year I drew Mrs. Swopes, a scrawny, hook-nosed woman of twenty-seven or twenty-eight, who the rest of the senior boys wanted to fuck. I couldn't figure it out. They all flirted with her and she flirted back, which got them going. I didn't participate. Moreover, I got restless, impatient with her giggle and her batty eyes. Expository writing was then one of the few things in school I liked, but Mrs. Swopes gave me a C- on anything I wrote. I could do my best and get a C-, or just write diddly squat on some scratch paper and get a C-. I theorized she was acting out her rejection by a senior boy, me.

We had to write a composition on *Macbeth*, and as luck would have it, Sissy had already written one just the month before. She was a senior, too, but at Washington University in St. Louis. She got an A+. I copied Sissy's paper verbatim as a control experiment, then turned it in and got a C- with a *no no no* and a few *awkward constructions* written in the margin by Mrs. Swopes. You can imagine Mrs. Swopes' denial when I told her she was not the right teacher for some students, me among them. She condescended instantly, driveling over whose place it was to determine appropriateness. You can imagine her chagrin when I showed her Sissy's paper and explained, "I didn't write this paper. My sister did. She's a senior at Washington University majoring in English literature. Washington University is much harder to get into than this high school."

Mrs. Swopes looked startled. Then, with disbelief, she said, "You plagiarized your composition?"

"No. I copied it word for word. This one got an A at Washington University. You gave it a C- here at Bullfrog High. You want to press the issue, that's fine by me. I think we should call in the principal and the English department and the goddamn school board. Or you can transfer me to a new teacher?" What a bitch. What a waste of time.

Fuck her, too, I thought on my grand exit. Mrs. Swopes said it would be best if we worked this problem out ourselves. I told her the work was done. I did it. She would be required to dispense As as necessary. To this day I don't understand her failure to read a composition with no bias for the writer's failure to flirt with her. It was so unfair; how could she not have known that some guys thought she was scrawny with a hook nose?

I got transferred to Mrs. Hussong, who was old even then, who taught me more that year than in all the years prior and graded me according to my accomplishment.

Mrs. Swopes just wanted the incident to go away. I tried, and never said anything to anyone afterward, but I could not resist giving her the eyeball, head to toe, then laughing once while shaking my head. Because I loved being right, loved being pissed off and right. That was my biggest problem, but it's been falling away for years. I'm still often right, but being nice about it takes more give than I ever imagined in the early days.

A rumble out front of Brother's house consigned all memories to proper proportion. It was trash day, and when the rumble reached 7.5 and sounded like it would come through the front wall of the house, I pulled back both curtains to see Brother's garbage men slinging hash, whistling and waving fists in truck lingo above the stink and tremor, letting the driver know: Stop, go, ease left, ease right, come on back. They used Brother's driveway to turn around in, pulling in past the limits of reasonable good taste until the big garbage truck windshield was nose to nose with Brother's big front window.

Alive and well, these guys stood out from the dull commute. Even in the razor-sharp cold of a Midwest winter they generated flies and stink—a million zillion flies, maybe two tons of stink. The guy at the wheel chewed a fat cigar that looked chewed a few times before. It wasn't lit. And he grinned in a combination of greeting and playful fun, like he knew the truth, because, well, just look at this evidence. His windshield was big as Brother's big window, and tucked down in front on the bottom edge of the windshield, spread open and taped to the glass was a centerfold from *Hustler* magazine, where a woman, also spread open, further spread her labia majora with her fingers so us guys could get a better look-see. A bunch of dead flies down between the magazine and the windshield made the picture perfect, underscored the garbage man's truth. The driver watched his side mirror, went on a whistle from his partner, eased left and came on back. It was enough to wake up everyone else in the house which that morning was Brother, his parrot, and his dogs. They barked and screeched and nearly pissed in their pants.

And with squealing air brakes and cans banging down the street, lids clanging like cymbals in a sunrise symphony, the garbage guys continued delivering their truth. You won't see a garbage man in a suit and a power tie. Power tie? Fuck—these guys got stray maggots on their shoulders, rotting grunge dripping off their gloves, old stogies shredded down to swamp pulp in their teeth.

Brother let the dogs take a leak, fed the bird, got coffee for himself and, still in his robe, since it was Saturday, shuffled into the guest/aquarium/TV room. Passing by he said, "It's the Smurfs. No talking, please."

Brother became a schoolteacher, inner-city, all black, elementary level. Father figure to thirty children without fathers, colleague to thirty teachers who knew all about white people, oh yeah. His days were filled with emotional disparity, racial hatred, political bullshit.

Maybe he was back in third grade to set things straight, I don't know. I went to school once, though, and he introduced me to his class as Ronald Reagan, President of the United States of America, because, he said, these children would most likely never be exposed to powerful men otherwise. The children asked, *Where is Nancy?* She's had a headache since last night, I told them. And I told them not to

worry, because soon the wealth and promise of America would trickle
down to them, too. They wanted to know when, and why not now,
and where's the ice cream, you honky fucker?

Maybe Brother went back to grade school to make it right because
it wasn't all right for him. He was among the first in our neighborhood to cop smokes behind the garage.

But that was in eighth grade, years after the worst of it. He didn't
like to fish—wouldn't even think of it, didn't like to talk about it or
hear about it. He'd eat it, if he had to, but he'd rather have chicken.
So when he got about fifty dollars' worth of fishing tackle from our
old man for his tenth birthday, because it was time for him to grow
up and be a man and learn how to fish already, he cried.

That was not acceptable behavior to our old man, who, in the eyes
of many others, Brother included, was not the cavalier rogue I perceived, but a rough, mean, often drunk and disagreeable man who
took out his failures and frustrations on those closest to him. Brother
cried. The old man yelled, all about being a man and crybabies and
fishing and growing up and getting out and not being so goddamn fat
your whole life, and how none of us were worth the powder to blow
us up, for chrissake.

That was the unromantic side of my old man that I forgot to mention, the side of him that reasoned fishing tackle as the perfect gift for
Brother, fishing tackle that had long been wanted by the old man, and
here was a perfect excuse to blow the money on it.

Then he smacked the shit out of Brother, but it was only a backhand, and we were used to that, and it didn't hurt that much and
didn't happen that often and wasn't nearly as bad as getting spanked
with a Socko paddle, which is what we got when we really fucked
up—like the time we wrecked all the hose bibs outside the house and
the water ran full bore all day, until the whole goddamn house looked
like a houseboat, afloat, and we got blood blisters on our asses for it,
and lay there whimpering in the dying afternoon as the ducks
quacked happily outside, and the yelling and shrieking reached new
heights down the hall.

Wait until I tell your father, Mother had said when the water began to rise. When he got home, she broke the news to him of the destruction and mess we had caused. Then we got whipped, and she screamed bloody murder at him and called him a lunatic and threatened to call the cops, so he split downtown for a reasonable drunk, after showing her what any goddamn fucking idiot over twelve ought to know: the shut-off valve. Three easy twists and the water was off, and so was the old man. Oh, Mother was not without blame, cursing him out the driveway for expecting her to know what no man would ever take a lousy minute to show her.

After the fishing-tackle, birthday-backhand fiasco, everything got back to normal, kind of. But that one hit Brother hard, and he decided to kill our old man. The old man had a tall Milk of Magnesia every night so he could take a good shit first thing in the morning, ditch all the steak and fried chicken that otherwise got stuck. His habit was so steady he got the giant-size Milk of Magnesia, so big and in such a dark blue bottle, he wouldn't notice the two ounces of iodine Brother dumped into it—this, in '57 or '58, when they still put a skull and crossbones on iodine bottles.

So Brother got focused, which took balls because it was just like Jack in the Beanstalk trying to steal the giant's harp; he could have died trying. He slipped into the bathroom just after the old man got home, while I was mixing up another highball, and he dumped the iodine into the Milk of Magnesia and shook it up.

Then he came back out and half smiled for the next five hours and stayed scarce, and tossed and turned and kept on sweating it out after we heard the old man in the bathroom pouring a long Milk of Magnesia. Brother figured that was it for sure, that the old man would be dead in the morning, and they'd find out Brother poisoned him, and then he'd get sent to reform school and prison and have to stay there forever.

He drifted off to sleep finally about four, but we were awakened about five by an unusually thunderous shit storm in the bathroom. Brother breathed easy, and in the next few minutes both he and the old man had something out of their systems that hadn't been out for a long time. The old man was in a better mood that sunrise than I ever remembered. Brother and I got up early and went out to play, and the old man didn't die for another three or four years.

Brother is a vegetarian now.

Above the cardboard box collection, near the hutch in the formal dining room at Brother's house, hanging on the wall in a corner is the photo gallery dedicated to me. First is an 8 x 10 of me at twenty on a motorcycle, with a goatee and sunglasses and a worn-out leather jacket from Goodwill. The profile is arrogance again, deadpan, just like Marlon Brando, but mine came across more uncertain, with a dash of fear. That was the summer of high speed across a distant continent. It was taken at the bottom of a long hill at the base of the Swiss Alps, after a blowout on a medium curve at sixty. Death got cheated those days, and though I couldn't hide the fear, I was still alive and willing to go again—crazy enough to fix the flat the same day and ride another four hours across a pass so high my fingers froze stiff, and another snapshot would have shown me more arrogant still, holding my hot exhaust pipes with my hands in ragtag gloves so my finger joints could thaw out. I didn't take no shit from no fucking Alps.

The next shot is another profile in arrogance with maybe a little bit more fear, maybe heading toward humility, or common sense. You can't be sure, and you wouldn't know by looking that the punk in the photo, me, is tripping hard, and it was a bummer. They don't teach you in college what it's like to stare nose to nose into the face of God. That was a lesson we had to teach ourselves. The acid wasn't really bad but was overdosed and padded with strychnine, maybe for the groovy death rush. We loved rushes then. And bad acid couldn't really kill you, most of the time.

Third in the photo gallery is a group shot of Lester and Moonpie and me, taken in sunny Florida in what looks like good times, what with the Porsche and the motor yacht, sunshine and palm trees and all. It was '77 or '78, and we'd just come down from Charleston, South

Carolina, a town with no life, only memory, pickled in Scotch, numbed out on what was, decked out in flowers, like a wake. But then cocaine hit Charleston like defibrillators on a flat-graph cardiac victim. That woke the town up. Lester was the guy to get it from. He flew down to South Florida for the photograph. Moonpie and I drove the Porsche.

Lester was holing up at my place at the time because my wife was soon to be my ex-wife and was gone. I was broke, unemployed, unemployable. I told Lester he could stay—not that he asked, he just started sleeping in the guest room after showing up with groceries and beer and sometimes women, and all the time good drugs. I had none of the above, so what could I say, no? I told him he could stay with a recreational stash, but I didn't want any pounds or kilos at my place. He said that was smart, and was, in fact, the cardinal rule of the surviving drug dealer. You need three places: a place for your stash, a place for your cash, a place to crash—because a dealer's biggest worry is getting busted, either by the cops or by crooks. And if he's with his stash and his cash, he loses everything. Spread out, he can deal again another day.

He'd noticed overall that, in fact, I was smart, and he could use a smart guy, if I wanted to work. He'd been telling me about these renegades in Florida who ran speedboats out to mother ships to off-load drugs and run them in, guys making a hundred grand in a month. I said sure, I'd work, I'd been on plenty boats before, used to have kind of a career on a shrimp boat, you know.

Lester was a lawyer and a CPA, but the law and the numbers bored him, so he started dealing cocaine, since he kind of knew the business, having worked his way through law school dealing reefer. He dealt cocaine in ounces mostly, which he bought by the pound or kilo from associates in South Florida—Colombians, who kept warehouses full of the stuff, and who one time asked Lester if he would run a warehouse himself, he was so well-suited to the job with his legal and accounting skills. Lester said no, he just wanted to work it on the Mom 'n Pop level. I think they scared the shit out of him, until a bunch of Cubans killed all the Colombians with machine guns and became the drug kings in South Florida; until a new bunch of Colombians killed all the Cubans with machine guns and took back what was rightfully theirs.

A kilo went about twenty grand then. Ounced out at a grand per, a kilo rolled over at about eight grand profit. Lester was moving a pound a week or so, and cocaine was still glamorous then, which was way before crack and gangs and epidemic drug abuse, so the guys who dealt it still seemed like lovable outlaws.

It was about that time a big bust went down near town, and a guy got busted who'd come up the dealer ranks from the auto-assembly line where he sold reefer to his fellow employees, so their mindless work could finally make sense. He'd kept rising in the industry to where he ran a sizable distribution network in the Southeast. He got popped with about twelve tons of reefer on three shrimp trawlers, and everybody on board got arrested, got separated and told that the others had made deals with the prosecution. It was plain to see that some outside organization was critical at this point, so somebody got a slew of lawyers to come in quick and counsel all the defendants with the same line, and to assure them that no one had made any deals. Lester maneuvered deftly and became counsel for the kingpin defendant, who was looking down the tube at twenty years in the federal slammer in Atlanta.

The kingpin had been in the import business long enough to make several tons of dough, which he had parlayed into real estate, boats, cars, and so on, all in his mother's or girlfriend's name.

Once all the boys made bail it was high times in town. They couldn't leave, so there was no recourse but to ship in enough drugs to sustain a continuous party until the trial. I was included, being Lester's landlord and a smart guy and all. Everybody was best of friends and just happy to be alive, all shaking hands and tooting it up and making plays for the women, who didn't seem to mind, as long as the toot held out. It was the kind of good times you see on TV, like at the Playboy Mansion, except that these people were even louder and coarser than that.

Lester got the kingpin to hand over the keys to his getaway car right after the trial. It was a black Porsche refitted with jet engines or something, so it screamed, even on a grocery run.

Then Lester drove very fast all over town working out the details for his next fiduciary trust with the kingpin; real estate liquidation. The kingpin needed money first for his defense, and then money for his federal slammer time, since you need significant dough in the Big House to keep your asshole intact, unstretched.

The kingpin had twenty acres of rocky scrub in Central Kentucky he wanted to unload. It was hardly worth a shit, much less the fifty grand he'd paid for it, but he bought this field in the glory days, when he and his band of merry men wanted a landing strip in the Midwest. They'd sent a young renegade up to Kentucky to do the deal; he flashed the cash with outlaw spirit, the local yokels lowered their eyes and said thank you—and called the Feds. So the empire crumbled.

A year later I got sent to liquidate, for the kingpin, via his lawyer, Lester. Lester got me some credit cards in my own name and gave me a hundred dollars in cash for road expenses. I was suddenly mobile and flush.

Lester said if I could get ten grand for the Kentucky property, he'd give me a grand, which was to me then the difference between penniless and a thousand dollars. Lester said don't worry about title complexities, because he'd work all that out in escrow. He was a lawyer, after all.

"How you do-een? Eddie N. Deep. Eddie N. Deep Century 21." Eddie N. Deep wore the piss-yellow blazer of a Century 21 associate. "Computer linked with over fourteen-thousand Century 21 associates worldwide." He offered his hand, telling me the field was worthless, that it held the state record for rattlesnakes per acre—"Ah shitchu not." He said we should have an auction. "Auction draws'm out, don't you know."

I told him I needed ten grand. He said, "Shit. Ain't nobody knows what she'll bring. They'll all be there, but everybody knows about the rocks and rattlesnakes. Shit."

The auction was set for one, just after dinner. Eddie banged the gavel and pleaded for a bid, any bid, and finally got one for five grand. Everybody laughed. Eddie N. Deep said he would have to take this unrealistic offer to the owner for advisement. Everybody looked at me. I shrugged. On the flight home I wondered if the deal would fly, and if I'd get my five hundred on the sale.

I flew south a week later, to the Bahamas, to sell seventy acres. If I could get fifty grand I could keep three. I'd advertised in Germany and France. Lester had paid for that, too.

I got letters from the Sultan of Oman and a few Germans and invited everyone down to Eleuthera for a showing. The Sultan couldn't make it, but the Germans did and wanted to buy it, but wouldn't go into escrow without seeing the title. I called Lester who told me I'd done good, he'd take it from there, come on home, he had another assignment for me.

I hung out a few more days watching the local boys chum sharks with chicken guts. They set a grappling hook with a whole chicken on a towline off the back of a rental jeep. They hooked a thirty-foot hammerhead who dragged the jeep into the water above the hubs, until the idiot at the wheel figured out that the shark was stronger than the jeep and disengaged the towline.

Club Med was just down the beach, so I eased on in and met a girl from Venezuela, but the place wasn't real. She came with me back to my motel for some barbecued chicken and then some funky chicken, and then I was broke again. I really wanted to stay a few more days and hang out with the Bahamians who danced by the pool every night. They laughed at me, I think because they never had seen a white guy who could move like they did, I think, like lumpy syrup, slow with just the right bumps. I wanted to stay there a long time because I couldn't imagine getting tired of the sensuality in the air, this in the days of no AIDS, the days that now seem long ago.

Those people understood the spirit of true fun, that it doesn't cost much, but I didn't even have that and had to come home.

The new assignment was driving the getaway car down to South Florida with Moonpie, Lester's little brother, who had a face more like a cowpie and a temper like a firecracker, or a string of firecrackers. Lester handed over the Porsche keys and four bills—and I suspected that he was a manipulating sonofabitch, keeping me broke so I'd have to run home to run more of his errands. I didn't complain though, because right behind the bills were two guns, .38s, so Moonpie and I could shoot our way out once we ran out of money, I guess. I asked if one gun was a spare and Lester said, "Don't worry, you ain't carrying." I asked why then we had guns. He grinned. "Moonpie likes guns. He needs two. You know, in case he runs out of ammo in one." He giggled. Moonpie grinned and fired off a few rounds, two-fisted, until Lester yelled, "Not here!" Moonpie frowned—Lester was so bossy, always telling him what he couldn't do.

Moonpie cheered up, though, when Lester decided to send him to parachute school over at the airfield in Savannah as part of a new strategy.

Lester was big on technology, and he could organize. He wanted to bypass all the Colombians and Cubans and other Latin maniacs shooting each other up for turf control. Why, Lester couldn't even trust one of those guys to set him up with a load and not turn him in just to get rid of him.

So he decided to follow up on a great efficiency that eliminated the mother ship, the courier ship, the crews and drivers and all that stuff that could go bad on you so easy. The plan was simple: You get your cocaine packaged flat, in inch-thick slabs, and you duct-tape it to your back, your chest—which of course you shave first if it has hair on it—your legs, your ass—or in this case, to Moonpie's back, chest, legs, ass. "Oh, fuck it," Moonpie giggled, "Just tape that shit everywhere." Moonpie loved the stuff, loved the action, and he trusted his brother Lester.

So Moonpie went to the five-day crash course in parachuting, then took a flight down to Colombia and bought sixty pounds of cocaine and got a pilot to fly him back over South Florida, at night, low. Without landing, the airplane couldn't be arrested—not without a dogfight—and at night Moonpie couldn't be seen. He jumped out at three thousand feet which gave him three seconds easy to gather his wits, pull his cord, and not die. He said later he kind of fucked up, snooting up so much of the stuff beforehand, you know, for the rush of it. It kind of messed up his timing, you know, and then all that spinning and dark bullshit. He missed his pick-up point by a mile or so and had to slog through the swamps and was scared to death of alligators and rattlesnakes, but he made it okay. And Lester gave him three grand, credit, on what he owed, which got his debt down to eight grand, and he said that felt a whole lot better than eleven grand.

Meanwhile, with Florida postponed two weeks, I was looking at two weeks penniless. Lester said sorry, he didn't have no money, since I fucked up in the Bahamas. Sure, I smelled a rat, but he came back quick, before I could ask, "What do you mean, fucked up?"

He said, "If you want to…" If I wanted to, I could run down to Hilton Head Island with five ounces he couldn't move, to see how I could do, gramming it out. He'd front me a hundred bucks and the toot, which he wouldn't front to anybody but me, but if I put my nose in the bag, I'd owe him. He laughed and said, "You might break even." Because toot dealers almost always fall into the bag.

I was to head out that night, because drug dealers always start their projects at night. I made a couple calls, call it market research, and was assured that yes, the market was strong on Hilton Head Island. Lester said at the door, "Three places. Stash, cash, crash." I said I'd heard that before.

Well, even a country Jew can't head down the road on a trip like that one without a headful of his mother's gnashing teeth and wringing hands and a big, quivering talk bubble full of *Oy Vay. My son, the toot man.* And my old man, who surfaced on new projects, would have cleaned my clock, cold cocked me right now, but… maybe not, he so understood how hard it is to turn a buck. And this was '77 or '78, before all the athletes and other great guys dropped dead from too much toot.

Oh, but you shudder, looking back on what you thought was spirited youth. I was lucky then, daring the phantoms in that fool's paradise, surviving what some of my friends did not survive.

I got down to Hilton Head Island about midnight, just as the clubs were finding high gear, and inside ten minutes the market found me, was throwing cash at me, wanting goods and services. I applied my degree, slowed way down, asked a friend if I could keep a bag at his house, asked another friend if I could keep another bag at her house. That was stash and cash taken care of, and I split and got settled and returned in an hour, hardly one, not even brunch time for the night people. As for crash, forget it. A sweet young female looked right through me, couldn't even see me but knew the deal of the hour. She looked like Daisy Mae and came on so strong I wanted to head out right then, but she said no, let's drink and dance some more. She said, "Relax, will you? We'll fuck all night if you want to, but I want to hang out here for awhile first, dig this buzz for awhile. Geez, you act like you're married. You are, aren't you?" I sluffed it off, shagged her a drink, gave her a line—then it didn't matter if I was a novitiate at the monastery.

Drug dealers were romantic renegades then, and love got boiled down to friction under modified consciousness. But love is never without its problems, its needs, its endless play of give and take. So Daisy Mae is down there honking my horn and complaining about us guys, always wanting the same old thing and acting like such big babies when we didn't get it. I was wrongly accused, but I didn't complain. I was getting it, thinking *La… di-da-di-da…* like Curly Joe used to sing in the shower.

I was still married but didn't feel guilty because my wife had already told me she didn't want to be the one to hold me back from anything—this, after she fucked a touring tennis pro after a computer lesson, or maybe it was a touring computer guy over a tennis game. I forget, so long ago. I called Daisy Mae for months after that, but she was out. I heard a year or so later she found Jesus—lucky Him.

Meanwhile, I sold four ounces, grammed out, brought one home, turned enough cash to pay for inventory, drinks, and gas and had fifty bucks left. Lester said, "It's hell, ain't it?"

The next week, Moonpie and I drove south in the getaway car with our four bills and two guns. Moonpie hated being passed—some cocksucker in a fucking Saab, of all chickenshit cars, passed us doing a hundred-five. Moonpie whimpered, stomping on it, reaching under his seat for his gun, cheek to the wheel, weaving at one-thirty. I said, "Jesus Christ, Moonpie."

"I got it. I got it." But he was only going to shoot the guy in the Saab if we couldn't pass him. We did. Moonpie said, "Turbo. Big motherfucking deal. Cocksuckers. Saabs. Ha!"

Lester was waiting for us dockside in Ft. Liquordale, as we called it then. He'd flown down. I gave him his change, around three-hundred-fifty bucks. He said, "You can keep it." I thanked him, but not too much, figuring I'd earned it, and maybe figuring Lester too, was priming my pump again. Moonpie and I parked the Porsche next to Lester's new yacht as a female who looked about thirty going on fifty came off the boat like a robot with basic programming.

She walked out front, aimed a camera at us and whined, "Smi-ull." She lowered the camera and told us to bunch together, because she had to get the car in there too. I shook my head and tried to look negative, so I could explain later, your honor, I had no idea what was going on down there. And there I hang on Brother's wall, looking negative. I swiped the film that night, of course.

The yacht belonged to the kingpin. We drank and tooted on board a day and a night, and then Lester laid out the plan; he told me he'd heavily insured the vessel. You didn't need to be a career criminal to see that one coming. He said it'd be easy, and he'd figured out the best way to do it was run the bitch hard aground in the entrance channel at low tide. If we got her going fast enough, we could run her up on the sandbar. The tide coming in fast with five-foot breakers on the sandbar would break her up quick if we could fracture the hull on impact. The explosion, from the gasoline poured over the decks, would finish it. Moonpie twitched for the fun of it. I sat back. Lester said, "Moonpie'll do all the work. You just tag along, jump off when he says jump off, and swim in with him."

"What makes you think Moonpie'll know when to jump off?" I asked.

"You'll be there," he said, smiling, and I knew he loved his brother after all, or at least he knew good help like Moonpie would be hard to replace.

"Ten grand," he said, just like he'd said a grand over Kentucky and three grand over Eleuthera. I was around five hundred bucks down since we'd started, and I'd broken enough Federal laws to get a few lifetimes in the slammer. I said I wanted to walk around the block and stretch out some. Lester smiled his weak smile, the smile that said *You can't run, because I'll find you.* I caught a taxi to the airport a few blocks down and bought a ticket home, cash. That was the last I saw of Moonpie and Lester.

Moonpie went alone and lived to talk about it. The boat they trashed was fifty years old and in perfect condition. Lester got thirty grand from the insurance claim.

About six months later, I got a call from another smuggler. He said a man in a suit and a new Lincoln with rental plates just dropped in, asking about me and Lester. The man worked for the kingpin, and they were looking for Lester, said he'd tried to steal all the kingpin's assets. "I told him you're just a dumbshit," the guy on the phone said. "I told him you didn't know nothing but running errands for Lester."

I said thank you, and that the profile was accurate. I woke up about three A.M. in front of test patterns, where I'd fallen asleep on the couch, frozen stiff, waiting for the suit. He never showed up, but he should have—I knew those guys, knew their profile; coarse, mean, aggressive, greedy with low-level speech patterns, a crude go-for-it mentality, and a keen sense of revenge.

These guys weren't romantic renegades, they were lowlifers who measured machismo in dollars, who surrounded themselves with women weak for cocaine. These guys had a hard time with complete sentences but maimed easy for a grand, killed for ten, and Lester had fucked the kingpin out of three hundred thousand.

I don't know if my old man had some kind of influence on the guy in the pinstripe suit, if a certain brain wave was bent just right, a degree or two in another direction. Maybe he did. That was '78 or '79. Maybe he rearranged the molecules in the bad acid that was choking me to death ten years earlier, so I wouldn't have to get popped at the hospital and have Mother remind me for the next thirty years. Maybe he kept my hind tire straight up and on the road after it blew out, or had a hand in letting the chains fall off my foot, so I wouldn't drown. I don't know. I only wonder sometimes at the long odds on the long stretch of close calls over the years.

I don't think I got casual or arrogant about thinking myself immortal, because every time I survived when I could have gone down for good left me drenched with fear. I only wonder if a protective spirit can alter events.

Like with Satan, the marsh stallion, who stood still so I could slip a bridle over his head, and swing a leg over his back and ease on up, before he made it clear as the clear blue sky that it would be him or me that day. I'd only walked across the pasture from the trailer Sue and I rented cheap, because the money was short in the early days of shrimping while the glory was still being sorted out—walked across to where Marie and Jack discussed whether Satan would be better off glue.

"Can I ride him?"

They looked up in wonder. "You can sure try," Jack said. I'd seen plenty guys ride bareback on TV, and hell, it was only ten years since I was going to be a champion jockey. I jumped on, all set to kiss the horse with my knees, but Satan tore out for a limb so low it scraped his neck and tried scraping me off his back. I'd seen Indians on TV hang off the blind side so the cowboys couldn't shoot them. That was easy. Getting back up wasn't so easy, until Satan sideswiped the barn. I got back up easy, nevermind my leg mashed into the barn—it was only severely bruised, and a better sacrifice than my head. We had a rough stalemate into the bucking phase, before Satan picked up steam, before he dropped through the trapdoor, leaving me nothing to hold on to, then shot out of it like a cannonball. I bailed out, let go and flew off as Satan hung a right and ran eight miles to the beach, where he could drown me.

I watched him go, from the dirt, bloody and dizzy and asking Jack and Marie, "Why didn't you tell me?"

"Tell you what?" Jack asked back.

Maybe my old man put a pinch on Satan's ear, or backed up Paul Kohman's hand five years later when Paul reached over the rail and grabbed my ankle and hauled me back aboard when the lifeline broke because I stood on it, fixing a tangle in the main sheet at the boom end, twenty miles out in eight-foot seas on a cold gray day, racing to Savannah. I don't know, and I don't know if it was only sheer blind luck that I survived another crossing in the Pacific, against thirty-foot waves breaking overhead and fifty knots of breeze that beat Kenny Bloom and me down to a whimper and a grunt and a knowing beyond hope that we would that night die.

I think people who lose their parents early, especially males from the hell-bent-for-leather school who lose their fathers right there in the crux of puberty, on the threshold of immortality, imagine a lingering spirit more easily, more naturally. And maybe a parent checking out too soon does linger, until the kid gets old enough to know the odds.

For years I felt accompanied in the clutch, a presence, a feeling leading to calmness, and maybe that saved me. Like at the funeral when nobody cried because my old man had shown every one of them the heavy hand at some time or other, but then I cried and then everybody else cried for the kid with no old man, down there crying, and everyone made a tighter circle then, and laid hands on each other and especially on me. And the crying didn't stop, but it changed.

Who knows about accompanying spirits or guardian angels? I don't, except for the one time that stands out, sure as shooting, when the room was full of my old man, which was the time soon after he was dead and buried, which is the time many spirits hang around. It was the half-second between Flossie's son raising his hand on his way to smacking my tender, impressionable face, which was the same half-second between poking another goober and flicking the wrist just so, twirling the fork over and around the thumb so that four movements, fingers, wrist, heart and head, converged on the next half-second, the one where I stabbed the aggressor with my fork.

That was thirty years ago, but the problem persists—that of the warm, good feeling head to toe, the goose bumps that rise quick sometimes like magic, with the satisfaction of tines breaking skin, sinking in.

❄   ❄   ❄

Blind Faith

I only know what Mother tells me about my early childhood. My own recollections come as snapshots, short on context or continuity, like the exhilaration of my first coonskin cap, just like Davy Crockett's, or getting bathed in the kitchen sink, or wearing my flannel jammies with the pooper flap and built-in mukluks while opening the front door on Brother coming home from his first day of school, or Mother's strange excitement the first time she dressed me as a little girl for Halloween.

She says I was attracted to danger. She says I was a wall climber, a difficult child. She said I made her look bad, like the time when I was only five, at dinner with the Meadrikes, the lovely new neighbors. We'd just moved into our fanciest house, before the decline, and she did so want to make a good impression. I stood on a chair so everyone could appreciate my cuteness, I was such a happy pup, then I pulled my dick out and said, "Look at this!" Of course Mother didn't call it a dick; she called it a *schmeckel*, every few years when she told the story again to remind me of the torture I'd put her through.

"I'll never forget that," she said. "I was so mortified."

"Are you still mortified?" She thought it over and slowly nodded. "Let's call the Meadrikes then," I said.

"They died," she said. "That was forty years ago."

"So it doesn't make any difference after all."

"You talk so crazy," she said, and we were back to where we started from.

Mother said I cheated death just past infancy, sticking fingers into electric sockets, heading across busy streets, headstrong at three, bringing home live rats and sometimes snakes, barehanded, that the neighborhood dogs had caught.

For me it was only natural, all fun. Yet a pattern formed, with a recurring theme of conflict, loss, transience, struggle. The pattern persisted until the profile of survivor was more than a credit, or less; it was a drive, a scrappy, unyielding, often harsh delineation of my soul. Survival became the product of my past. My single blessing was that I was still alive. Survival was all I had to show for all my effort. More of the same looked to be in store by the time twenty rolled around.

The college years helped, because of all the drugs that so effectively diffused my floating hostilities.

I didn't attend my college graduation, it was such an empty exercise. For years I could not claim graduation from the great U, because of the loans I wouldn't pay back. They wanted me to pay, but after a while they couldn't find me.

I rationalized the default, because rationale is what you learn in college; I would have quit college if not for the Vietnam War, and I couldn't afford to stay in college unless the Feds loaned me money. It was extortion, plain and simple; a loan scam. *Look here, Kid. Borrow the money or hit the swamps. See?*

My rationale was another foolish exercise, this one in sophistry, another lesson learned by college students in the humanities.

My college degree said that I was a bachelor of arts in creative writing. They mailed it to Mother. She hung it over the TV. Then she married a couple more times, moved south and back north and way south and way north to Flossie's place. Now it hangs over Brother's TV.

It's dated 1970 and certifies that I successfully avoided military service four years in a row. The choice was simple; reefer, acid, easy sex, or a hot swamp with diseases, snakes, land-mines and millions of strangers trying to kill you. You didn't need a college degree to figure that one.

The decadent fun did not justify the waste of time. Yet college in the sixties was a rare chance to explore realities outside the prescribed social path, outside yourself, always stoned, always postponing the willfulness that gets a person ahead, looking constantly for ways out, any way out of anything.

Besides the Vietnam War, I had to factor the Social Security benefits paid to college students under twenty-two with deceased parents who'd paid in. My old man had died long ago after a life of minimal payments into the system. But the $140 a month I got from the government—as long as I stayed in college, until I was twenty-two—was enough to cover my $35 rent, $45 new-car payment (a Volkswagon bug with peace symbols on the windows) and $35 for groceries, leaving, let's see, 35 and 35 are 70, plus 45 is 105, no, 115, wait, yeah, that's it—115, leaving $30 a month for my reefer, acid and easy sex habit. And $30 a month was significant dough then, with draft beer at 25¢ and decent Mexican lids running around $12. Of course, it's never enough, and I was always $5 short.

Even short on cash and wasting time, abusing drugs and liquor and seeking new heights of anarchy, college was still a better choice than the hot swamp, the bullets, snakes, diseases, and madness. It was the lesser of two evils, the choice least likely to end in death, where far more time can be wasted. Those of us in college then, especially those of us in the arts, knew college was snug harbor, never mind that it was bullshit and worthless, a beautiful backdrop for stagnation and discussion.

The degree in creative writing for sale then at the University of Missouri required eight short stories written during the fourth year—about one a month, which didn't seriously inconvenience our social life. Student stories were discussed so the student writers could "develop their craft."

The first three years required forty forgettable courses that fit nicely with the hallucination of those days. One standout was 17th Century Metaphysical Poetry and Prose, taught by a professor of aggressively modest demeanor, a small fellow who wore suits, with vests to set a tone, and bow ties for singularity. His name and message are gone; only his voice survives, slowing time down to slag and drool like two seconals and a tallboy, like all the world was down from 78 to 33⅓. I attended two classes, the first day and the last day.

The first day was to check it out, you know, for chicks, goofs, laughs. First days were ritual, higher times, because time was marked in semesters that were four months long and monumental, like decades to a person marking the stages in life. The Bible said you got three score and ten years; the university gave you eight semesters. The hot swamp waited, with the bullets, the snakes, the diseases.

The first day of a semester was a celebration of sorts, a grim, happy time, kind of like a funeral in New Orleans with horns playing and dancing in the street, kind of like coming on to heavy acid.

It was a joke, every aspect of it—the courses, the teachers, the agricultural students right off the farm in their 4-H Club jackets, the long hairs in ragtag blue jeans rolling joints at the Student Commons in wheat-straw papers, then asking ag students for a light.

What a laugh. Ha.

The last day of class was the day of the final exam, four months later. I got my composition blue book—25¢ at the university bookstore—and walked in stone-cold but stoned enough and recently hallucinated enough to feel confident, if not secure.

Choose 3 of the following 6, the final exam said, *for comparison intrinsically to each other and/or themselves and/or to a single iota of the real world,* or some shit. *Please annotate.* The six were 17th Century metaphysical poets, must have been. I sat there thinking, Ho boy, scratching my nuts. *Please scrotate,* I wrote on the final, but this was no time to choke; the hot swamp waited, its sickening humidity and cloying, teeming itch, its potential for instant resolution of all problems seeming more present in the tick... tick... tick... stillness of that stuffy little room, in which we refugees from reality hunched over our little blue books and spewed bullshit.

I took the bold move—had no choice, surrounded like that; it was make a break and run, swerving the hips, ducking, rolling, moving quick for the clear, or fold up in the clutch and die. *Do you solemnly swear....*

I shined the question as written—fuck three; I never heard of these guys. I picked one, Andrew Marvell. I remember his name, it was such a marvel that I was going to fill a blue book on his life, his work, his intrinsicality to himself. I compared the works of Andrew Marvell to *Bonanza*, showing how Hoss Cartwright, Little Joe, Lorne Greene, Shoo Fly and Frog Dick were, in fact, practically, if not pragmatically, intrinsically—possibly, potentially, innately linked one and the same to the overriding theme and/or motif of Marvell's dominant love-hate, or, rather, approach-avoidance processing of poetry, or, as far as we know, of prose, too, after all.

I filled the little blue book—that was the main thing, especially getting down to the last two pages where your writing has to shrink so you can cram all the important stuff in. And it wasn't all that bad, because the episode of *Bonanza* I used to compare and contrast was so fresh in my mind, still clouded by hash smoke, sure, but hardly twelve hours old. A few of us watched it together, with ice cream, pizza, cookies, pickles, beer, soda, chips—the usual. We all had finals that week, so we didn't take any psychedelic drugs. It wasn't like we were completely irresponsible.

I got a C-. The little professor understood. If I had to waste four years it wasn't his fault, well, not entirely.

But I learned a big lesson in college, or maybe college only confirmed what I already knew, what I'd grown up with but had yet to define, that those who commit to risk are the only ones who win or lose; the rest stay lukewarm, cradle to grave.

I've known many smart people who never went to college, most of whom suspect they would be smarter if they had gone to college. Doesn't college make you smarter? Maybe knowing the answer to that is for those who went.

I learned the truth from Ted Moffett, a teaching assistant, also a writer who taught Narration 50.

Narration 50 was prerequisite for Short Story 404, in which you would actually write short stories under the tutelage of William Heyden, fiction heavy.

Bill Heyden wasn't a heavy writer, he'd been a heavy editor at *Story* magazine, and the legend mill that operates full-time on any campus held that Bill Heyden gave first breaks to Ernest Hemingway, Scott Fitzgerald, John Steinbeck—anybody you could possibly think of who was heavy probably got a first break from Bill Heyden at *Story* magazine. He was that heavy.

He wasn't a bad guy, even if his tutelage in a nutshell was, we are here, we have requirements, let us proceed. I learned nothing, in accordance with the unwritten curriculum.

Ted Moffett, on the other hand, was a different kind of fiction heavy. Ted Moffett had no past, no money to speak of, no prospects beyond the bottle and the blind faith that one day his writing would emerge, would endure. He was twenty-nine then, old already, and he didn't mind drinking with us, getting drunk with us on occasion, and talking with us about writing. He had a beard and a girlfriend and, most importantly, he told me what was good about my stories, what was bad, what needed fixing, a few things to consider. He worked on his writing every day. He said, "I don't know," when he didn't know.

Ted Moffett knew what he liked and what he didn't like. He was a stylist, a man with a real life, who reflected on what he saw and took insight to his writing. He didn't assume the common voice of so many "writers" burdened by the ponderous, imposing, otherness of narration. He was to Bill Heyden like Vincent Van Gogh was to Lucky Pierre.

My college short stories grew dusty but not all that moldy on top of Brother's dining room hutch. I leafed through the stack, browsing what had come from my cloudy young mind in that rarefied atmosphere of tuition and grades, ponderous assessments, too much thinking, too little action. A page at random dealt with a twenty-one-year-old boy in sensual encounter with an exotic, older women who was thirty-five already. Another dealt with a man who took too many drugs and grew permanently morose, then went insane.

My last year, '69-'70, was the first year of the draft lottery. The concept was frightening as Russian roulette; who would want to play but someone attracted to death? The drawing was televised, prime time, and the 365 ping-pong balls with all the birthdays on them got pulled out of a fishbowl by an old white man in a cheap suit. We watched, smoking joints and drinking hard liquor. Near the end of that year, and the end of Short Story 404, Bill Heyden came to class with an announcement. He always spoke slow, Virginia aristocratic, like the fictional character he'd chosen for himself, so even though he never said much, it took awhile and was more pleasant than a monotone.

"I want you all to consider the Ph.D.," he began and ended, filling in the middle with advantages of the Ph.D. Most of us didn't know what to do next, he said, maybe indicating that he understood our recent waste of time, the coming predicament. But most importantly, he said, was the serious commitment to fiction. We would either make it or not make it. He said we'd reached the age of playing for keeps, and a commitment to fiction would include the Ph.D. Eighty percent of all National Book Award winners, he said, held the Ph.D. Maybe it was eighty-seven, or seventy-two, I can't remember, but it was way up there.

I hadn't considered the Ph.D. I thought, well, shit, this isn't a *bad* life. I wasn't employable for anything but manual labor, because I didn't know how to do anything else. I was about to get drafted, so I thought maybe I'd get the Ph.D. in San Francisco while waiting for my trial on my refusal for induction—Yes! College students love two birds, one stone. I could get a graduate teaching job for money, teach six hours a week and squeeze another three years through the wringer while waiting for my trial—maybe four.

We had a couple other heavyweights on the writing staff, two poets whose ages were hard to tell but who both looked sixty or sixty-five. They were probably late forties, they drank so hard and smoked so many Camel straights. One looked like a hippopotamus— too much flesh on his tired frame and especially in his face. I had the other one, the long, skinny, bedraggled one, Tom McAfee, for Poetry 402. Affable Tom McAfee was a fair poet and decent guy. We read our poems in his class while he hunched over a crumpled pack of Camels, his shoulders severely stooped, sometimes nodding, sometimes smiling halfway, sometimes laughing short for a single exhale.

Tom McAfee spoke in class once when one of my poems was on the floor. He said it should have read *I wish I were there,* instead of *I wish I was there;* another still life from time at the great U.

He drank coffee and smoked more cigarettes in the Student Commons with the philosophy guys, but he never joined their polemics, their tirades, their animated gesticulations over the sequential causality of events in a precognizant yet post-deliberate series of events, a series, yes, and not a single event; because how can a single event be? Or some shit. Tom McAfee only watched, smoking, hunching, half-laughing every few minutes, or was that a cough? No, I couldn't ask him what he thought about the Ph.D. He was busy, working on a poem about nothingness, decay, life with no meaning, convoluted volitions leading to the same result in every endeavor. Ah, the great U.

I found Ted Moffett at the Hoffbrau House, maybe another chance meeting in a series of sequential causalities.

"Oh, fuck no!" he said.

"But ninety-one percent of all National Book Award winners hold the Ph.D.," I said.

"Sure, they do!" he said. "And look at the books they write! They're boring! Well-written, technically, but do you want to write books like that? Boring books? Books that make you sleepy?"

"Then why do they win?"

"Look who the judges are! Ph.D.s!"

He was right. Moreover, truth delivered over a cold beer on a rainy afternoon in a dark bar was akin to my past.

Ted Moffett was, well, one of us.

We drank some more, talked and pondered. I recalled that Bill Heyden had written some short stories, and that he'd read one in class once, about a little girl who goes to the fair and becomes dizzy and amazed by the dizzying amazement of reality, and the fair. I missed the last half of the story, dazed, unamazed. Ted Moffett said, "No comment."

Bill Heyden was not dazzled by me, either. I got a B, which is like an F at that level. Who reads B writers?

My friend Arnold got an A. I reflected on the nature of rejection, of failure in the single area where meaning resides. Arnold helped assuage the pain by reminding me how little in that life had meaning. "Writing professor," Arnold said. "It sounds contradictory, like passion theory, or something."

Yeah, I thought. How can you grade an art form, unless the artist is so bad you give him an F. But a B? Isn't that more a measure of the reader's taste? I thought these things but didn't say them. I only stewed on Bill Heyden's taste and the potential of second-rate writing.

I told myself that Bill Heyden was academic, that his stories were analytical, and so were his tastes and inclinations. I told myself that he'd never been anywhere, never teased death or walked the edge, and that Ted Moffett was right. With the benefit of hindsight— twenty-five years of it—I think I was right; I gave Bill Heyden a B. But then, rationalization could never fully ease that early sting.

Arnold became a dentist. I fell into writing, writing all the time, like a junky shoots up all the time. I pushed myself to write with discipline, every day, or every now and then, or every something. Then I stopped trying, stopped banging my head against the typewriter, stopped knowing that the stuff was supposed to spurt from my brain onto the page, because, after all, I'd spent years in college, learning how.

The theory of commitment was just another round of bullshit. I laughed with regularity, if not with discipline, wondering how often my old man and Uncle Sammy would have spent entire days in their meditation and mantra, lakeside, casting and reeling, casting and reeling, if they'd approached it as a discipline. No, they did not hope for the record fish, the mystery fish, the fish that would change fishing— well, their hope was not what drove them; they went for the contact, for a line in the water. The fish was ethereal, caught in the simple act of fishing.

College was wrong, not just an overwhelming waste of time, but dangerous too. College was for thinking very hard, for developing a mentality, for becoming aloof from the physical world. College is where *writer's block* has gained currency, because all mind, no body, gets the thoughts backed up, constipated.

Considerations of the Ph.D. ended quickly. And so did college, ending insulation from the hot swamp. I was prime for an invitation.

I drew a 198. They said projections that year went to 195, but they couldn't be certain. It depended on the body count from the hot swamp; if more guys got killed than projected, well then, they'd need more guys to go over. It was another summer down the rat hole, waiting for my physical. I ditched thirty pounds—down to 120—on some heavy dex Brother scored. He thought they were tens, oops, they were thirties, so I got hot-wired in three days instead of three months, charting new highs in drug-induced frenetics, new lows in personal filth, stink, contagion.

I had an inspiration. All the guys were growing long hair and pulling the hippy number at their physicals. I went against the grain, got skinny as a death camp survivor, applied all the techniques I'd heard about, like chipping my buttons and my fingernails, wearing long sleeves and gloves to turn pale white all over, getting a crew cut and keeping a four-day stubble, no tooth brushing or ass wiping, with a little shit residue under my chipped fingernails. And I was so strung out, starving, the nervous tic was no longer an act.

The army doctor said, "Next." But they stopped at 195.

Whoever said I wasn't stable or sane? I wanted to fail the physical but couldn't. But the numbers worked out.

Life began after that. I still believe civil strife could have been avoided if the question was not general: *Should we fight?*, but personal: *Will you go?* Each war would generate enough people willing to fight, or we'd call it off.

I saw a woman on TV ranting about moral imperative for sending ground troops into the latest region in need of American troops. She wore a full-flounced number in flaming red with shoulder pads. But would she have changed into cammies and an M-16 and gone? I don't think so, not with her importance, not with her agenda.

The first year out in the real world I worked too many shitty jobs to count, dirt labor, shrimp nets, crab pots, longlines, digging, heaving, hauling, humping it, hating it, but doing it. I hit the road for about five thousand miles, got arrested, got out, worked the boats again and finally got a line on a job with a metro daily paper out of Savannah, just up the road from where I'd been shrimping with Jeffrey Baxter.

The first story I sold was about Jeffrey and *Edith* and shrimping, to a little, local monthly magazine. I got fifty bucks and a lead from the editor, Big Bart Bartholomew, on the newspaper job—"I'll tell you what, Kid, you got no experience and you're a little bit rough. But goddamn it, you write a mean stick!" Big Bart Bartholomew was good for continuing advice when I didn't get the job, because I had no experience and was a little bit rough. "Aw hell, Kid, just write the goddamn copy! They got nobody over here! They got presidential candidates coming in! They got the goddamn governors coming in! Bob Hope for chrissake! Just show up and do the work. They got egg all over their faces! They got to take whatever you feed them!"

I showed up, did the work, and after three weeks of feeding stringer copy for next to no pay, I went back over and got on the payroll, formally—a hundred-fifty bucks a week. Hallelujah. I'd written more the first week than I'd written in four years of college and never got asked if I had a college degree.

And the less I got asked the better, I'd got so short-fused from all the heat, the grind, the goddamn umph required of every day just to get by in a brutally indifferent world. I saw other guys whose fathers set them up with a little help, say twenty grand or fifty. I was envious, I'd grown so efficient, so keen on maximum utilization of every shred, every breath of resource available, as if I, too, was stuck in the Great Depression.

A metro daily is the best place for a new writer with a college degree, with experience severely limited to eight short stories in four years, suffering an overdose of sensitive give-and-take. No waiting on a metro daily, no ambiance, no mood, no setting, temperature, inspiration, none of that stuff, just hack it out. You got your sheriff's report first thing, rapes and murders, accidental deaths and dismemberments. The grotesque brutality, meanness, and ignorance of human beings is a novelty at first, sunrise, over coffee, until it sinks in, no joke.

But no time for reflection either, because you got two or three hard news stories to cover, write, and transmit by three o'clock, and if news is slow, you get an assignment, along with the Sunday feature you got to stroke from 3:00 to 5:00.

Those were good days for writing, productive days of increasing efficiency, of more skill across the keyboard. But they all led to a single depressing difficulty, which was the next day, beginning with rapes and murders. The novelty wore off very fast, the crimes moving more quickly from the calamitous nature of humans to the intimate pain and prolonged agony of those only brutally raped and/or dismembered but not murdered. Follow-ups were required, so I became a nuisance at the hospitals too, on critical-condition victims, because the public had a right to know.

It came down to the ultimate crime, which was another mauling, another rape, another brutal assault on the simple notion of good manners. Restraint, silence, goodwill, healing sentiment was so much flotsam on the roadside, cast into the dirt with yesterday's paper.

"Well sir, we got us a grand theft auto, assault with a d.w. and... two... no, three rapes... hell, I can't tell if it was three bucks on a gang rape or one buck on three rapes. Hold on here, Bub, I be right back atcha."

Rape and murder led straight into a caffeine boost and the sugar-coated, happy horseshit bad newspapers love to fill with. I hated it when no heavyweights came to town. They were news; without them we had only ourselves, only our rapes, our murders, our recipes and gardening and our increasing resort development.

My first big event was the Southern Governor's Conference, with a bunch of governors and a vice president and candidates for the presidency of the United States of America. All the networks and kingpins converged on my first day on the job on the resort that was my beat. They had a pressroom set up for The Working Press. I know

now that phrase is a compensation for low self-esteem, an announcement that it's a job, not a cakewalk. What else can they say? The Drinking Press? The Obnoxious, Hostile, Aggressive, In Your Face Press? That would be more accurate, they've so forsaken style and manners in the spirit of the fray, then they drink like fish, the smart ones, because it's such bullshit.

The pressroom had about a hundred typewriters with telephones nearby, paper, pens, the works. All these guys are banging away, and I thought, What? It hasn't even started. And they looked so intent; I sat down, loaded up a clean sheet and typed a letter to Mother. I did want to make a go of this one. I wanted to fit in.

Dear Mother,

The guy next to me looks tired and alcoholic. I think he's trying to see my work. I think he's homosexual.... I've been so hungry lately....

All the newspaper stories now reside in a loose-leaf binder beside the college stories. My newsroom letter to Mother is on page one. She asked for several months after receiving it, "Is this it? I mean this... what do you call it? Writing?"

I didn't call it writing. I got free lunch at the Rotary Club and met all the stuffed shirts and got to interview a bunch of governors and presidental candidates and movie stars and assorted famous assholes, but it wasn't the kind of writing I longed for, with breaking waves and sunken treasure and all the fantasy of lost youth. I stayed with it for the brief but steep learning curve, and a hundred-fifty bucks a week was a brave new world. I kept up with monthly contributions to the local magazine, too, because Big Bart Bartholomew took a liking and let me cover nearly any topic I wanted.

That was good for another fifty bucks a month, sheer mad money, and more than that was the sense of family down at the magazine office. I made friends with the women who worked there, who'd had to drum up far more filler before I came along.

I was gratified by life itself with my first magazine bylines; this was what I'd worked toward, the ideal—this was the great beginning at last, on my way toward literature. Those women taught me that all ideals are surrounded by real life; no matter how lofty our concepts, we still delve into bodily function, daily.

Front-and-center at the magazine office sat a receptionist, Linda, who had a set of jugs on her you would not believe, so big and round and gravity-scoffing. She had a hard body but a lumpy husband who waited at home every day at 5:15, where, by decree, she had to stand still while he slid his hands up her dress, pulled the leg hole of her panties to the side, slid his finger up her pussy, wiggled it around a little bit, pulled it out and smelled it. Checking for stray spermatozoa he was, because he just knew knew knew how bad all the guys wanted to fuck his wife, and goddamn it, she was such a... such a... Well, goddamn it, he wasn't about to sit around doing nothing while she was slipping out for lunch every day and having some guy slip her the big salami.

Linda worked in front. We talked things over when I came in with stories and had to wait to see Big Bart Bartholomew. We talked about life, love, the mall, comings and goings, stuff like that. I thought she was only sweet—and dull as a post. I didn't mind talking to her, because I had to wait anyway, and though I couldn't get over the size and shape and anti-gravity characteristics of her breasts, I didn't think she minded my staring. I couldn't help it anyway. She began telling me one month to the next that she'd read my latest story. She told me unemotionally that I was the best writer around, no question about it, maybe one of the best she'd read. She made me weak, she understood so much.

Then she told me about her husband and the finger check. I experienced a sudden hot flash on the first hearing, proceeding in the next moment to strategizing on proof of her husband's theory. Why else could she have brought me into the maze? I longed for experience, for the stuff of great stories.

I started coming by weekly, coming by when the office was empty, except for Linda and me. She was so simple, so open, so abused, so perceptive, so stacked. I got to where I wanted to fuck Linda more

than I wanted to make it big in New York, just as her husband suspected, and I really wanted to leave a little slug o' maple syrup down
there—*Whu!... What in a hell? Why... Issiz maple syrup!* Or, as they say
in the Carolina Lowcountry, *maypull surp.*

I thought maple syrup would make it colorful, worthy of a good
story. Our moment came one late afternoon when I stopped in on my
way to the post office. Linda was an hour or so from locking up, and
she was alone. I needed a manila envelope, because I knew she kept
them in the back room—no windows, only one door. In the back
room, she bent over. I steadied myself, went to touch her, chickened
out, backed off, and she stood up and turned around with a stack of
envelopes and a confused blush. "You cain't make a omelette...," she
said. She looked down. She looked up. I knew. I stepped up. We
embraced. We kissed. I felt her breasts, trembling as I unbuttoned her
blouse and then disengaged the turnbuckles and grappling hooks that
held all the canvas and wire that held her bosom just so.

She's only human, I thought, *only lonely and confused and maybe a little bit
dreamy like so many good people are.* I paused for sweetness, on the verge
of every man's dream, then peeled away her bondage. I gazed upon
nature's bounty, thinking she was a dream, even when she pushed me
down, releasing my privates calmly and finished the dream; it was wet
and loud, the heavy audio garbled by a mouthful of sausage and hateful invective. She hated the bastard, just hated him. In the aftermath
and silence, when men wonder what's for dinner and try to remember what got them so excited, Linda said. "I'm glad we did that. I
really wanted you to have it. God, if he ever found out."

"What would he do?" I asked.

"He wouldn't do anything to me. He'd kill you. I mean it. The man
is such a... such a maniac. He's insane. I don't even care. I want to
do it again. I want to do it all the time."

"Yes," I said. "Again. Sometime. You have to be home soon."

"I can't wait. I'm going to breathe on him."

Oh, God.

"I'm going to tell him I got this weird coating on my tongue."

And I'd thought she was sweet and simple, a mere victim of circumstance.

I wonder where she is now, Linda. I'd call her, but I can't remember her last name, and she must have gone back to her maiden name by now. I mean that was in '71 or '72, and what female today would put up with pussy check at 5:15? I want to tell her that she comes to mind every time I recall my literary beginning. More importantly, she taught me that art imitating life is most often awkward, unedited, graceless.

I quit newspaper work and little, local magazine writing a year later with a big sportfishing tournament held near where I was living. The newspaper editors didn't want me on the story, but the boats were so big, so fancy, so expensive, and prospects for action so good I went anyway and wrote the story and sold it two days later to a New York magazine for $500. That was ten months of local magazine writing, more than three weeks of newspaper work, but that was my last week. I had other fish to fry.

It's easy to think you made $500 in a single day when you're only twenty-four, easy to think that working five or ten days a month could put you way up into the money—easy to think you got it figured out at last, that this is what you'll do, what you'll be, what you had in mind all along.

The next eighteen months were bleak on money and writing—a dozen more scores out of New York would have been good work for good pay for twelve days, but you had to work a few weeks before and after each one, kissing ass all the way and for what? Five bills? And that was a cast-iron maybe. I'd be better off writing a novel, I thought.

Bleak got worse. The wife split. And who could blame her? There she was in her prime, hooked up with a dreamer, a guy who thought that work was for losers, for non-dreamers, for people who'd accepted their lot, thrown in the towel, and on and on; work was not for a guy like me. She shared my perception, with a twist; she saw me as a guy with his head in the sand when it wasn't in the clouds, a guy for whom contact with the world of rent, groceries and attendant liabilities was a pain in the ass, a guy who didn't exactly fit, a guy with no money, no prospects except for the hundred-to-one shot, on the nose, of *Once upon a time....*

I didn't blame her, but then I did. Sue knew the risk/reward ratio of blind faith in an artistic medium, or she said she did. But she wanted the return now. I saw her eyes go wide when other guys came around, guys with new cars and real jobs and disposable income, guys who came on to her even though she was married, shamelessly, the way many guys will. I wanted to give her more of the good, here and now, but wasn't I working on the most important thing in the world, truth and beauty? And don't forget the flourish, the drama, the turn of phrase, the word, the gesture, the wickedly twisted syntax.

She read Margaret Mead's autobiography. It said that life is made up of parts, each part with a different fortune, a different husband. We drifted further apart until the day came when the words as yet unspoken got spoken. She thought that maybe it would be best after all if we separated. She was willing to go, because, frankly, she was all used up by the little burg we lived in, all done with that phase of life with its small-town limitations, small-town thinking. I let her go, because, frankly, I could work infinitely better without the overwhelming distraction of her life, her appetites, her needs.

So began another phase of still lifes in dirt. It got down to eight bucks, cash on hand, one February afternoon frosted opaque from dawn to dusk, then turning dark, like prospects for the future, with no fuel in the furnace nor food on the table, the rent a month late, dead sick with the Siberian flu, both cats under the covers crying *milk*. Wondering who would die first, me or them, I wondered when would come the good. But don't you know the novel was coming along famously.

Anyone could solicit an agent in the mid-'70s, but to hit up a publisher direct—to actually speak, in person, live, to one of the great goddesses who made decisions in the industry, you needed a reference, heavy moxy, considerable good luck. I finished my book and made many calls, sent many manuscripts, began another series of shitty jobs, starved and drank, just like Ted Moffett and my old man.

One day a letter came from New York, not a form rejection but a letter from a literary agent who saw tremendous literary merit in my manuscript and tremendous potential in my literary career. I scanned quick to the bottom, for the kill, for the farewell forever and best of luck in placing your manuscript elsewhere. But it only said yes.

And they're off! Yahoo.

Her name was Barbara Nance, and she was in the formative years of her own career. For the next three years she pounded the Manhattan pavement, talking, selling, lunching, schmoozing with a different editor or publisher every week or two. Each meeting led to the same bullshit; the various editors and publishers thought the manuscript was great, fabulous, fantastic, but it wasn't exactly right for their lists. Lists are the publishers' specialty, their claim to a market share of a particular niche. Saying that a book is good, but it's not right for a list is like saying, *You know I love you, I really do. But I don't.*

It was bullshit again, of a measure and consequence that can make an independent thinker wonder how control of something like literature got so centralized, like it was in the Soviet Union. The literary market was an extension of university life, peopled by those who revered the advance degree, for whom critical assessment was rote, was academic. The line on lists got tiresome and paradoxical. List appropriateness appeared prearranged, in accordance with market demand—the approach responsible for so many sequels and look-alikes. I told my agent that lists were a euphemism for a reality based on whom was taking it in the ass from whom, and when. She asked, "Is that nice? Or necessary?"

"It's not nice," I said. "None of it's nice. And I can't tell what's necessary."

"I can," she said. "Why don't you forget about this. Let me worry. You should be starting something new."

The best thing about Barbara Nance was that I could share my disgust with her over the phone, and she understood, and I didn't have to offend anyone in New York in person. I ranted and raved; she said I reminded her of Scott Fitzgerald. She silenced me that easily.

She went all around town and began again, seeing some editors for the second and third time, because turnover averages about fourteen months in the industry, so she'd call again in case the manuscript might fit better on the new list at the new place where the old person now worked.

She wrote me after each rejection, tirelessly reiterating the manuscript's value, how easily its tremendous potential was recognized.

After the first year, Barbara Nance quit the big agency where she'd been and hung her own shingle. The decision then came to me, she said. I could stay Big, because I was under contract, and they would assign me a new agent, she didn't know who, but maybe I would get someone who gave a good goddamn. Or I could roll the bones, which would make her happy, even though her new teeny tiny agency was strictly nonfiction; she was willing to keep one fiction client, who alone in the whole wide world could tell a story as well as F. Scott Fitzgerald and write it even better.

Shit, I finally realized. She thinks I'm better than I think I am. That kind of faith is uncommon, sometimes coming only from Mother. I didn't have to think it over, because I knew even then that bigness is a function of the heart, that if another heart is as open for your prospects as your own heart is, well then, that's big. Calling the big agency one day to speak to Barbara, I was told she'd moved into her own office. I asked for the number.

The aggressive voice at the big agency wanted to know: *Who are you? Are you a client of hers? Does she know you?* And then, slowly, suspiciously: *Are you fiction?*

It was a laugh and a milestone, offering insight to the immutable course of nature, the foolishness of considering changes in what was so intrinsically natural. That is, the conventional approach to life had never been available to me or to my father before me. For years you can delude yourself that this unfair situation will one day be corrected. A theory that took years to mature, began on that day of allegiance to Barbara Nance. It was that conventional modes were never wanted, never missed, that racing forms were for those bettors who didn't know Mr. Billberry, that the allegiance was not to Barbara Nance, but to the end run, to the most direct route to the back room. The family legacy classified many social conventions—sometimes for better, sometimes not—as more bullshit.

I called the new number and Barbara answered—no secretary, only the simple warmth of a friendly voice there in the center of New York.

In six-month intervals we had rock-solid deals at St. Martins, where it died in Paperback; at Elizabeth Von Schnitt, who vanished into thin air; one more with Margaret Snowden, who was doing much better now at her new job with whoever was new for her then, but then she relapsed, poor thing. We were on-again, off-again, the bullshit factor mutating into what looked like a personal curse. "Don't think that," Barbara said. "It's like that here. I'm supposed to worry about that stuff. Not you. Start another book."

Finally, after three years, maybe a dozen outline synopses for those editors and publishers who wanted to know if, possibly, perhaps, maybe a different slant could occur here or there or everywhere, after as many rewrites—this, in the days of no computers, when a clean, crisp page got typed manual, top to bottom with minimal White-Out—after a marriage failed, insolvency, aging, anxiety, neurosis, neuritis, neuralgia, Barbara Nance called.

"Okay, Booby," she said. "We're on."

"But are we high?"

"Are you doubting me?"

"No!"

"Okay, look. I can't talk now. I didn't tell you about this one because, well, you know."

"I know."

"She read it. She loves it. She's young, and she's red-hot. She's scored on every list so far and anything she touches is a go."

That meant that those manuscripts this editor had chosen for development and publication on each of her employer's lists so far had made money. Her employer was Seaview Books. "It's the hardcover, literary arm of Playboy Books." The hot young editor used to be there, but now she was here, instead of there, and everything was different now, and she was on a roll.

It was one of those moments you hope will arrive, but the numbness that fills you when it does cannot be imagined. Sure it was like the call my old man got on the last loan coming through to save the oil wells. Sure my eyes opened wide as my old man's did, hearing the news that yes, the dream would be fulfilled. But this was different. Wasn't it?

Barbara couldn't talk—she was at a pay phone on the street in New York, but she just had to call with the news. We said goodbye.

I didn't believe it for three days, until Barbara called again and spoke of our deal as if nothing could go wrong. So, I believed it. I was on, sucked through the black hole, as it were.

"Should I come to New York?" I asked.

"I don't think so," she said. "Don't worry about that crap. Plenty time for that. You're going to be very busy on rewrites, new angles, all that."

"I love rewrites, new angles, all that."

"Hey. Congratulations," Barbara said. "I'll generate two-hundred-fifty thousand dollars this year and your book counts for less than one percent of it, and I think you're my hottest property."

I couldn't speak.

"I'll call you," she said. She would forward directly all Sheila's preliminary notes, suggestions, considerations for my perusal, contemplation, meditation. Sheila was the red-hot young editor.

I flew to New York the following week because I just couldn't stand it, the fame and money and everything, going on right there, and I'm sitting in Bumfuck, South Carolina. Besides, I'd had it with South Carolina, too. The place was easy socially, but it had no imagination, no new thinking, no nothing but high tide, low tide, Scotch and history, until everything was pickled. The place was supposed to be a continuing saga, but it wasn't, not for me.

I was moving to San Francisco at last, so now would be the time to visit New York.

I arrived in the afternoon, checked into a cheap hotel and went to dinner with Barbara Nance—after three years of letters and phone talks. Physical presence was good. I was thirty or so. She was a few years younger, but older in a way, city smart, and business smart, too, a product of New York. She was a hustler, a mover, an inside operator, a closer. She was much nicer than I was, yet tougher, too, a viable city mouse.

We became friends in a few minutes, forgetting business for the first time in three years and getting to know each other over dinner and wine.

I told her adventure stories. She loved that, listening to the country mouse recall the giant cats of the country. She loosened up, into the wine, perceiving a friendship, a rare commodity there, in The Apple. She said her name wasn't always Barbara Nance. Nor had she always been the person sitting there before me. She'd been a far different person, a person named Rhoda Gershenstein.

"How far can you get on a name like that?" she asked, making a few jokes about the Rhoda Gershenstein Agency.

I didn't know why she told me that she'd changed her name—why she appeared compelled to tell me. I said I didn't think either name was bad, and that she'd be as far along as she is by any name.

"Barbara Nance is much stronger," she said. And besides, she wanted away from Rhoda Gershenstein, whose life had been riddled with sadness and horror.

Oh boy, I thought, another one of us but worse. I relaxed, poured more wine, because now it was her turn for stories from the city.

As a child, she'd been chained to the steam radiator by her stepfather, diddled, tweaked, burned, fucked, tortured, the works—this, fifteen years before child abuse became a major media event. She made my past look like the teddy bear's picnic.

I poured more wine, but relaxation and getting to know each other better began giving way to a discomfort, a burden, a mortal weakness she needed to unload, to share as soon as possible with, well, someone like me, I thought.

She survived her childhood well enough, and restored herself, especially when the bastard died. But her mother never recovered and committed suicide when Rhoda was still a teen. That was only a year before her brother, the big-hearted, dim-witted, puppy dog of a guy, got drafted and went, the fool, to Vietnam, where he stepped off the airplane into a chestful of shrapnel, leaving only Rhoda, who was soon changed to Barbara.

My boyish adventures seemed long ago and inconsequential, the casual tales of youth that might be shared over dinner and wine. But this past, these images sprawled across our little table and our common experience like a Grand Canyon of vulnerability, and I realized that someone like me had nothing to do with catching this earful. Her sense of intimacy was unfounded, even in the light of our three-year campaign and two bottles of wine—but then what sense of intimacy could have survived the tortuous youth she'd laid out before me?

Now she was choked up, couldn't speak, except to apologize for the emotion, to explain that she didn't share her background ever, but she thought I should know it. She hoped we would be together forever. I held her hand and said that nobody but my mother had ever had as much faith in me as she did. I told her I treasured it, and no matter what happened, her faith would be a lesson to me forever.

It was too sentimental for comfort, our first meeting, on the verge of greatness and all. I'd come to New York to meet this woman whose confidence in me was greater than my own. And here she was, telling me that she needed a friend to share the future with more than anything else in the world. I liked her—I loved her for what she'd given me, yet it was amiss.

We said goodnight with a hug that was maybe our first real contact. For me the hug encapsulated the years of trying, for her it was an embrace with a non-threatening human being who might not betray her. She'd cried at dinner, and she cried again, saying she thought I was the most terrific writer alive today.

You want to believe that stuff, but the other stuff can get in the way; at any rate I believed that she believed it, that in spite of her difficulties she was good at her profession. And I was comfortable with prospects for knowing her forever. That was most important; tomorrow we would try to close a deal.

We met the next day for the hallowed New York rite: lunch. It was a cheesy little deli with paper plates and cheese sandwiches and sodas. Who could eat? We were talking greatness. Barbara had changed from the night before, back to hard-nosed business. Sheila wore a matching keen edge, and consensus around our little table was greatness, a presence no less than… Literary History in the Making. Sheila was Possibly the Greatest Young Editor on the Scene; Barbara was the Miracle Story of the Year—a quarter-mil in contracts her first year out; and I was the Sizzling Secret, the writer who would not wait for his third or fifth novel to realize his coming out, but would break through on his debut. That's what lunch is good for, for taking the general street level bullshit and pumping it up to headlines. People in New York often imagine themselves as headlines, maybe confusing collective consciousness with mob rule.

"I'm thinking front page," Sheila said. She meant on the *New York Times Book Review.*

"Oh, yes," Barbara said. "I'm not even worried about that. The important thing is, this will be your coming-out novel."

I sat there like a bumpkin—New Yorkers love bumpkins, they're so refreshingly unbloodthirsty. For me it was all love, the greatness and tremendous potential, all of it comprising the first day of life as ordered as the universe. Unfortunately, everything needed to be rewritten, re-angled, reconsidered, before Sheila could actually sit down and structure the deal, but don't worry, it was as good as done.

I flew home the next day, wondering why I'd gone to New York, wondering about stability and greatness and the bullshit phantom that lurked in every corner, every shadow, every voice and volition in The Apple. Barbara needed me every bit as much as I needed her, I thought. I wondered why she'd chosen to open her soul to someone flying out in hours. I determined to speak with her about more than my potential, my writing, my success.

The following week I moved to California, drove there in an ancient Ford Falcon station wagon, battered but not beat and I was ready for action—I had my ratchet, my sockets, a bag of reasonable reefer, a cooler, my typewriter, a change of clothing and enough bedding for roadside sleeping down to thirty degrees or so.

Two days after arriving at the house of an old sailing friend in California I got a Christmas card from Barbara. The wish was for joy, for now and always.

A week after that Sheila called, tearfully. Barbara had committed suicide. "It was so awful," Sheila said. Barbara overdosed on pills on Christmas Eve, after telling everyone she was off to the Hamptons or somewhere "for holiday." New Yorkers sometimes talk British, maybe in compensation for their cloying accents.

Barbara wasn't found until ten days later—that was what Sheila was gasping over, the awfulness of ten days later.

I sat on the far edge of the continent, where only that morning I had begun my new life as an author. I'd set up a card table and a chair, so I could begin, because great authors can't be bothered with finding a place to live and unpacking and mundane chores; that stuff works itself out. We needed to get to work, me and the greatness.

The numbness this time made the numbness last time look tame. This time was like a roundhouse right to the nose, in the split second after impact, before pain. This numbness throbbed, wound up and whacked again and again. I sat there, hearing the end of the world. I sat there another three days wondering what people close to a suicide wonder, if I had been remiss, if I could have changed things.

I sat there hearing Sheila's voice ditch the emotional quiver and take on new resonance as she proceeded to the business aspects of life: She had resigned her position as red-hot editor. Maybe it was this thing with Barbara; maybe it was only time. Who knew? But the time had come, it was bigger than she was, and it couldn't be put off any longer. She quit, to write, to be a writer, to answer the call of her own greatness.

Maybe her greatness was presumed. Maybe she was clear on it. Maybe she was well enough connected to score a contact with the Publishing Success Juggernaut that pays obscene advances and then hypes headlines whether or not the book is good. I don't know, didn't know anything except that she'd slammed me against the wall of oblivion in less than a minute. She said I was on my own.

I knew that. That's the way it was, since forever.

She said I could call her any time if I needed help on anything—any time in the next week, during which she would be wrapping up, after which she would be *out of pocket*.

In the next year I moved five times, scaling down, spending a grand on phone bills to New York, spending another thousand hours in rewriting, re-angling, re-outlining, reconsidering my manuscript from the perspective of a dozen different New Yorkers, all of whom had heard of the tragedy of Barbara Nance, all of whom said that if Barbara believed in me, then something about me was right, all of whom smelled money on the table.

I still don't think too many people can prevent a suicide, but I think if anyone could have prevented Barbara's, it would most likely have been a nonresident of New York. I played out a few scenarios in my imagination, from visiting a month later to a mere phone call at a certain hour. I came up empty, again and again.

For money I wrote promotional brochures for an investment real estate company—rent caps, depreciation, tax credits and worse. And I joined the army after all, the San Francisco army of waiters, waitresses, copywriters, maids, cab-drivers, bellhops, you-name-its—the foot-soldiers of failure in the arts, the frontline faithful, blind to the reality of day in, day out.

It came to nothing and worse; poverty and burn out. I asked the agents of literature, please, to run me around the block. They said, Sure! The manuscript generated another consensus, that it was not quite right for that year's list.

That was in '80 or '81. I'd written ten or twelve thousand pages since college. I wrote another thirty thousand pages in the next fifteen years. I got beat and tired from too many times round the bend; maybe that's what a guy with too much piss and vinegar needs to get, so he can get wise in knowing what not to do, which is more important than being young and oh so smart.

Then you got the luck to factor in; Mr. Billberry either shows up or he doesn't.

In the tropics people love to stare at fish while sucking air through plastic tubes. The hustle that finally worked made some money and didn't hurt anyone and was clean and pure and free of the bullshit that ultimately oppresses aging rebels. And it was that simple, as if it was there all along, if only the smart-ass punk could get out of the way, ditch the vinegar, showcase the attitude, make them laugh, give them the contact they've longed for, which is contact with other beings more colorful, more orderly, more graceful than themselves.

And it worked with no hustle, no scramble, no pro forma, just some relaxation, some red wine and a bit of magic remembered from so long ago that the past seemed like another planet.

Maybe success hinges on magic, and childhood is the best time to store it up. I remember the day my old man bought me my first cheap mask, and a snorkel with a ping-pong ball on top, and frog fins made of plastic with straps that cut into your heels. But who cared? Because a subtle other world opened up, opened eyes wider than any news of success could do.

I remember when I was much younger, looking out to sea as a storm set in, or passing a haunted house as night fell. I let the fear in, saw myself swallowed in darkness, then shuddered in relief that I didn't have to swim into the monstered deep or enter the ghostly shadows.

I sometimes thought: *But what if they offered a million bucks?* Then I would go, resolutely. For the million bucks I would set fear aside and change life forever.

Life changes forever with or without the money. Money is everything, if you don't have any. If you get some, you might wish you

could face the fear again, just to see if you could come up with a better reason to set the fear aside.

I realized that it was set aside long ago, no fantasy required. I had
walked in the shadow of death to scratch an itch, to satisfy a need, to
survive, until it got to be just another walk in the park. I learned that
failure is my friend. That's when times got good.

Mother says I didn't learn to write in high school or college but
from early childhood, from the earliest days of wanting to be somewhere else, like in a story. She said I wasn't a bad child, but I wasn't
a good child. She said I never sat on the furniture, I climbed it, often
mortifying her with a spectacle of unrestrained energy.

Along the way, across the continent, the oceans, the years, I lost
the manuscript that I'd followed to New York. I believe such losses
are neither accidental nor bad. The manuscript represented years of
work, but those years were lost long before the manuscript was. It was
a Jonah—*let it go*, I thought. And I let it go, except for once a year
when I would riffle every file searching for it. It had to be there, somewhere. But it was gone. I had found a few of the best rejection letters and a single rewrite of the first hundred-twenty-five pages, but
the other four hundred pages were gone.

Well, the manuscript wasn't that good, poorly written, unstruc-
tured, with a few memorable passages. I scanned the first hundred-
twenty-five pages; overwritten, rhapsodic, too descriptive, heavy-
handed, immature. One rejection letter said, *You are a fine writer indeed,
and rereading your manuscript reminds me how much I love the parts that I love.
I just don't feel confident that I could place this now on the lists… blah blah
blah….*

A little money in your life can help, can soothe the pain, ease the
regret, the resentment, the loss. And so what? They'll fool you, you
know, the people telling you how great you are. Because you do want
to believe them, and if you're unlucky you will believe them.

The greatness can only be in the story, and a story needs time to
gather readers who live outside commercial trends. I never stopped
writing, even when the stacks of manuscripts got too dusty dirty to

send off, even when the money coming in was less than a little bit—
even ten or fifteen years after leaving the great U, when I wrote a letter to William Heyden seeking guidance at this juncture of my
commitment. He never answered, most likely having the same trouble with his own commitment.

I called New York last year, called the big agency where Barbara
Nance worked fifteen, sixteen years ago. I asked if they knew Sheila,
the red-hot editor. The woman on the line said, "I know of her. One
of her clients just quit her, to come to me, for better service."

I got Sheila's new phone number and dialed her up. She'd become
a literary agent. Maybe she'd given up writing, greatness being as elu-
sive and difficult as it is.

The front-line-defense voice at Sheila's office wanted to know,
"Who are you? Are you a client of hers?"

"It's a long story," I said.

"She's extremely busy," the voice said. "She can't just talk. Besides
she's on another line. Hold on." Hold hold hold hold hold hold…
hold hold hold hold hold hold hold. "She's talking to California!"

People in New York are sometimes taken by the length of the long
distance. I told this person a summary version of my acquaintance
with Sheila. I wanted to ask Sheila if she knew of anyone in New York
who had known Barbara, anyone I could call to see if the old manuscripts were still around.

"Fifteen years? Impossible!"

"At least remote," I said. "I'd like to talk to Sheila, if it's not too
much to ask."

"It's not too much to ask. Hold on." Hold hold hold hold hold…
hold hold… hold. "She doesn't know. She knows nothing. I'm sure
she doesn't know."

"Can I please speak with her?"

"She's very busy. She might be busy… ten minutes—or twelve!"

"I'll hold."

Hold hold hold hold hold hold hold hold hold hold hold hold
hold hold hold hold hold… hold hold hold…

…hold…

…hold hold hold hold hold hold hold. "Hello."

"Hello."

"Look. She doesn't know, okay? She says she was never friends with Barbara Nance. Okay?"

"Okay," I said, setting the phone down.

"Have a nice day," called the voice from New York.

So I let go again the old, troublesome manuscript, let go of any hope that anyone in New York was listening to anything but themselves and a distant echo that sounded like greatness.

I think my old man understood this dilemma, understood the remedy. I think he was a seasoned veteran of the intensive approach, of the life available to those who avoid the prescription, to those willing to risk everything. Because a free life rewards only those who take risk, and if you risk enough, then victory is assured, since total defeat leads to the same gratification as success, which is relief, peace of mind, commitment to survival. Because in the end the only thing you can lose is peace of mind.

My old man understood the still, deep currents running formidably in town and in the river, understood the sudden undertows and whirlpools that could surface in the scheme of things, knew what rocky shoals could run you aground. The old man knew all about that stuff and that it all came to the same thing. Sure it would be a better life with some regular good luck that would lead to some money. But if it didn't, so what? What else could you do, but put it out there one more time? What else could you do? Sell insurance?

Ha. That was another laugh, stopping quickly when I realized the one place in the world where my long lost manuscript could be—in the archives atop Brother's hutch.

I stacked phone books on a chair and began offloading while Brother made new coffee and prepared for his morning routine. I had only arrived in St. Louis last night, but the time lag and long morning made it seem long ago.

It was a Saturday, just another Saturday at Brother's. It officially began with a low-budget cartoon on television, one with space monsters and a popular music idol, followed by another cartoon about another music goddess who achieved fame by accentuating her breasts and quivering her lips, like the blow jobs never stopped. The cartoon version was idiotic; she was sweet and simple-minded. The next cartoon was The Smurfs or The Duffs, or The Plunks, or something, and it sounded like dog turds would sound, if dog turds talked. I looked outside again, where Lucy and Ethel had just finished pissing six times each, offing a couple major dumps, and now they whined and howled to get back in, out of the cold, back to the Saturday morning lineup. "How can you watch that shit?" I called in.

Brother shushed, stoked up his bhang and explained in a cloud of smoke, "It's Saturday." What a kid.

He came out of his trance long enough to get pissed off at the mess I'd made. I told him I needed an old manuscript. He said I'd asked about it twice before, or three times, and he'd looked each time, "It's not there."

So I let it go once more, dressed, and went outside for some free-form movement, arms and legs, away from the kaleidoscopic avalanche of reminders in Brother's house. I needed some air, but the air had turned to cold steel; it stuck to your skin and wouldn't come off, so a walk around the block was painful. I considered other pain, wondering why all pain, all discomfort, all dissatisfaction could not be dispensed as easily as the stinging cold, by simply letting it go.

I had come to St. Louis for justice after thirty years of waiting. Sure Flossie's son was a bad person, but his badness was his spiritual dysfunction, not mine, unless I got down there with him and wallowed in it. My old man's advice was more practical then, because I could have popped Flossie's son in the nose, could have stood over him and claimed dominance. But then I wondered; dominance over what?

I had seen Flossie's son a year or two earlier, getting into the Mercedes (leased) that The Devilment had needed all these years to round out her rightful claim to the social ladder's highest rung. I was in town then, too, on another visit, picking Mother up for another furlough. Mother had waited on the front steps outside Flossie's condo, because she knew if I went inside it could lead to trouble. Flossie's son was leaving just as I pulled up.

He was shrinking fast even then, a couple years earlier, withering at last to proper proportion to the size of his soul; body follows mind every time. He'd become a mushy target. That could be a problem. These thoughts drifted like snowflakes around Brother's block, and I finished my walk as Mother and Sissy arrived, rounding opposite corners, pulling up and parking. I waited, thinking this is the future, thinking that prospects for a Saturday morning with the family seemed as different from thirty-five years ago as the Midwest is different from the tropics.

Then again maybe not; Brother had the cartoons on, Mother would try to force-feed us, Sissy would be tense and busy, and I was happy to be free of school.

Inside, after the dogs stopped yapping and the coats got hung, and Brother asked everyone to please shut the fuck up so he could watch his goddamn cartoons, and Mother reviewed the menu out loud and ended up dejected with only three bagels to toast, and Sissy said she didn't have time, not now, she had to be somewhere and then she had to be somewhere else, we reached a lull. It lasted about thirty seconds.

"I don't want to dwell on anything morbid," Mother said out of the blue. "But I *am* meeting next week with the rabbi to talk about a plot for myself. They're not easy to get anymore, and I have to know now how many to ask for, I mean, together."

With no hesitation, casually, she presented this question of eternity. It was only another Saturday morning, but maybe a good one for Mother, so easily did she approach the bones, the dust. She looked at me first, expectant maybe, with a smooth, subtle turn of her head more free of anxiety than I'd thought possible for her. Chronic urgency was a part of her; she was the cause of her own effect, the action preceding her own reaction. *How many baked potatoes will you eat? I need to know now. Will you eat two? I must know.* This series could come hours or days before dinner and could repeat itself at random.

But now her calmness was as contagious as her neurosis had been for so many years. I smiled. "I'm actually very comfortable in the tropics," I said.

"Okay," she said, with an ease, an acceptance, an approval as profound as that of a mother knowing that her child would be fed, clothed, educated, watched over, made happy, and then properly buried. She turned to Sissy and waited.

"Mother, I can't! Not now!" Sissy was too pressed at the moment with expenses. This was a chronic condition for her, poverty as a function of acquisition. And on the topic of death and burial, Sissy got upset. Why did we have to talk about something so morbid? But she too was having her fair share of adjustments in life; with three beautiful, over-educated children of her own now gone from the nest, Sissy looked ahead with uncertainty, looked back with curiosity.

Sissy had succumbed to the dangerous notion that her children should have everything she never had, in this case meaning stability in the suburbs. Her three children didn't have a clue to the nature of instability. They were generally healthy, except for their susceptibility to colds and flus, because their immune systems were weak from franchise food. Maybe Sissy never cooked *because* Mother had cooked like no tomorrow, and Sissy didn't want to make that mistake. Sissy was pressured, unwittingly, like Mother; pressured over enough money for more. The years of strident stability and assuring success for her children by suburban standards had taken a toll on her calmness, on her ability to relax with the family, our family, on the old level.

Sissy had taken up a new hobby—miniature cars. I tried to understand what it gave her, but I could not. I thought I was missing something. Brother had clued me in: "It's all these people who are boring," he said. "They get together with their toy cars and talk about them. And they're out in public with other people, talking about something. It's like life, for them."

Ethel, the dog, was perhaps a catalyst for Sissy and the family— Sissy came to Brother's house on Saturdays. Mother said Sissy came to see Ethel, to hug and romp with Ethel, because people have far fewer emotional problems with dogs than with other people.

"And you think she only comes over to see Ethel?" I had asked.

"Yes," Mother had said. "I do." Mother's response was unexpectedly unemotional, factual and cold. She'd scaled a learning curve steeper than Machu Picchu in recent months, but she still had not reconciled to the possibility that Sissy's blind filial devotion would be less than her own, that this was actually what the world had come to.

"Looks like a two-pack'll do it at the cemetery, Ma," Brother said, arriving from the next room to end our rare talk of eternity. He announced his aquarium was finally on self-maintenance. "I can leave town if I want to and they're okay. First one that croaks feeds the rest for a week. It's balanced. They're the perfect size."

He drank his coffee from a cup that said *I ♡ being Black*. The cups were given free to all the teachers at the school where Brother was a teacher. He said that just for fun he'd ordered up a case of cups for those teachers in the minority at his school that said *I ♡ being White*. He had to meet with his lawyer to make sure he couldn't be fired before handing out his cups.

Brother said his position at school was more secure now, since last month when the assistant superintendent of the district told all faculty and staff to forget old prejudices and animosities and simply get along. The assistant superintendent said she wasn't kidding around, and that goes for the blacks, the whites, *and* the Jews.

❄   ❄   ❄

Freeze Frame

So the morning passed with another six-course meal, talk of burial sites, self-tending aquaria, three hours of mind-numbing television, and hardly any mention of the trial next week, because the truth was still sensitive and sore for Mother. Just after noon, when everyone got tired and tired of it, just when Sissy said she didn't appreciate one bit Brother and I plying her son with drugs, and Brother asked if she expected us to smoke the dirt weed that little punk brought home from college, I announced a side trip, two days. Mother could join me.

She looked up. Sissy looked up, interrupted and impatient. Brother smiled and nodded, because he knew too about events and dates and unspoken histories. I would travel to Southern Indiana tomorrow, in Mother's car. Mother asked, "Why? We have so much to do."

We had nothing to do, except plan out the next seven days times three meals times six courses times a different grocery store for coupons and specials for each course. Mother said it would be a mad rush as it was, without gallivanting around the countryside. So why now?

"It's thirty years," Brother said. Mother had forgot. Sissy either forgot or would have kept it to herself. Thirty years Monday since our old man died, thirty years since I'd been back. Brother went back once after eighteen years, after he started his sorting-out phase. I don't know what he did there, or what he got from his visit. I didn't know any more about my intention, except that a homing instinct, converted to words, went something like: *It's time.*

Mother could in no way be ready for that kind of trip without planning ahead—it could take a few weeks. I told her fine, I'd go without her. Or, she could call Flossie's son and let him know that Flossie could croak tomorrow with no asswipe at hand, and Mother could join me, gallivanting around the country. I would stay at Aunt Aileen's, because some places are still okay to drop in for a stay after thirty years.

"I don't know," Mother said rhetorically, obliquely, mentally on her way.

Mother called Aunt Aileen an hour later, in a huff and a rush and a yak over swooping down on Southern Indiana. Aunt Aileen said, slow and easy, "Okay. I'll have some of the girls over for lunch."

"How can you plan a luncheon in one day?"

"Be here by noon," Aunt Aileen said, slow and easy, just like thirty years ago.

"She's crazy," Mother said. "She thinks she can plan a luncheon in one day."

"Do you think she can?" I asked.

"We have to be there by noon!" Mother said. "Now move!"

And twenty hours and eighteen courses later, after six phone calls between Mother's and Brother's on logistics, Mother and I were on the road. We had eggs, lox, bagel, jelly, cream cheese and famous coffee cake that sunrise. Mother said we were looking at a long, strenuous day, so I better *eat!* She packed several bags of fruit, chips, cookies, and fried chicken she'd prepared last night, so it would be just like old times, when we rode the train to Flossie's in St. Louis from Southern Indiana. That was in the way back when, when we got a baby duck or two every year at springtime, when a day could hardly be better spent, if you're five or eight or eleven years old, than playing with baby ducks. We made houses for them, fed them, and gave them swimming lessons in the kitchen sink. We took them along with us on the train because you can't leave a baby duck all alone and even though my old man never came with us, we couldn't very well expect him to take care of baby ducks, after the ducks had stolen so many of his baits, and we knew how he stood on ducks.

Brother and I put them in shoe boxes with some grass and a jar lid of water and another jar lid of duck food and then put the boxes in the baggage car, as baggage, because no pets were allowed on the train. And once the train left the station, we headed back to the baggage car and found our shoe box of crying baby ducks, all the water and food shmushed into the grass. But they eep-eep-eeped happily when we took them out and played with them in the aisles of the baggage car and sometimes, if the conductor was nice, we took them up front to our seats for some cookies and soda—and fried chicken, carrot and celery sticks, deviled eggs and potato chips and olives, and about six other courses all spread out on a continuous tablecloth of overlapping napkins with a baby duck somewhere in there, under or over or burrowing in for a nap or a stray chip.

A couple-three ducks stood out over the years as most memorable for their personalities and strong character, like Duck-a-luck, who would follow a kid anywhere and get upset as a puppy not allowed to play when his kids rode off on bicycles. And Matzo Ball, who scarfed one down and got his name. And maybe most famous of the ducks was Quacky, who lived in the kitchen as a duckling, in a box with windows. He stuck his head out the windows to see the world and once saw a crate of strawberries. The old man swapped a mess of bass for the strawberries with a guy who had a strawberry farm and a lake. Quacky stretched his neck for what could have been the last time, reaching happily for a two-pint snack.

He looked like a duck with his head cut off, blood-red down to his belly, his little quack remorseful from the bulge and bellyache. It was curtains for Quacky for sure, but we jumped to, uncrated the strawberries, ditched the shmushed ones, cleaned and cut up the rest quick for the shortcake Mother was already kneading on the counter. We didn't fool anyone—"Goddamn fucking ducks," my old man said, coming into the kitchen and seeing Quacky all red in the face and

green in the gills. But with fresh strawberries over hot shortcake coming right up, moods could hardly stay harsh.

Quacky got a reprieve but had to move outside, which was only
natural and fine with him, since the cesspool out back was way over-
due for pumping but that cost money, and Quacky thought it was a
pond, special for him, because we loved him. And though the red
stains gave way to brownish greens in only an hour or two we still
loved him, and every now and then he'd get hosed off and brought
back inside to play when the old man was gone fishing or drinking or
trying to hustle a buck or two.

We lost our lake in '57 or '59. So we had to take our grown ducks
out to one lake or another where other ducks lived. Our ducks had
a hard time the first few days, down in pecking order, but they
adapted and got along. My old man scored a .22 rifle when I was
eleven, swapped a guy for a diamond, because it was a good deal and
he figured his boys should learn to shoot. We took the gun with us
one summer day, along with our ducks, out to a distant lake, a lake so
big it was known for monster catfish, giant bass, bluegill big as your
hand, many ducks.

I proved to be a natural shot, could hit a half-dollar propped on a
dandelion at thirty yards, could hit a bottle on the fly, couldn't miss;
and so the old man lit up when I got a yen for a real moving target
and asked him if I could shoot a duck.

"Sure!" he said, happily recognizing a new and valuable ally in the
never-ending war against his nemesis, the ducks. They were maybe
sixty yards out, just off a far bank, and I slid one into my notched V
and brought her even with my barrel tip, exhaled nearly all the way
and soft as a whisper squeezed the trigger. It was as if shooting a duck
was nothing, no different than the breeze bending a cattail. The gun
held about 18 rounds of long rifle bullets, but I must have shot every
one because the hammer clicked empty, which in the moment of
hearing was more resounding than the shot would have been.

I think God planned it, or set me up for it, or emptied the cham-
ber, or something, because I lowered that rifle in a rush and a hot

flash, feeling faint with an overpowering wave of realization that I'd just nearly killed someone. My old man pulled out more bullets and reloaded and handed it back and said, "Come on, Hotshot, let's see what you can do."

But I said no, I didn't want to. He yelled that I shouldn't worry, our ducks were over to the left, come on. But I said no, I didn't want to. It wasn't the sort of thing my old man would easily accept, unless it was mixed in quick with the idea of shooting another half-dollar while Brother held it out for me—*I know I can do it, I know I can, I won't miss, pullleeeze!* I got the old man to come around to my negative frame of mind. "No," he said. "We better not." So we went home, Brother and I breathing a sigh of relief.

That was the last time I aimed anything at an animal, realizing that people with guns are like people with paint brushes, eyeballing everything for the once over, once momentum gets worked up.

Maybe I realized as well that I liked most animals much more than I liked most people. Just look what the people had done on every mile of the road back to Southern Indiana. The trip back wasn't like old times. The train was long gone, replaced by four-lane highway, and the countryside, too, was a darker shade of pale, displaced by franchise food signs so garish, so ugly that they scream in your face. Joining them in the devastation were more gasoline pumps than could be healthy, or necessary, calling obscene attention to themselves in the frozen, deciduous landscape. Mother and I talked of how it used to be, and we ate.

We arrived late so the girls had a head start on us, three cups ahead on the drug of choice in Southern Indiana, caffeine. The yak was mile a minute and nonstop, like the train used to be, or maybe more like the stock car races on the figure-8 track. The girls were early seventies to mid-eighties, had been the women of my early youth. They surrounded Mother, said she looked beautiful, lovely, wonderful, great, and on and on. Mother soaked it up. I watched, knowing this first minute would be a freebie. Then they would turn to me, turn on me, for the inquisition.

Rose Sugarman, who'd been married to Al for a few hundred years, until he split one day, and then he died one day, had become eighty-three. She looked like George Burns and could have passed for his twin if she had a cigar. Brother went steady in eighth grade with her daughter, Ruth. That was when Al was president of the congregation, and the rabbi got busted for fucking a woman at the Holiday Inn every Wednesday for several years, covering with a story about study with the monks at St. Meinrad's Monastery. Yeah, studying steady pussy—this was the rabbi who got the ax right before my old man died, so the rabbi at the funeral was a new rabbi. The old rabbi's five-o'clock shadow made eighty-grit sandpaper look like a baby's ass. He further charmed us by chewing on old stogie stumps, staying pissed off and mumbling, always mumbling. He was strictly a bullshit artist, a spiritual fake, and nobody knew it but the kids. The Sunday school teacher he humped gift-wrapped it and served it on a platter, motivated by revenge, because she hadn't been born Jewish but had married into it. She'd converted—even down to the ritual baths. But did the other women accept her as one of their own? Well, not exactly, there was just something about her. So she fucked the rabbi.

Everyone found out how worthless he was when he got the third degree at Rose and Al's house, when Al was president. The Sunday school teacher who wasn't Jewish, not really Jewish, confessed her motivation. Everyone suspected she liked the ride though, especially the rabbi's wife, Bernice, who asked rhetorically, in the real Jewish idiom, "Monks? What, with the monks? So what does he need from the monks, every Wednesday like clockwork, what? Three years?" She'd sent a private detective to follow him, to the Holiday Inn. Bernice cried her eyes out over this and other misfortunes.

It all came back in waves, back to the most fun of all, which was giggling over the gossip and sweet revenge for having this jerk held up as a role model.

"Remember Ruthie?" Rose said. "She's married. Divorced. Married with a few kids." I couldn't follow. It didn't matter. Rose turned quick to make another point, like she was pissed off or something, waving a finger for emphasis. "No no no! It was a serving dish, a glass one!" Most of the girls didn't look at her. She wasn't talking to anyone but she got more excited, so Dora stepped over and listened. Rose married Mannie Levitz after Al split and Mannie's wife died. Mannie was Dora's brother, so after klatching sixty years Rose and Dora became sisters-in-law. So Dora listened, because Rose took good care of her brother, Mannie.

"She married a very wealthy man from Terre Haute," Rose said.

"Was he Jewish?" Dora asked, shrugging aside, sharing with me that she, too, had no clue to what Rose was talking about.

"Oh, yeah!" Rose said. "She never had no trouble." And in a wink Rose turned from Dora, laid her eyes on me for the second time in two minutes, but it was the first time in thirty years, this time. She stepped up toe to toe and said, "He knew about that basement. You think I'd let him get away with that?" This, out of the blue, with no context, no reference, no meaning; like a hallucination, Rose broke into nonsense like it was a real subject, like thirty years was three seconds and this was the second half of a sentence started way back when. I understood. I'd experienced alternate realities.

"Not for a minute," I said.

She nodded, "Uh huh. That bastard Al tried it more than once."

"Hard to believe," I said.

"I told her, they got that big fellow out there to take care of her. You know who I mean... Jack... Jack... Jack..."

Dora came to the rescue, "Nobody knows what you're talking about." Dora turned to me, "You look wonderful!" It was the sentiment of survival in a small town; those who had not yet died told each other they looked wonderful. She made me feel old. None of these women had ever once in my youth told me that I looked wonderful.

"Jack... Big fellow."

"Jake," I said. "Big Jake."

"Yeah! That's the one! Jake! Big Jake! I told her!" Rose laughed loud to underscore her point, "Ha!" And she strolled with purpose to the far perimeter where Mother soaked up praise, and when the praise went full circle for the way her children turned out, Mother primed the pump again, with her wonderful grandchildren.

Dora had only become seventy-two. "I'm so glad you're here," she said. "Rose is driving me crazy. I can't be with her by myself." Dora was ready with her own interrogation, but Rose's move to the far side prompted Henrietta Nussbaum to come my way, with a walking cane but spritely. And she cut a pixie figure, too, at eighty pounds and a head of orange-gold hair spun loose and round and big as the cotton candy you used to get back when.

She moved between Dora and me and said, "I got a girl for you. Twenty-nine, and all of a sudden, available. Nice, huh? And is she a little beauty? Let me tell you something. My granddaughter graduated college and went back and got her master's degree, because she's smart, that one. Then she went down to Texas and was in a bar and saw this fellow and liked his looks, you know, and then saw he had on a pin from SDT, and so she goes up and asks him if he's Jewish. Oh, it matters. Well, it does to my grandchildren..."

They got married, had babies, and the Jewish fellow died slowly of lymphoma over the next ten minutes. Now the granddaughter was available. Any interest?

"You said twenty-nine," I said. "Now she's thirty-one and has two kids. That's way too old, and who needs the baggage?" I was born in the region, spoke the language; a problem solved quick and neat would more likely stay solved.

Rose laughed hard from across the room, "Ha! That's right. Who needs it? Listen, Mannie taught me everything about sex! That bastard Al didn't do nothing!" And luncheon was served.

And a lovely time it was, once initial concerns were dispatched over Jennifer, who was dishwasher and server, whose mama had worked for Aunt Aileen for years and years and now Jennifer had followed in her mama's footsteps with two kids and another due in a month. Jennifer was twenty and too big, and the girls doubted that she'd washed her hands—*I don't think she's washed her hands! No! No, I don't either. What? Washed her hands. No, she didn't. She didn't wash her hands. But* they shut up when Aunt Aileen called into the kitchen, "Jennifer? Wash your hands, Honey."

More coffee sustained the high-level exchange and I had to admire the girls, still strong in spirit, still at each other's throats after all these years. I eased back into my chair as the girls wound up for the lovely-grandchildren competition, and the Instamatic snapshots flew like two-deck pinochle in the old days.

Then came gee-it's-great-to-see-you-you-look-terrific and good-bye. Aunt Less left first. She married Nardy, Adolph's son. Adolph died before I was born, so all I ever knew was that he was the oldest of my old man's brothers. But Less wasn't Jewish, didn't speak the language of cutthroat love, never had, nor had she cared about acceptance but was instead imbued through life with a smile, a warmth, a benign independence, so when she left no one had much to say.

Rose and Dora left next, in a dither and a spew with many hugs and kisses and compliments on physical fitness, and boy oh boy oh boy you oughta see this one or that one or the other one now! That exit, too, was followed by a silence, but it lasted only the length of a sigh. Henrietta Nussbaum said, "I don't know if she's got all her marbles."

"They're different colors, that's for sure," said Aunt Aileen.

"You ought to talk to her," Mother said. "Tell her. Tell her slow and nice. Tell her we don't know what she's talking about."

"She don't hear a damn thing," Aunt Aileen said.

"And I don't talk to her," Henrietta Nussbaum said.

"Then talk to Dora," Mother said. "Maybe I could talk to Dora."

"Oh no!" Sylvia said. "You say one word to Dora, she'll blow up. Not one word."

"Let me tell you something," Henrietta Nussbaum said. "Rose and I are the same age. We were born the same day. We're eighty-three. She was born in the morning, I was in the afternoon, and I tell you I look at her and I think, 'Am I like that?' And I don't think so. I'm intelligent..."

...mmm...yes... Yes... Yes, you are.... The refrain was mumbled, consensual, polite; Henrietta was granted intelligence.

"And I have conversations with people," Henri said. "She's nuts!"
...mmm...yes... nuts... She is....

But soon, it was Henrietta Nussbaum's time to leave. She told me
to get the door for her and carry her things to her car and get that
door, too. At the car she said I could call her granddaughter, if I
wanted to. I told her I'd be back in Hawaii in a few days and her
granddaughter could call me there. Her farewell was a scoff and a
flourish of her cotton-candy head. I waved goodbye, because it was
a small town, after all.

I got back inside just as Aunt Aileen was saying, "She's a mean one."

Mother nodded and Sylvia concurred with a vignette of Henrietta's
meanness that had occurred about the time of Milton's death last year.
It was brief and had to do with Henrietta's failure to offer a ride to a
social function, when she knew as plain as the nose on her face that
Sylvia was going, too, and needed a ride, what with Milton being sick
and about to die.

Sylvia eased up to the edge of the sofa and eased into wearisome
monotone for the last days, weeks, months of Milton's demise, up to
the unfortunate decision to inject him ten days running with lethal
antibiotics at home. He died, but the story continued because he did
not die of a common brain tumor or any other run-of-the-mill debil-
itating disease but rather of a rare and exotic strain the doctors knew
nothing about. So they asked permission to remove Milton's brain,
for greater knowledge. The whole family convened and concurred.

The story went on, amazingly, another ten minutes, following
Milton's brain on its farewell tour, drawing crowds here and there and
everywhere—crowds of doctors, those greatest of all men, in their
white robes, their omnipotence, their Godliness, their Cadillacs and
club memberships. Eventually Milton's brain got to Cincinnati, where
the phone rang. Mother nodded off, Aunt Aileen answered the
phone, I ducked out for a whiz on cue. Sylvia went on a few more
minutes on keeping a kosher home, which she did for years and years,
for Milton, but now she didn't and didn't care. She still slept till ten,
but it wasn't the same, waking up without her toast and OJ waiting
there on the nightstand—oh yes, Milton did that for her for all those

years. Finally, with that cross to bear, Sylvia stood up. Mother woke up. Aunt Aileen got off the phone. I came back. Sylvia said a sad farewell and left.

"She's so full of shit," Aunt Aileen said. "I swear."

I laughed. Aunt Aileen isn't an aunt in our family, nor was Uncle Louie an uncle, not in the blood sense anyway. But we called them Aunt Aileen and Uncle Louie since before I was old enough to remember coherent speech because their house was also home. I don't know how we got so intertwined with them, except that maybe it was a chemical need of Mother's, Aunt Aileen stayed cold when Mother got hot, stayed calm when Mother got excited, balanced out with alkalinity when Mother got acidic: She was the yin to Mother's yang. And Aunt Aileen stayed even-keeled; she had no moods, except for an occasional craving for buttermilk or fried chicken.

Aunt Aileen's house hadn't changed, a little place in a country neighborhood with a barn, a garden, a blackberry patch, some giant trees. And I laughed because the years had not diluted her ability to call a spade a spade.

"I have an idea for dinner," I said. Mother and Aunt Aileen waited. "I'll take you both out, somewhere where we won't be seen." They laughed too, and Mother and I had finally arrived.

The afternoon was short and gray, cold and misty. Night fell quick and cold as dirt into a hole. Dinner was a push, too much to eat, but Mother and Aunt Aileen so enjoyed going out, and how often did I come to town? I stayed up late, reading, recalling the old times, names, faces, fun and games, in a casual audit of my youth, looking maybe the way pilgrims do, for some spiritual connection between long ago or far away and what it all came to.

I'd played Hide and Seek in this house a hundred times—hid under this very bed—complained over Red Rover and Crack the Whip because I was too small. Red Rover was only capture capture capture for me, and I always had to be on the tail end of the whip, I snapped so good. Freeze Tag and Piggy Wants a Wave seemed so much more fair.

We caught lightning bugs by the dozens and put them in jars and then let them go later, inside this room in the dark.

But when I doused the light it stayed dark, the very air so different from those times, that the recall itself was a disinterment. An image here, a yelp or a call there, then stillness. And all the recollection sorted out like an exhibit in a museum, preserved but no longer alive.

I remembered tomorrow, thirty years ago.

Mother was up at six, because she likes to get an early start. She stood in the door of the room I slept in, until I opened my eyes. "Are you up?" she asked. "Let's go. Did you bring warm clothes? What do you want for breakfast?"

"Yes, I did," I said. "But it won't be that cold."

"That's what you think," she said, heading off down the hall as if she knew exactly what I needed for breakfast. "It's cold in the summertime in a cemetery." Pearls of wisdom, idiosyncrasies of nature like this, she still imparted unto me, lo though she leaned hard on seventy-four.

And here it was January, as sadly, somberly gray as any day stillborn in the frozen north ever was. It was a day of dormancy, crushed with cold, flecked with sleet on a fluky breeze that couldn't hold steady but wheezed and coughed as if it, too, would give up the ghost by sundown. Sunrise looked like dusk, and so did midmorning when we finally found Mt. Sinai Cemetery on the far side of town, where the old families settled at the turn of the last century, where the new families never went anymore, not since '65, since the new, modern cemetery on the developing side of town gained popularity.

I had known what I would do that morning, kind of, so I'd brought a folding chair from Brother's house in St. Louis. I got it out of the trunk of the car while Mother and Aunt Aileen watched me, after Mother looked over the short wall at her first husband's grave. She said she could not go near it because they had been divorced, and the Law forbids a divorced woman to approach her ex-husband's grave.

"You approached it thirty years ago," I said.

"I didn't know then," she said. "Besides, I couldn't let you kids go alone."

"So now you know," I said. "So what. If your heart is clear and you want to approach, then you can." I spoke about this like I knew more about it than she did, and she accepted that; she finally recognized the man in me, even though I had to reach middle age before she could let go of the child. But no, no...she could not approach the grave.

And watching me pull out my folding chair from the trunk, she asked, "What are you doing?"

I knew what I was doing, but the process was one I'd learned far from home. It was nothing, it was everything. I would meditate. I would empty the vessel. I would allow contact, not between specific things or beings or events, but contact that would become the *all*. I would relinquish rationale, modify the coordinates of place and time, then join those places and all time, after removing those things from their thingness. How could I explain this to Mother? I knew what she would think, what she would say.

I smiled. She waited for an answer. An answer was required, just as my presence was required, requiring all the aggravation of modern travel, because you feel compelled to be certain places at certain times, so you run the gauntlet of long flights, long drives, excessive nostalgia, wasted hours, harsh weather. Snow began to fall. Frost formed on the car windows. A chill rushed inward, causing Mother and I to tremble. It was time to proceed, time to stay warm in the heart, just like the people who lived on the ice.

"I'm going to see the Ice King," I said. I didn't think Mother would understand, but I hoped she'd let it pass, one more crazy notion. She scoffed as she'd scoffed at so many of my ideas over the years. *You talk so crazy,* she was about to say and would have said it. But she remembered the morning thirty years ago that the dam broke in my eyes, flooding all of Mt. Sinai and all the hearts and eyes that were gathered in that spot. She remembered her baby's pain, and she sought again to comfort. This time she used a new facial expression, not scorn but confused tolerance.

"The Ice King," I repeated, unwilling to give in to distraction at that point, since a good meditation begins before it begins. And I'd taken my first step, folding chair in hand, seeking calmness already, because the cold was urgent and letting it go required focus. "I'm going to see the king of the frozen north, where the spirits live. The Ice King rules the land of spirits." I got the look again, but with a twist, a struggle maybe; I think it could have been Mother's attempt at understanding, or maybe it was only the limit of her tolerance.

"To express gratitude," I explained, but sometimes explanations only compound confusion. Aunt Aileen laughed short, maybe because she remembered my old man like Mother did, as a rough, sometimes dangerous person. Maybe Aunt Aileen thought the gratitude would be for surviving a childhood with my old man. She and Uncle Louie had helped Mother on the day of the Exodus, out of the land of bondage in '61, had picked Brother and me up at school and taken us to the new house. Then she and Uncle Louie had gone home and turned all the lights out, knowing what the wrath of my old man could mean. Maybe that was all she knew. It didn't matter.

Uncle Louie understood a side of my old man that few people understood in those days, which was the volatile side, the side that would go off if you shook it up. They weren't close friends, Uncle Louie and my old man, but they shared the idiom of that small world and got along. Uncle Louie was as big as my old man, but where the old man was thick and powerful, Uncle Louie was fat. He smoked cigars and called my old man Puddin', which my old man hated, but he never punched Uncle Louie, maybe because Uncle Louie was a master of stirring up just a little bit o'shit. The old man called him Puddin' back and let the peace be. Mother said Uncle Louie was as much of a troublemaker as my old man was crazy.

Country Jew was the identity they shared, homeboys who grew up with the grim rule of history. Country Jews do not fit the stereotype, do not kvetch for identity, do not cling to the *oy yoy yoy!*, the *Vayezmere!*, the *What, are you nuts?*, or *Maybe it's a nice cup of soup you would like.* Country Jews go back farther than the three or four centuries of *shtetl* life so ardently recalled by urban Jews in America. They reach back to what came before, around fifty-five hundred years of it.

Most people don't know about country Jews because of the media-fed profile of New York Jews and Hollywood Jews, too, with the shirt open down the front, all six buttons, exposing the hairy chest and gold-plated *Chai*. But Judaism in Southern Indiana was not the song and dance, the idiom and accent, the inflection that announces your heritage. What survived there is a soft approach to life based on education, hard work mixed with smart work, and faith, without the glitz. And along with faith now thrives the iron rule all Jews understand: *Never again.*

What survived was a community of Jews, rich and poor, who know what the world will do to them if given a chance, simply because it's what the world has always done.

The Judaism that was lived there conformed to historical context. Abraham was a prophet who had a vision. I don't know what drugs were available then, but I too have had visions. Anyway, Bob Dylan put it best in *Highway 61 Revisited*:

> God told Abraham, kill me a son.
> Abe said, Man you must be puttin' me on.
> God said, Abe.
> Abe said, What?
> God said, You can do what you want Abe but,
>   next time you see me comin', you better run.
> Abe said, Where you want this...killin' done?
> God said, Out on Highway...61...
>   (ba dom ba dom ba dom...)

God tested Abraham's faith with a heavy hand, and Abraham passed the test. So God said, *Okay, okay, don't kill your son. I'm not that kind of God. Kill a goat instead.*

It was a first; direct word from God that human sacrifice is bad. God wanted sins expunged by way of sacrifice—not a human sacrifice but, say, a goat. So the Chosen People imparted their troubles to a scapegoat.

But other people scorned the Jews, they were so soft, so easily contained, and in time so convenient as scapegoats themselves. A pogrom could nearly always solve economic unrest, restore the kings's popularity, vent the pressure, or at least soothe the populace.

Then came the big test in our own century.

The reality that country Jews share is the old reality of softness and pliability mixed with the modern rule. As a Jewish child in Southern Indiana in the '50s, I only knew that I didn't have to kneel down in school, and that the shit could hit the fan anytime. It could be little shit, like Jew-baiting on the playground. Or it could be big shit, like all humanity being told to form two lines, and one of those lines is for Jews, and it leads to some waiting trains, and they ain't bound for Madagascar.

My old man was that Jewish—Jewish enough to know the score and be comfortable with it, to discuss it in any form you like. Uncle Louie was more Jewish than that, and though I never thought much about Uncle Louie's spiritual connection, I thought about it after he died, when Aunt Aileen told us how he got up from his deathbed and raised holy hell because they wanted to shave him on Saturday. He never shaved on Saturday. Many Jews don't. I don't, since I heard that story. It's a reminder, what most of Judaism is; reminders, lest we forget.

I guess country Jews don't need to remind themselves and everyone else nearly as often, or with so much showbiz flourish. They know, and the knowing, unspoken, undramatized, always impressed me as a stronger, calmer knowing, not fading like a weak pulse, not requiring constant resuscitation.

Aunt Aileen watched my naive attempt to introduce Mother to another cockamamie idea, *the Ice King, ruler of the frozen north*. She laughed, shaking her head—she and Uncle Louie said thirty and thirty-five and forty years ago, "That boy's wild. You'll never keep him home." The prophecy had come to pass. So what. I loved the notion then, am happy with it still.

And there I was, gone out and into the world and now back thirty years later to the day, more full of piss and vinegar than the day I left, telling the old folks what was. And what the hell, I didn't need pressing on an issue, like what I would do at my old man's grave thirty years after the funeral. *What do you mean, what am I going to do?* is what

I could have said. *I'm going to meditate!* And Mother would have said, *What do you mean, meditate?* And I would have had to yell, just like the old man had to do, because he never figured it out like I did.

I carried my chair down the wall to the entrance and then back to my old man's place. I opened it at the foot and I sat, feet on the ground, back straight, chest open, shoulders floating, hands together in a common Buddhist mudra.

Thirty years ago, I'd stood by my old man's final resting spot in the shade. And even though I now wore as much clothing as I had worn in heavy weather at sea, sitting in that place of death I could not keep the cold from coming through, embracing my naked body like clothing was the weakest defense of all. The cold continued its penetration to the bone and on in for a flash freeze on the marrow. Of course, a living body reacts to that kind of shock, fights the sudden death with heavy shakes. I brought the universe into my center by half, and then half and half again with my mind in that same spot, took it out of its rational mode and put it down where intuition and instinct reside. And once free of the burden of cause and effect I let go the pain, let the cold course through. So what. I imagined myself frozen, frozen and relaxed, with some success.

But you can't apply a simple technique to some things and expect simple results; the heavy shakes got so bad I looked like an old agitator washing machine, off-balance, and the real, living, rational pain cloyed in until the entity, Death, was present among the living, with insistence, with an eager, playful question: *Is it time?* It felt natural, maybe because Death is the perfect host in a cemetery.

But then, surrounded by forebears whose legacy and hope is me, I could more easily accept my host without fear. You cannot stop its grip and jolt and rattle any more than you can sit on a folding chair at graveside and reach communion; not in a minute or two anyway, and anyone who ever felt pain and a pang of fear or the presence of Death, encroaching, will tell you a minute can be far past the dimensions of normal time. But I sat and sat and sought nothing, nothing in the positive sense. I'd come so far over the road and years.

Breathing deep, in through the nose, out through the mouth, deep and slow and then slower still, until it calmed, until it was slowest of all, I eased the shakes down some. In a while, the host was placated. The shakes came down from violent to steady, then they went away. The host stayed on, not with warmth or physical comfort, because Death is not that kind of host, but with a neutral presence, beyond pain even for me, the living, and with curiosity too, maybe, since living bodies sitting still as the dead bodies is a novelty. Flesh and bones eased then into a better stillness, until all the ripples faded away.

But the stillness changed again, and the communion that approached was yet another neutral presence, in which things that can be known are there for the taking, in which omniscience becomes the air you breathe, in which questions and answers are one and the same.

I became a man watching a man on a folding chair, by his father's grave for the first time since the cold, wet day thirty years ago when the boy got slammed into the real world. With posture straight, hands folded, tears rolling down his cheeks, he could easily be perceived as the main player in a scene of sorrow.

But the bitter cold and terrible shakes are what made the tears, not sadness, and then the shakes became so perfectly timed with the frozen gusts, that cold and sorrow too became one and the same.

Some men don't want to be seen crying, not now, because forty-three is far gone from thirteen, so it was a comfort to feel the tears slow down, and then another small pain followed their tracks; they froze in a crooked trail to where icicles formed. And there it was; lines open, free and clear, anything you wanted, forward or back, audience with the Ice King.

Consequence is for the living, if they want it—that was the gist of it. The dead are gone, but spirits do linger, or at least you sense they do, and you can imagine imparting information at such a time: *I sailed across the ocean.* Or, *I rode a motorcycle across Europe.* Or, *Mother is taken care of. I got a chicken named Flossie, and a farm in the country, a few acres of nonstop beauty with avocado trees and mangos, papayas, lemons, bananas, oranges, grapefruit, tangerines, macadamia nuts, lichee, guava—and trees yielding color like it was fruit, like color was a cash crop too; screaming yellow crotons with blood-red in half-inch veins, bauphinia, jethropa, euphorbia, giant white birds of paradise, little blue and orange birds, pink hibiscus and red and white, red, white, orange and orange-red and red-orange and more blood-red, gardenias, pikake, plumeria and jasmine with enough sweet scent to bend your knees, and ducks and more chickens and trees, palm trees, and...and a good life, good weather, and the ocean... And sometimes you got to get out of there, it's all so nice you just want to hang out there, but if you're too young to be a hermit, you realize after a few days that you ain't been out in a while. So I head out. I thought I'd stop by....*

Things surface quickly from the years, like the momentous events or situations you feel most proud of, would most like to share with a dead parent if given, say, only another few minutes in life together.

Or, harking back to other events, other situations, you could offer consolation. I remembered one time in '59 or '60, my old man came home late one afternoon and lay down on the bed looking as down and beat as I ever saw him before or after. He had two years left to live. I stood by the bed and showed him a new toy I'd invented or something, and he said I should come on and lay down there with him. I did, and he just lay there, and I knew better than to talk, and he finally moaned and said, "Oh... I got to find some money. I got to get some money. I just don't know what to do anymore."

This to a child of eleven, who sat up quick and said, "I know! I heard a guy on the radio who said no matter what, he'd lend anybody twenty-five hundred dollars for any reason, no matter what!"

My old man half-smiled and looked sadder still, and in a minute I understood that the guy on the radio was only another lying sonofabitch. *Shit, I'd give you the dough right now if...if...you know....*

Of course the money didn't matter, not now. But the idea was big, of conveying news at his grave that I had scrambled as hard as he had, had fallen down plenty and got back up like he did, had brushed myself off and jumped back in the ring, because what else can you do in our line of work? I got lucky—yes, lucky; had scored a few winners and parlayed and waited and held steady and gone inside at the right moment and scored again. And now I lived in enviable conditions that, if seen thirty years ago, would have looked like those of a very wealthy man, but, well, that too did not matter.

My old man was a romantic in the rough-and-tumble tradition, a man who loved westerns, good guys and bad guys, right and wrong; a man who didn't need to pussyfoot around, not with simple truths so close at hand. My old man loved adventure and nature—that was the legacy. I remembered scuba diving in strong currents at a hundred-twenty feet among ten-foot sharks, remembered the feeling of the depths, recalled the sibilant groan and creaking bones down there that sound like the ocean itself looking for a comfortable position to lie in. I remembered, as if the memory and feeling could be shared. Who would have thought we could scuba dive together, me and my old man?

Who could have imagined that, or any of the adventures in store for me, all those years ago? And with so many memories of so many adventures crowding forward then for communing, from the mon-stered depths to nights that looked unsurvivable on the storm-tossed surface, with waves whose faces stretched so long and looked so haggard, drooling froth from the corners of their evermore gaping grins, as if they were pleased at last with prospects for gobbling you up—a memory surfaced from other depths, which was the time my old man taught me how to swim in '55.

We drove down to Miami Beach, Florida, because that's where Mother and he went on their honeymoon in '41, and still got glassy-eyed recollecting that first and last time of fun in their life together. They brought home a picture of Mother posing, shy but proud, up next to a sizable sailfish she'd caught. Actually, the old man saw the fish, called up to the captain, teased the bait, and set the hook, just as Mother puked over the rail. Then he played the fish in halfway before calling to Mother to *get on over here and land your goddamn fish*. She pulled and reeled, pulled and reeled, pulled and reeled, then handed the rig back to him so she could reel and heave. He played the big fish slow and easy and then landed him like he'd always dreamed he would.

Maybe he savored all the myriad gifts of life then, too; blue skies, sunshine, pretty new wife.

Mother posed leaning on the strung-up fish, smiling flat-footed with her eyes closed and her fishing rod erect. She said for years later he made her do it. I think she meant the pose; I know he made her go fishing. She was twenty-three. He was forty-one. I don't know how he looked in the picture, because she cut him out with a razor blade, probably sometime in '60 or '61. I asked her why she did that, even though the answer was obvious. She said she couldn't help it, as if what had passed between them was bigger than both of them, was more than she could bear. She hung her head, so I only asked her to send any other pictures to me, uncut, if she couldn't stand having them around anymore.

It was her first marriage, his third. I asked her again why she bit, if the bait was all that bad—asked several times over the years to see if time and insight might dilute her bitterness. But she only reiterated his incessant pursuit. She said he just kept coming. He wouldn't take no.

But I think the romance of the thing—that first week in '41—got to her, never mind the seasick and fishy smell. The old man got a couple highballs down her that trip, and they remembered the fun and glory for fourteen years.

We drove down in '55 in our '53 Packard Clipper—a two-year-old car being fairly used up in those days—down through a southland fairly strewn with roadside stands selling rubber tomahawks, back scratchers, and stuffed baby alligators. You could get live baby alligators at most stops then for only a buck, but Mother said no.

We stayed at the Gould Hotel right there on Collins Avenue in Miami Beach, the old man overwhelmed by the madness that had destroyed the place. He'd reviled the miracle-mile development from two hundred miles out—"It was paradise. Paradise. It's not worth the powder to blow it up now." It had been real, like every place in the world once was, two-lane roads, a few people here and there, little businesses and places to eat that were unique and uncloned. And it had turned to shit, homogenized, with a speech pattern and value sys-

tem coming at you from every point of the compass, six lanes of traffic by '55 and oversized, ugly buildings that looked alike.

By the end of our week, the sentiment was ironclad; Miami Beach,
Florida was gone. We had to agree—the asshole of creation. Brother
and I giggled in the back seat. I got poison ivy on the way home in
some woods behind a motel and got painted twice a day with
calamine lotion, once in the morning, just before daybreak and once
at night, just after the grueling double-time drive of the day so we
could get farther away from the asshole of creation and get back
home. Calamine lotion goes on like paint and dries flat, and then
cracks and feels so creepy you'd just as soon scratch.

But any trip a thousand miles from home is an adventure, if you're
seven. And one of the two high points for me was my old man teaching me to swim. I'd futzed around two whole days down at the baby
end and then couldn't find any more tiles to chip off or anyone to
splash or anything. The old man was standing in the shade in long
pants and shoes having a highball, grumbling over the goddamn heat
and all the fucking hotels, when I walked up dripping wet and told
him I was ready to learn to swim. He liked straightforward guys like
that, even at three-six, thirty-eight pounds.

He looked down and said, "Okay, go on down there." He nodded
toward the deep end. I went. He said, "Get closer." I stepped up.
"Now, jump in." I jumped. "Now, swim."

That was it, clean and concise as the old one-two. Mother looked
up, then jumped up, then screamed bloody murder, then spent the
rest of the day doing her little mumbling number about crazy, looking down the whole time. But if it was left up to her I'd still be in the
shallow end, and hell, the old man would have jumped in and saved
me. But no need; I was a natural. I swam. All I needed was a clean,
crisp lead. And hell, he didn't throw me in the deep end, he only gave
me my own two feet to stand on.

I don't think my old man was crazy, no more than, say, anyone who
isn't dull. The irrational, sometimes violent behavior Mother called
crazy wasn't so much a loss of touch with reality, but was rather a per-

fect reflection of it. Just like sweet, plump, succulent oysters will kill you one day, not because they're crazy, but because the sewage treatment plant got overloaded from too many people taking too many shits, and the shit got pumped into the bay.

My old man didn't want to kill anyone, he only gave back some of the toxins coming his way from a society that lost its moral responsibility, lost its sense of right and wrong, went whole hog for the money, losing the only thing of value along the way. The only thing of value was nature, and though he smoked enough Pall Mall straights to kill lesser men much sooner, and he ate fried foods and steaks all the time, and he'd just as soon throw a punch as not, my old man loved nature. He calmed down in nature, didn't count the hours spent in nature, because nature was where he felt at home, where nobody came at him, turned on him, or failed to deliver.

An acute, compulsive sense of right and wrong was my old man's MO. It was into the face of the wrong that he often flew, quick with a jab. I've thought about hot temper as an inherited characteristic, and with some effort have toned mine down—but then he had responsibilities, the wife, the kids, the shelter, groceries. How do you feel when the world is digging into your pockets, you're pedaling full speed, your wife keeps yelling that she needs more money for milk for her children, you need a drink, and here comes another sonofabitch to try to do you in?

My old man was big on luck. He said nothing mattered one way or another, if your luck ran out. I believe that. But luck, like anything else, needs a chance, a receptive frame of mind where you can let go, relax, achieve calmness, get lucky. The old man found that frame of mind in fishing, but he never could apply it in business. And he sure couldn't bring it home.

Maybe Mother didn't let him, but I don't think so. I think he was wrapped as tight as she was. I think crazy was one of their common chords, then it became one of the phantoms Mother nurtured. The major phantoms were crazy, liquor and strange women. And maybe things could look a little bit crazy to the casual observer who didn't take the trouble to see what was beneath the surface, like compassion—they both had it, but not for each other. Like when the old man started up in diamonds and started carrying a gun again, a .45, for the protection, for the diamonds. Mother called that crazy, too.

But I was with him the night he pulled over onto the shoulder behind some drunk boys and their stalled car. My old man liked helping people, and these boys had their hood up like they needed help, maybe a lift or something. One of them yelled back at us, hostile and drunk, and then walked back toward us with the tire iron, but got very polite looking down the little black hole of eternity. My old man didn't lay any shit on the guy for yelling or for coming at us with the tire iron. He only said, "Thought we'd help you boys out. Need a lift?" The drunk boy said nothing. "Suit yourself," my old man said, and we pulled back out onto the road. I was only a kid, but I got the picture; crazy and compassionate, with maybe a slight edge on the crazy, but you get the idea, too.

Maybe it was the perspective allowed by the years that I missed most sharing, standing there thirty years after the last day shared. My old man wasn't crazy, and the women weren't strange. They were the women of those days, that's all. Mother never minded them when she got taken along, like to the Trocadero sometimes, and she could feel young in that netherworld of drink and smoke and the power of the night. Then the women were only present, in their slinky dresses and polite smiles. I think Mother knew how those women changed as soon as the wife wasn't there. But it wasn't all that much, hardly more than a caress up and down an arm, a wink and a nod. And hell, what's a few highballs?

Mother wasn't the only one who thought my old man was crazy, but many people who shared her conviction had been proselytized by her. She couldn't figure an easy way out of her predicament, her life, any easier than he could, and maybe I cannot reconcile the desperation of those years they went at each other, trapped, cornered, each unwilling to give any margin at all for the sake of the peace.

Like the time in '55, down in Miami Beach, Florida, at the Gould Hotel, right down from the Fountain Blue, or whatever it was, where rich people stayed. Some guy who worked at the Gould Hotel became our friend, maybe because he was taken by the novelty of country Jews after such a flood of New York Jews. His name was Vince and he showed us all around the block one day, showing us how to cross a street in Miami Beach, Florida, where traffic isn't all that different from New York, you know. Vince held his nose and stuck his thumb up his ass and high-stepped it full speed across Collins Avenue, which was thick with traffic then. He was about the funniest guy I'd ever seen and we all laughed a long time, except for the old man.

A few days later, when Mother told everyone in the hotel how crazy the old man was for allowing her baby to jump in the deep end, Vince offered to give me swimming lessons, real swimming lessons. I told him I'd give him a few swimming lessons. My old man loved that, and he laughed, and he finally relaxed enough to share his reason for disliking Vince. Vince had a moustache. The old man put it this way: "Now why would a man want around his mouth what he's got all over his *pupik?*"

I nodded slow, thinking that one over, maybe wondering when I'd get hair on my pupik, maybe wincing at the thought of pupik hair on my face. My old man must have liked the way the ponder looked on me, because he took me down to Walgreen's, now that I could swim, and bought me a face mask, frog fins and a snorkel. Then we went down to the beach where I sloshed around in three feet of water, as amazed with the mud minnows and sand crabs darting across the bottom as I've ever been amazed with any wonder of the universe. The reality available in that shallow water was more awesome than stick pretzels or Nickel Nips.

I'm fairly certain the old man got a charge out of it, too, because his wingtips got soaked and he only grinned, no goddamns or sonofabitches on the beach. He only wanted to know, "What do you see, Hotshot?"

I told him; just about everything.

I remember once in '56, around in there, my old man asked me if I wanted to go fishing with him, which was a commitment because he liked to stay eight or ten hours and a kid could get bored after two or three. But I said I would because he sorely liked the company, and he wanted to go to a particular lake that covered several acres and had its own overflow spillway where, for some reason, the biggest bull-frogs in Southern Indiana lived. I wanted one badly and had come close to catching one twice, but they were so big you could hardly hold on; three-pounders, some of them, and when you finally did get a grip on one, which was two-handed and way slimy, he'd practically turn to you and open wide, like he was about to swallow your head or something. I shunned the three-pronged frog gig because who wants a frog that's all messed up? My old man finally caught me one with a fly rod and a fly, cast for it like it was a bass, and the frog took it. I was happy as a clam, and I think that made it as good as a major bass for my old man.

But anyway, that day we headed way out of town, and so we stopped at a country store for sodas and chips and bread and mustard and the excellent cheap lunch meat we never got at home. I paid at the counter, to get me comfortable handling money, and the old guy at the cash register looked at me—I went about fifty pounds then—and then looked at my old man, and the guy said, "Well, sonny, out with Grampa today?"

Oh, Christ, I thought, as my old man stepped forward, reached across the counter, gently grasped a fistful of the guy's shirt, raised him off the floor and said, "I'll Grampa you, you sonofabitch." He was testy like that, sensitive about all the stuff he'd done wrong, like hav-ing a kid when he was pushing fifty and going broke. He reacted with violence—Mother called it crazy.

Maybe she was right. Maybe I repressed the indictment due him; maybe I forgave him for no other reason than I was the only one left who could, because it was a time for resolution, and that required for-giveness for him, in whose spirit I stood there, breathing, alive, on top of the world.

I don't know why the guy at the grocery store surfaced then, a gen-eration later, graveside, but it was a laugh, a short one, maybe at the foolishness of that kind of piss and vinegar always on the simmer in my old man, and in me too, like the kind I harbored so fiercely for Flossie's son. The shakes came again and were let go again, and I remembered a phrase my old man used whenever he got into a jam, that he was between a shit and sweat. That was a laugh too.

It was about that same time when I was a kid, when I was nine or ten, that I spent a few intense days knowing beyond all else that, no matter what, I would grow up to be a fireman. Sure, it was the red, the hat, the big hoses, the long rubber coat and, my God, *the trucks*. And don't forget the kind of action in store for a fireman. That would be tough to beat—saving people, squirting water all over the place, *driving the trucks*.

This insight was valid, much more plausible than the conviction I had a couple years earlier that the very, very best thing to be when you grew up was an elephant. That goal lasted a few months, and maybe I would have pursued it if not for the practical difficulties. But that was only in second grade, and though second graders might have more magic to call on, they don't know much—not like fifth graders.

The fireman passion was as strong as the elephant passion but didn't last nearly as long, maybe because we got to see a movie about firemen in school, and there was all this smoke and coughing and everything got ruined, and then this fireman had to give mouth-to-mouth to this big old fat lady. Yuk.

I let the future go for awhile then until another dream took hold between my ears, which was to head out, into the woods across from my house farther than anyone had ever been. I would find the Indians and join them. I had already joined in my mind; my trek across the continent waiting across the street would be a homecoming. How. Ugh. I had a headdress and a tomahawk made of really hard rubber and a bow and arrow and plenty wampum; no squaws allowed.

Sure it was kid stuff, but the idea was unlimited, like magic, or a dream, and maybe I'd be happier now on the open plains with a nomadic life on horseback, as a buffalo hunter and gatherer. But maybe not, I've so learned to love taxis, hotels, cafes.

My old man wouldn't recognize the world today, and he'd surely have a harder time in it, with his rambunctious spirit. I suppose he was one of the most pissed-off guys I ever knew; *just pop him in the nose* was his prescription for diplomacy, flashing fists quick and easy as some guys blink.

He died on the lam, I think. Nobody knows for sure if he was running a hustle in Oklahoma City when the last heart attack took him—that is, nobody knows if he was breaking the law. I know that the law of nature had him broke again, and that Aunt Florence and Uncle John had taken up in Oklahoma City for some reason, and had taken my old man in, because he was her brother. That was the year after Mother called it quits, which was a good year for speculating on illegal hustles too; Uncle John was so recently returned from *building bridges in South America,* which was easier to explain to children like us than saying he was in the slammer for bilking widows and orphans on an aluminum-siding scam.

I saw Aunt Florence in '71 or '73, a few years before she died. She sent me down to a jewelry store to pick out a watch for myself, *a real nice one, Honey, because a man should have a nice-looking watch so people can know.* Then she gave me fifty bucks in cash and called it mad money and made me promise not to save it or spend it on anything sensible. She didn't say, *Go ahead and piss it down the drain* like my old man would have said, but that's what she meant, that was the family spirit. I think she appreciated the visit we shared for its spirit of forgiveness. I think she was confused, thinking she'd done something wrong. But then Mother put out a vibe back then that was heavy enough to last a few generations. Mother held every blood relative of my old man accountable for the way things turned out. I know Mother was justified in her own mind, but even then I held other culprits accountable.

Aunt Florence said I was quiet and strong, like her mother. I didn't ask her about the time my old man died in Oklahoma City, because it didn't matter—didn't matter any more than the bridges Uncle John never built.

Uncle John had sold aluminum siding to old people for years before he brought my old man into the business, before he went to *South America*. He made decent money at it, but he broke the law, too, and got sent to *South America* for most of my youth.

Uncle John was a hustler, a scammer, a bullshitter who would rob you blind in a heartbeat. I rationalized his behavior because he wasn't just a bullshitter, he was a great bullshitter, a high roller and high liver, here today, gone tomorrow, easy come, easy go. And I knew he'd never rob me; I was family, after all, and besides, if he did, my old man would beat the shit out of him.

Uncle John didn't just love to play the horses, he loved driving his brand-new Cadillac twenty-four hours straight all the way down to Miami, Florida to play the horses at Hialeah, where the real horses ran and the real action was to be had and a man could get up next to players as heavy as he was. He thought Brother and me going to the track in Kentucky and playing the horses was a perfect way for kids to start out and about as great as being Eagle Scouts. He always drove Cadillacs, new ones, and always had the most marvelous restaurants to tell you about—*It was marvelous. Marvelous I tell you. And the cheese bull...intzes! They were marvelous, simply marvelous.* Uncle John always talked about bull...intzes! and said things were marvelous or called places *gargeous*—*The place...was...gargeous!* He was so full of the blarney he didn't drop a note when his brassy inflections set Brother and me off like hyenas; he thought we were nuts for his material, that we'd never heard anything like this guy. He thought we were right there with him, neck and neck, in the spirit of the photo finish.

Uncle John kept about a half ream of 11 x 14 cheap prints of the Last Supper in the trunk of his Cadillac, and if he met someone he liked, really liked, someone with moxie and chutzpah, who knew how to give a little, how to take a little, like a mensch, then that person would get a cheap print of the Last Supper. At the bottom, Uncle John would write:

1/1/1

Dear Irving,

The herring in cream sauce was delicious! The bagels had to be from New York. The knishes were like Mama's, the matzoballs lighter than goose feathers. The kreplach was out of this world, the tsimmes and farfel divine. Oy gott! The brisket! Not since Miami Beach have I tasted kugel like that. And the cheese blintzes... Oy vay-izmere!

Your pal,

Jesus H. Christ

A tremendous guffaw accompanied the presentation, maybe three or four seconds after the recipient had a chance to get the joke—"Haaa! Ha! Ha! Ha! Ha! So? Does a Jew know about good deli, or doesn't he? Haaaa!" I saw Uncle John present several dozen prints of the Last Supper. He was known for it. He never got tired of writing the schtick at the bottom.

Uncle John was a renegade, an outlaw who wore stolen jewelry and drove fancy cars on the brink of repossession. But he had color—call it garish and loud, call it unethical, immoral. I didn't know; I don't care. He exposed us to bullshit as a second language, a fluency that eased my way in strange lands.

Uncle John came home, too. He RIPs just over yonder, second row, beside Aunt Florence. He wasn't a bad guy, always in a good mood. And if my old man would have understood some of the mud puddles I had to wade across to get to the money on the other side, well then, I forgave him as well for selling aluminum siding in Oklahoma City, or selling the promise of aluminum siding. Down to seeds and stems, Uncle John and my old man did what they did. It wasn't right. It was all they had left. Many people didn't like Uncle John. I did. I didn't see him as right or wrong; that was foregone. But he never held a gun to anybody's head, and whether he beat you or you beat him, he'd make you laugh. I never saw him in a bad mood. And I met plenty guys of his ilk in moods, hurtful, unstable moods.

My old man knew who among them had a sense of humor or compassion, who among them was criminally mean. It was no different than when he went a few bucks up and had a hard time keeping that to himself, too. Oh, he spread it around. He popped a few people in the nose, but he'd pull over to give you a lift, or lend you a hand.

It was only last week, thirty years ago, that Brother and Sissy and I got home from school, and I felt Mother watching us in a strange, prolonged way as I set my books down and went through my routine of sluffing off the constraint and compression of another whole day wasted. She let a sad, sad smile stretch her face into that most difficult border between compassion and crying, and I knew. I knew. "You're father died," she said. But I already knew.

Maybe things have been sorting out ever since.

And sitting there in the bone-cold morning in January in the Midwest, it was plain to see how being dead thirty years could mellow a guy out, could allow him possibly the same opportunity for personal development available to us, the living.

And there was a new common ground, no more anger, no revenge, no fists, no fight. A day of reckoning approached. We would surround it with compassion, with dispatch; any scalps would be taken quick and clean. War cries would be from the heart, to the sky. He knew. They all knew, Izzy, Rudy, Sammy and his wife, Aunt Hazel, who told me, the last time I saw her in '70 or '71, that I reminded her of Glen Campbell, "And, Honey, a man doesn't get any finer than that." Next to Hazel were Adolph, Ben, Florence and John, and then the parents—Haddie and Joe.

But the knowing that emanated then from the ground up wasn't a knowing like people know after they hear the news. It was peace. And it was final, passed away at last; the kid is on his own now, and that's okay, because he knows how to throw a punch and, more important, he knows how to take one.

The knowing there at Mt. Sinai was resolute as words in stone; youth is over, it said. Gone is the time of protection, the safe passage provided by a guardian angel, the spirits of the family. That felt good, as transitions from birth to life should feel. It felt natural, like the healthy fatigue that calms the body and spirit at the end of a long hike, rife with adventure, along a precipice with a view reserved only for the adventurous, with insight to what lies over the edge.

Clarity came down to a phrase: *Now is the time.* Now is the time to fend for yourself, because now you can. The child becomes father to the man. Go now. Rest in peace.

The shakes came in flurries then, the breeze filling in until the shakes jolted again, as if the host grew restless for a check-in, because I, the living, had hung around, had come closer to the place of Death, had stayed colder than a living person should stay for forty minutes. I stood up, and with a heavy voice let go the words nobody residing in the cemetery needed, but that the living feel compelled to say: Thank you.

And then I'd been there long enough for resolution to be foregone. Mother and Aunt Aileen waited in the car with the heater on, but they were restless enough to go, just go, and let me go too, without the usual line of questions. We drove to Newburgh, to the riverfront, where thirty years ago you could buy crawdads, crickets, night crawlers, minnows, meal worms, hooks, line, nets, Nehi Soda, lunch meat, white bread, Moonpies, stick pretzels, jaw breakers, rope licorice, bubble gum, and more stuff than a kid could take in. Then you could walk down to the rocky banks of the Ohio River and watch the old guys who knew the river coming and going. They fished for carp and river cats, sometimes talking about the monster river cats they all knew were out there, and you could have about as much fun as you wanted to have.

Now you got a semi-chic bistro open for lunch and a couple wannabe-chic antique stores and some generic-chic boutiques. I looked up and down the street for a chic bait shop, with svelte craw-dads, pastel crickets, fashionable nightcrawlers and maybe some mud minnows just like the ones in Hollywood. But the bait shops are gone, and so is the decrepit hovel that sold Nehi Soda and Moonpies, cat-fish stew and black coffee, mustard, bread and lunch meat for a day out in the real world. Maybe it's best my old man never saw this.

But the bistro was still in Southern Indiana, so it was Hoosier chic, with catfish on the menu and a view from the second floor that overlooked the widest, deepest, muddiest, swiftest-flowing river in the whole wide world of my youth. The river went way back and way yonder all at once. Its banks were frozen in January, its swirls and eddies rushing southwest. Reduced to brown and gray and darker gray and muddier brown, the river looked dead but alive, freezing but boiling, still hell-bent for leather like some of us boys who grew up nearby.

Then we took Aunt Aileen home and backtracked to St. Louis over reflections on the past, and another hard lesson for Mother from her most demanding teacher, me.

She remembered again, as befit the moment, as if so much filial duty and sentiment might lead poor, naive me to the wrong assessment; she said it was rough in the extreme back then, that she had no money for milk for her children, because my old man wouldn't give it to her, because he was blowing it all on strange women and liquor.

I had to lay the law down, say what you will. I told her she plain couldn't understand that blood won't come from stones or turnips, that a man with no money has no money, and that a man with no money can still come up with a drink, especially in the face of so much pressure, because a man reaches a point in life with money or without, and he can count on a drink more than he can count on most other things. And moreover, *whether you realize it or not, there is absolutely no difference, zero, between the occupations of my father and me. The only difference is that he never got lucky with money, and I did. You should see this; that I owe everything, the will, the wits, the drive, the tooth and nail, to him. Not to sell you short, to you I owe the sustenance and nurturing. But I cannot tolerate your indictment any longer, because I take it personal. I always have. So it must stop.*

We rode another couple hours in silence. She fell asleep. Maybe she dreamed of the day I would forgive her her shortcomings as completely as I'd forgiven my old man; maybe she longed for a generosity in me that she'd longed for ever since she was a girl and first cleaned up the messes of those people around her—it would indeed be a generosity I had not yet practiced, one that would allow her her own brand of idiosyncrasy, of insanity, of no sense, of shrill, comical lunacy without a word of criticism from me. But doesn't the greatest burden fall to the living? She was Mother to me, after all, and I did so want her to get it right.

And I realized that sometimes a grown person can watch an old parent sleep the same way a young parent watches a child sleep, in awe and wonder and hope for good fortune ahead, in the unknown. We got home late.

❄   ❄   ❄

utter Side Up

Two days later was the trial.

I'd thought about it so much, pondered its meaning, savored the face-off from so many angles, considered so many consequences that it had become anticlimactic. Maybe that would be good. Maybe analysis *ad nauseam* would let me spend the anger, use up the fight festering in me all these years. Maybe not, I was so steeled for it, so ready to flash like a live wire and fry the sonofabitch, so ready to advance him spiritually, to within an inch of his life.

I wore a suit I had made in Bangkok maybe ten, twelve pounds ago, so that the suit, like the bile enveloping my soul, strained for a break, a release, a sundering to the realm of freer living, easier breathing. It was navy blue with faint pin stripes an inch apart, sedate and conservative—an effective camouflage for the seething ire inside it.

And maybe it was only coincidentally double-breasted, so the color and cut of it matched the suit my old man wore in the only photograph I have of him in real clothing, taken in '44 or '45, about the time he managed to borrow a hundred grand or so on a hunch and some obscure lead on the moderate potential of oil fields in Southern Illinois, not too far from home. A hundred grand then was the same as a mil or two now, and his posture in the photo was that of a confident man, straight and broad-chested, with a cashmere overcoat and a Stetson hat and a cigar; he stood on the barren, frozen field where his first two wells would go, looking as free of doubt as a man who already had the money in his pocket.

The money came in, too, with the oil, moderate flows of oil, tremendous flows of cash, but not to him or his, because the hundred grand wasn't enough and neither was four hundred grand, so he lost his hold on what became the biggest oil company in Illinois, lost it to some men who paid off half his debt and then spent another fifty grand and hit the black juice that reaped millions of dollars a year, forever.

My old man sluffed it off, brushed it off and got started up as a building contractor, knew enough about building houses to learn the rest, and then scrambled one more time all over town with all new loans secured by bigger shares of the new action, all leading to the next line of work, the racetrack. Then came diamonds and then newer lines of work, up to the package liquor store on Diamond Avenue, where, the old man was assured by the old friends left, they would buy their liquor from him. Lines blurred from there, between the half-pint sales, into the steady, struggling hustle that would last for the duration.

My old man could put a project together like nobody's business—and with a seventh-grade education, he was a natural. I learned early, when my head was full of poetry and prose, that natural runs in the family, that deal-cutting for our clan came as easy as dirt farming for the rest of the Hoosiers in Southern Indiana. And maybe I owe my good luck to my old man, who never could recognize the downside before it was too late, never could build a back door into a deal, never could save his ass or his shirt, or bail out with the few bucks that were rightfully his for setting a thing up on the right track in the first place, no matter how undercapitalized he always was. Down in flames was how he went. Losses were always total.

The photo from the oilfields was the last one to survive him. You can only see the man in that shot, not the fatal defect that let him get so badly burned when a deal went less than perfect, which every deal in history has done. The old man was a natural on the street, in business, like a broken-field runner with only one defender to get past for the score. That lone last defender comes up every time, just before the pay out, with a voice that says, *Okay, everything now changes—no money for you.*

The difference between a scrambler who makes the score and one who gets tackled inside the ten-yard line is that the one who makes the score knows the biggest challenge comes moments before the pay out, because nothing changes human intent, morality, integrity like money on the table. My old man got inside the ten-yard line with the best of them, then he lost his chance to score, because he was naive at the wrong time, because he expected men to behave and perform as he would have done. If he'd lent money to someone for an oilfield, and the project looked strong, but needed more money, he would have helped the guy out. If a friend opened a liquor store, he would have bought a few cases of liquor. If a friend sold diamonds, he would have bought a bunch of jewelry. If a friend was a building contractor, he would have signed up for a house. He expected people who were friends to behave that way, because it was natural. They didn't, because other behaviors got in the way.

The lesson wasn't lost on me, nor was the second nature that went hand in hand with a childhood on the move to twelve different homes, heading downscale, in ten years. That taught me the truth about stability; there ain't so much to go around at street level, so you keep your eyes open, your mouth shut, and practice movement at all times, even when you look like you're sitting still. They got to him, because he didn't think they would. I learned early what can happen any time.

I knew where I'd been. My old man grew up in a secure, stable family, just like so many people who can't cut a good deal, because a comfortable childhood can leave you unexposed to downside reality.

I hadn't worn or even owned a suit in thirty years, not since double-breasted was long gone, not since it was considered a laughable cut, suitable only for old, corny movies. I hadn't worn this one since the day I bought it, on a whim. I'd remained oblivious to the perfect occasion now approaching for its debut. And moving in long strides, I was mindful of posture myself. An association with the past crept in, an idea that times had changed, but maybe some of the characters were still around. I was a long way from fifty-three pounds and four feet tall, but everything else was the same. I didn't go five-ten, two-twenty like the old man, but I matched his stride, stood up straight, broad-chested, relaxed and proportionately just as thick. And I stepped through the big double doors of the courtroom like a representative, like an old character with a new agenda. I too had borrowed big and rolled the bones. I'd fared better than my old man, and I realized I had come to a point, a convergence of past and future, at that moment becoming the person my old man had been.

I strode into the room of great ceilings and walls ornately covered in tooled hardwood, where a mortal being in dark robes would be elevated to look down on those in need of certain justice. I looked everywhere at once.

And everything did change. The bile went away. I didn't have a good feeling about Flossie's son, but seeing him stooped over, frail, trying to keep up with his concrete-faced, lard-assed wife, eased the tension, reduced my need for justice, or violence. He'd got his, and how. I wanted it to end; it was already over. This round was incidental. I'd nurtured the spirit of revenge for thirty years, and there before me was a sorry sonofabitch I hoped I would never resemble. I wished him an easy, painless death. I laughed and shook my head; to think I had planned to knock down a pitiful old guy like that.

The Devilment was close enough to cackle low, "Don't laugh!" as if she'd far outdone me in nurturing the evil spirit, as if today would be hers, as if victory could still be hers.

"How did you get so ugly?" I asked. "And how did your ass get so big?" The plaster covering the front of her skull cracked and flaked and nearly fell away, frighteningly, slagged down to a new hardness, cheek by jowl, high in the eyebrows and bulging the eyeballs like her namesake, the goat-headed Satan, she broke down to a new low in hatred emissions. She wanted to breathe fire. Oh, God, did she. Bad breath was all it came to. And she stepped forward, seething ill will more intensively than I'd ever imagined doing—she stepped up, daring me to respond.

It was curious behavior, until Sissy thrust a hand in front of me like a patrol girl blocking a foolish child from crossing without looking both ways. The Devilment had attempted to draw me in for a sucker punch; I'd scored a good hit on her ass, but she soaked it up like she knew, and she stepped up with a duck and weave of her own, maybe she planned an aspersion on my old man, but Sissy read the action, knew I'd take the bait, maybe blow the whole campaign. Maybe Sissy saved the day.

Who knows if I would have taken a whack at The Devilment? I think I wouldn't have. But then again, someone should. Round one ended, and each camp eyed the other from neutral corners.

Mother said, "She's the cause of it all"—she meaning The Devilment, it all meaning anything bad that ever happened to or came between Flossie and Flossie's children. But by then, Mother's assessments of family and reality in general had lost considerable credibility, and we plain knew better.

Mother pressed her case, insisting that sundown would find Flossie's son still hungry—Mother meant hungry, as in wanting something to eat. "Because that bitch still won't cook for him, or take care of him at all, if you want to know the truth." She was livid, just thinking about all the years The Devilment had failed to scrub floors for, make little sandwiches for, wash and dry for, scrimp and save for, worship and fear Flossie's son.

Neither Brother nor Sissy nor I said anything; Mother's mind warp was worse than we'd thought.

For a brief time some years earlier, Sissy had shown apprehension that family roles would repeat—that Brother and I would become as vile as Flossie's son, and that we would hate her children. She got over it because Brother and I have nothing in common with Flossie's son.

Still something existed like an itch between your shoulder blades, the...thing that no one could describe or define, but it nonetheless encompassed all the perversion, the warp, the magnification and shrinking, the diseases, the strange behaviors, the greed, the vibration and bad luck emanating from Flossie and her clan.

Brother scratched the itch by giving the thing a name, by summing it up so we could understand it as a single item, rather than a range of quirks too vast for a single reference. He called it The Curse. Brother and Sissy and I were convinced by then that blood ties with these strange people equaled zero. And once named, The Curse became easier to sort. That day, The Curse became clear. Brother said the most obvious symptom of The Curse was anal retention, in the literal sense; severe constipation was chronic with Flossie, her son, her son's family, all of whom knew in their hearts that if they took a shit, the world could cheat them yet again, out of something, somewhere, of value. They couldn't let go, couldn't relax, couldn't take a shit. And look what they clung to now.

Flossie's son was possibly the perfect date for The Devilment, his long, pointed chin running parallel to his beak now, maybe from so many lies over so many years. Rawhide lips, that looked stretched thin from grimace and licking, now lay complacently folded over teeth gnashed too long, so the mouth hole had lost its bite but could maybe muster a few more months of gumming the world at large. He must have been seventy-something, an old, tired seventy-something, with a stooped, colorless body that looked flat wore-out from so much hostility and distrust. He looked pitiful, like an old rattler still requiring gingerly treatment until a few hours after he was dead.

We waited.

We sat while the lawyers lawyered, arguing spuriously for show, for the benefit of clients, insisting that their numbers, their claims, their inaccurately stated cases were the truth. We spoke softly of other things in the stifling, low-oxygen atmosphere of life indoors in the Midwest with no windows; as if the view outside wasn't worth the look.

Brother said he had to be home by four to unplug his food dehydrator or he'd lose the whole load, because the stuff tastes like shit if you take it down to leather. And he'd paid seven dollars extra for rush shipping on his new Snack'n Sandwich Maker for making hot snacks and tasty sandwiches and, well, forget it, because he would most likely miss the UPS driver today anyway.

You could breathe fine in the courthouse, if you didn't move around or breathe too much. We waited and waited and declined a low-ball offer, three grand or so, and we didn't whoop or holler at having them on the run. We were tired and tired of it, going for a hundred-five and finality, maybe sensing the lifeless potential of justice. Back in His Majesty's chambers was where justice hid that day, and it would come out once His Majesty was good and goddamn ready—after coffee, the paper, toe jams, a dump. We retired to the corridor, where we sat, we paced. I approached the enemy camp with death threats in my eyes, and the clocks went tick, tick, tick...

That's all it came to. I could still envision the moment in which I would step around him, apologize, and take him down. I could easily see that aggressive motivation as a fixation, a frailty, a character defect in myself, but one I could accept, it felt so natural. And maybe as I stood staring at him, he read my thoughts, which couldn't have been so difficult to do, since it was a pure moment of no love; none, not a pinch of it.

He called the bailiff and, maybe sensing another potential like all the potentials he'd sensed in his life, he called again and again, each time more urgently, more desperate, as if the threat were real and approaching. I stood and stared. The ancient bailiff and two stray lawyers in department-store suits hurried to the rescue, to contain me, but I hadn't moved.

The old bailiff yelled for everyone to settle down as the lawyers came out from another conference, another offer, this one for fifty grand. We said no, all of us but Mother, who was maybe the wacki-est of her lot, who asked, "Will it be over? Will that be the end of it?"

Oh, she could push my buttons. I reminded her that I'd spent sev-eral thousand dollars and the last few years, then a few more grand and seventeen hours bouncing through airports, breathing bad air, that we'd pressed this issue for this chance, now, maybe three hours from her just reward, a hundred-and-five grand that had been stolen from her as surely as if it was plucked from her pocket. If we could simply stay strong, simply maintain the resolve of years, simply relax, with fortitude, then we could be true to ourselves. Then we would deserve justice.

She hung her head in contemplation, in the weakness that had kept her in the yoke so many years, and she said, "After all, he is my brother."

I quit. So, it ended. We drove home at dusk ruminating on victory, however diluted, because fifty grand was still a good sting, a TKO at any rate, and besides, Sissy said, the money was small potatoes compared to what the community would think once it heard that Flossie's son got sued by his sister for stealing her money, and lost. And what the community would think would be pocket change compared to consensus at the Club. "You wouldn't," Mother said. But Sissy would and did, and Brother and I nodded sanguinely, as if death by gossip was possibly a refined and, for them, more grotesque form of justice.

Mother was instantly and severely distraught over this gruesome prospect, but Brother distracted her with a question to help her through her purge. "When did it start?" he asked, like Mr. Rogers might ask a toddler. "When did it all start?"

"Nineteen twenty-nine," Mother said, staring obliquely off, as if the past hovered there in the air, as if a certain moment was still fresh and plump sixty-five years after it happened; 1929, when she was eleven and Flossie's son was seven. "We got five cents a week and I went and got a Hershey Bar. And he took it. He took it!" She got stuck there on the first injustice, where it all began.

"He took it," Brother narrated to the invisible crowd gathered round the ancient moment. "But did she complain?"

"No," Mother said. "I gave it gladly..." Mother seemed to seek subsequent moments, but they all jumbled up, so many of them of so many different shapes and colors.

"She gave it gladly," Brother said, helping her move her story along. "And then she asked him how his BM looked. Did he chew good, or could you see the nuts?"

Mother nodded woefully, a giver to a fault, and a fatal fault it would have been, had not her weakness been recompensed by our side of the family.

At Brother's house, adding another zero to her store of lessons in life, Mother called Flossie to make sure everything was in order, to make sure Flossie had been given her enema and served her dinner. They spoke for a minute or two of bodily functions. I asked if I could say hello. I hadn't spoken to Flossie in years. Mother would have been suspicious, but at that moment she could only grasp the prospect of restoring her family to its united front against the world, at last. "Thank God!" I bellowed into the phone. "Thank God, the money is still in the family!"

Mother grabbed the phone back and in a sleepy voice said, "Well, I'll be home later." She listened another few seconds, then she hung up. "She wants to know when. Sonofabitch."

"Which sonofabitch?" I asked.

"Why doesn't she call her son?" Mother asked.

"Yes," Brother said. "That's a good question. Why doesn't she call her son?"

We had wine with dinner that night, two bottles. Mother didn't get home until way after ten, with an entire glass of wine under her belt.

The following month Flossie got checked into a home, where she still complained about the enemas, too much rushing, not enough grease on the nozzle, as if they just didn't care enough to slow down and do it right.

Mother got her own condo with her victory money and some help from her children.

Sissy became one of the most renowned collectors of toy cars in the United States of America, and more of the good daughter Mother always wanted her to be, if not the best daughter Mother could have imagined, Sissy was so late in catching on to a daughter's filial obligations.

Still, Mother was grateful and asked what took Sissy so long. I tried explaining that Sissy wanted to be good long ago, and it wasn't a personality issue, well, not entirely. Sissy's notion of what a good daughter should be was diametrically opposed to what she observed, in Mother. That is, Sissy rejected the subservience that kept Mother in the harness for her whole life. Sissy wanted to be good, but not on the same terms Mother had chosen.

Mother didn't respond, although I sensed she considered my analysis crazy. It was one more go round, teaching up the line.

I was not confident, but I tried again, explaining to Mother that Brother, Sissy, and I wanted to help her, wanted to make her life easier, wanted to exalt her to her rightful place as matriarch of a vibrant family achieving success on every level, in spite of monumental odds. But every time we tried, we could only feel like we had shit rubbed in our faces, because she would be at Flossie's feet in the next hour, scrubbing the floors, or fixing a six-course lunch for Flossie and her son, then excusing herself to clean the toilets, while Flossie and her son discussed business.

"I don't do that anymore," Mother said.

I sighed. "Do you understand my point?"

"No, I don't. If you want to be good to me, then do it," Mother said. Mother was adept at presenting challenges at least as difficult as those presented to her. I pressed the issue. I explained that she had lived a role since childhood, played out a script cast in stone that was morally corrupt. She was no more than a convenient maid to Flossie.

"I know you understand this," I said. "But I'm not so sure you can change. Because you may think you've changed, but you haven't. And it's very difficult being as good to someone you can't respect, than you can if you do respect them."

"So?"

"So how could Sissy ever respect you," I asked, "if you never respected yourself?"

"You talk crazy," Mother finally said.

I said, "Yes. I suppose I do."

Flossie finally died early on the morning of her ninety-seventh birthday. Mother was distraught, not so much by her mother's death or the shock of liberation, but because Mother had planned a party, a luncheon, with all the aunts and cousins and everyone, and all the cooking was done, the cakes were baked. "And she was looking forward to it," Mother said.

"So?" Brother said. "She croaked with a party to look forward to. How bad could that be?"

Mother only mumbled, "Well... She... You know..."

I didn't travel from Hawaii to St. Louis for Flossie's funeral. It was the principle of the thing. But I went in a few days later, to help ease the transition if I could. Mother, after all, had become seventy-five. She'd held up well, ready for a life of her own, but as uncertain as a woman of the East whose feet can flex only after a lifetime in bindings. I said that now would be a good time for her to come for a visit, to the tropics.

She hesitated, mumbled some more about visits, and her adjustment was complete. She said, "I can now. I'm free now, you know."

Brother then told me the story of the day we'd all waited for. He said everyone got excited when Flossie went into a fit, breathless and convulsing, even those who'd seen it before. Sure, the idea of another melodrama was in the air, but Flossie was convincing. So the ambulance was called, and the whole dog-and-pony parade began, with the stretcher, the machines, the graphs, the drugs. They got Flossie stabilized in the ambulance and drove to St. Luke's. But two blocks out a medic said, *No, not St. Luke's. She goes to St. John. Her doctor is at St. John.* The other medic said, *No, not St. John, St. Luke. I'm sure of it.* But they turned around and drove cross town to St. John, because the first medic was that certain, but they got advised on the radio that they were late at St. Luke's. So they turned around again and drove back across town to St. Luke's, their blaring siren of marginal effect in thickening traffic. DOA.

I think it's cruel to view Flossie's last moments as karmic retribution, surrounded by the same chaos and runaround she so thoroughly surrounded Mother with. But the thought crossed my mind, along with the image of medics arguing directions and blame over the sirens: What a way to go, especially for someone so righteous.

Brother had also changed, opened up. He was pleased with his Snack'n Sandwich Maker, and surprised—it made waffles, excellent waffles that even the dogs liked with cartoons on Saturday mornings. He resolved to work the waffles off on the Nordic Track Machine he sent for, as seen on TV, which would allow him to ski cross-country over the polar ice cap while watching old movies—and while having a nice jolt from his new 2-in-1 Espresso/Cappuccino Machine. He cut loose, whole hog, and got the fancy grinder, too.

I came home from that visit pondering time and the few short years to '00 which was the same year my old man was born. It had been two years since the pilgrimage and the trial, and I still felt the spirits of the clan linger, go away but linger at the same time, because spirits can do that, like smoke.

Mother let me take some of the old photos. She gave me the oil-field photo, the one of my old man in the double-breasted suit standing straight and tall. Placing it in the envelope, she reminded me once more that the bravado was false, and so was the promise; that the money never came, and all that photo showed was the hollow confidence responsible for my poverty-struck childhood, in case I'd forgot. I told her she could maybe go have a tongue sandwich and use her own tongue, which she hadn't heard for years, not since she last got shrill as a harpy on my old man.

Maybe she didn't realize that I remembered him saying it, that I didn't just make it up, like my father's son, so I said, "Ha ha. Gotcha."

She didn't laugh. But she asked me if I needed silverware and gave me a set of flatware for eight, "God-awful ugly stuff," she called it— so bad she never used it. He gave it to her as a gift when they were engaged, fifty-six years ago.

Then Mother wailed that Passover was in less than a week, and it was crazy that I was leaving, crazy, since I was there already, and Passover was only next week. I didn't explain to her that I had a life, a home with responsibilities, because I knew the look I'd get, knew what she would have told me—"This is your home!"

I only said, "You know what you must do when it's time to go. Don't you?" She called me morbid, but she shut up and let me go.

I had to stop in San Francisco for two days and was there for the beginning of Passover and the first-night Seder, a many-coursed affair overlaid with poetry, song and the general lyric of Judaism, which strives for love, with everyone talking at once. I would have stayed in St. Louis, but I had a shot at a deal worth considerable points in San Francisco, so I went. The next day was Passover, so I stayed, after calling an old friend in San Francisco, a professor who said yes, most definitely, join her at the home of friends in Marin.

Oy, I thought, Yidloch, in Marin; that sounds like chic meets kvetch. But the real eye-opener was the serendipitous lesson learned that night, over the many courses, the songs and bitter reminders of oppression, when we were slaves in the land of Egypt. Everyone had opinions on oppression, both historic and recent, both general and personal. All opinions were expressed at once, while the kids lamented, "Go down, Moses. Te-ell oh-old Phay-ayro-oh-oh..." I've seen other groups get down with passion and conviction, but none with as much razor-sharp, neurotic humor as Jews on Passover.

But the insight for me was seeing, in action, families with children who played music with a feeling beyond their years, children who discussed concepts and literature without trying to outscore anyone, without falling behind. The horn and piano recital came before dinner. I tolerated the idea of it, until I heard it. Then I loved it—these kids understood jazz. I wondered how that happened. And who taught them to exchange ideas without insisting on being right?

It was a way of life, a phase of life lost to me, of children evolving on a level so much more delicate than the scrimp and scratch, the scrap and scramble—children with two parents who grew up in one place. Imagine that. I wondered if that sort of thing happens often.

And then, between the soup and the brisket, attention came my way. "Tell us," said the mother. "Tell us something."

I had just come from St. Louis, I said, from a visit with my family there. Mother had let me take some photos, I said. They were in the car, actually, but I could get them, if anyone wanted to see them...

"We do! We do!"

"Well, they're not regular photos," I said. "I mean they are, but they're old, some of them sixty, seventy years old. They're of my family."

"You mean your grandparents?"

"No. My old... My father was old—nearly fifty when I was born." They got excited, politely, so I fetched my small collection.

I showed them the oilfield photo—they loved the suit, the background, the...the...the something about it, maybe it was what it captured, yes, that was it. It captured the feeling of those times. "It captured more than that," I said.

And I saw that Mother had thrown in a couple more photos I'd never seen. One was of my old man in ridiculous, antique football gear—lumpy pads, leather helmet, funky jersey, like in the old Gipper movies. They laughed, wanting to know if that, too, was my father, and if he was dressed up for Halloween.

"That's him," I said. "And he's dressed up for real life."

I told them about the '23-'24 season when my old man played left guard for the Cleveland Tigers, which was either a farm club for the Cleveland Browns or an independent, semi-pro team, I don't know; but in his three-point stance he looked at the camera like he'd just as soon take it out as not, the overconfident grin in its first phases then at twenty-three, pushing twenty-four.

The next one was a surprise, showing my old man in wrestling trunks, ready to rumble.

"You're father was a professional wrestler?" Todd asked. He was another guest. He had two children, one who played trumpet and one who wanted to be a writer. He sold insurance. He was about my age.

I said, "Yes, he was. It was different then."

"Oh, I know," Todd said.

"They were real then," I said.

"Well, they were more like what they appeared to be," he said.

We were called to the table then, the brisket was served. Todd said, "I wanted to be a wrestler. Then I got into insurance. It's kind of similar." We laughed, remembering what we wanted to be. Then things quieted down, with so much to eat, all opinions displaced.

Later that night in my hotel room I pulled back the curtain for a better view of the alley. It seemed bigger than alleys used to be, and the far wall made more sense now, its windows framing the dimensions of an evening in the city. I thought about the next few weeks and the last few weeks, and I felt the world come around to a place I'd been in before, where a highball made sense. I hung my clothes and straightened my stuff and mixed one up, bourbon over, with a splash. I sat at the table just off the end of the bed and took another look at the few shots of ancient history Mother had sent along, seeing a few angles for the very first time.

The wrestling picture was from '32 or '35. You could easily see why Mother would need to hide that one way back in Southern Indiana, because professional wrestling wasn't the high-paying showbiz it is today, and it was a long shot from the refinement she tried to give us. That picture showed what professional wrestling was about then. It was a bunch of tough guys grappling for a few bucks, which was fairly consistent with my old man's career, and maybe with my own. I think he liked those guys, the wrestlers, and moreover he understood that they lived where he lived. And if they came into life less equipped than some men, they entered the ring on even terms. He kept up with those guys for years.

None of the kids I knew in Southern Indiana would ever believe that I went into the locker room down at the *Channel 7 Wrestling* place and met, in person, and shook hands with Johnny Valentine, the champ, master of the elbow smash.

Just over in the next row of lockers was Rip Hawk, one of the first bad guys—platinum blond flat-top and black eyebrows—who ruffled my hair and threw a soft punch at my shoulder and told me not to take any shit, Kid, just don't take any shit.

Down at the end was Bobo Brazil, the black giant with hands that could cover a grown man's head, and they did, just before he delivered the Cocobutt. But Bobo Brazil only shook my hand and leaned way down to my level and asked, "How do you do, Sir?"

And way over alone in a corner, with a single locker that looked separate from the others in every way, was Dick the Bruiser, the original wrestling psychopath who bled buckets of blood and kept coming at you, who maybe wasn't ever entirely out of character, who didn't ruffle a kid's hair or shake hands or anything, but he didn't ignore my old man either. He stood up straight and faced my old man with his whole body and grunted and nodded and said, "Hey, How's it going?"—*Dick the Bruiser!*

My old man liked staying in touch with that action, like it was more pure and easier to take than what came at you outside. He's thick as a redwood in his wrestling shot, the big grin full-blown to all-out love of the moment, fists clenched, energy coming at you, like the click of the camera was all the time left before the knuckles hit your nose.

❄   ❄   ❄

The Ice King

Design and composition by Gael Stirler, Tucson, Arizona

Text composed in Weiss, a classic, elegantly crafted typeface
exhibiting balance and readability. Title composed in Benguait.

Printed and bound by R.R. Donnelley & Sons,
Harrisonburg, Virginia

❄